SYREN'S
SONG

SYREN'S

A CONNOR STARK NOVEL

SONG

CLAUDE BERUBE

NAVAL INSTITUTE PRESS
ANNAPOLIS, MARYLAND

Naval Institute Press
291 Wood Road
Annapolis, MD 21402

Library of Congress Cataloging-in-Publication Data

Berube, Claude G.
  Syren's song : a Connor Stark novel / Claude Berube.
    pages ; cm
  ISBN 978-1-61251-915-9 (alk. paper) — ISBN 978-1-61251-914-2 (ebook)
  I. Title.
  PS3602.E7693S97 2015
  813'.6—dc23
                        2015023494

♾ Print editions meet the requirements of ANSI/NISO z39.48-1992
(Permanence of Paper).

Printed in the United States of America.

23 22 21 20 19 18 17 16 15   9 8 7 6 5 4 3 2 1
First printing

Book design and composition: David Alcorn, Alcorn Publication Design

IN MEMORY OF
JIM ST. JOHN AND JACKIE PASCARELLA

Break, break, break,

On thy cold gray stones, O Sea!

And I would that my tongue could utter

The thoughts that arise in me.

Break, break, break

At the foot of thy crags, O Sea

But the tender grace of a day that is dead

Will never come back to me.

—ALFRED, LORD TENNYSON

ACRONYMS

CFO	chief financial officer
CIC	combat information center
CO	commanding officer
CONN	conning officer
DS	Diplomatic Security
EMP	electromagnetic pulse
FLETC	Federal Law Enforcement Training Center
FLIR	forward-looking infrared radar
GAO	Government Accountability Office
GPS	Global Positioning System
HSI	Department of Homeland Security Investigations
LCS	littoral combat ship; little crappy ship
LSO	landing signals officer
NAV	navigation officer
NAVSSI	Navigation Sensor System Interface
NCIS	Naval Criminal Investigative Service
NVG	night vision goggles
OOD	officer of the deck
OPS	operations officer
PC	patrol coastal ship
RHIB	rigid-hulled inflatable boat
ROE	rules of engagement
RSO	regional security officer
SWATH	small waterplane-area twin-hull
TAO	tactical action officer
UAV	unmanned aerial vehicle
URE	unintended radiated emissions
VBSS	visit, board, search, and seizure
XO	executive officer

PART I

DAY 1

Trincomalee, Sri Lanka

"The sun is setting. Maybe they won't come. Maybe they lied," the younger naval officer said to his admiral.

"No. They have never lied before," the admiral said wearily. "They will attack." He turned his pipe upside down and tapped out the ashes against the steel railing of the bridge wing. The embers fizzled into the calm water below. The Sri Lankan admiral had taken every precaution possible in the eighteen hours since the warning had been issued. The notice had been short, clear, and concise: "Our fleet will attack your ports tomorrow."

Like his counterparts to the south in Galle and in the west coast port of Colombo, he took immediate action, closing the harbor of Trincomalee, Sri Lanka's northeasternmost naval port. Safely sealed inside were scores of small boats, several fishing vessels undergoing repair, and a few sailboats fitted out for global cruising with navigational radar and small, wind-powered generators attached to the stern. These were likely Western retirees fulfilling a life dream to sail the world. He had often seen their like sailing around the Bay of Bengal, intent on their pleasure and oblivious to danger. Some had even defied warnings in the western Indian Ocean during the height of the Somali piracy attacks and had been captured and ransomed; a few were killed. The admiral viewed their irresponsibility as the arrogance of a fading Western culture. They expected the world to be theirs—free of the dangers others had to face daily. The Westerners' elegant sailboats were easy to distinguish from the local sailboats that dotted the second largest natural harbor in the world.

The harbor—and northeastern Sri Lanka in general—had long been under the influence of Europeans, but the region was on the cusp of a major change. It was the admiral's job to prepare Trincomalee for that change as Chinese workers cleared hundreds of acres for a major new shipping terminal. His staff had only two days before given him the itinerary for a series of meetings between representatives of Sri Lanka and China to determine how security would be established and maintained. They had not even had the first introductory meeting.

He looked around the vast harbor, focusing on the piers where several merchant ships remained, denied departure from the harbor. The shipping companies were outraged about his decision; every unnecessary day in port meant a loss in profits. A dozen more inbound merchant ships, mostly freighters, had chosen to wait out the threat by anchoring outside the harbor. The Sri Lankan government had issued an advisory to all vessels approaching the nation's ports of the threat, but many fishing boats, trawlers, and merchant ships had continued on course for Trincomalee. Each would have to be inspected before they were allowed to enter the harbor, but he had too few ships and men to adequately search them. They would simply have to wait outside until the threat ended.

Three of the smaller patrol craft in his squadron maneuvered back and forth along the five-hundred-yard-wide harbor opening. The admiral had ordered one of his Sa'ar 4–class boats to remain on station half a mile outside the harbor entrance while his own ship, SLNS *Sayura*, operated with the patrol craft. His helicopters remained on standby. He knew this enemy and the type of ships they had used in the past, and he had defeated them then. No invaders would enter Trincomalee on his watch.

The cloudbank behind him blazed orange and then faded to pink as the sun sank behind the hillside. His tension grew. Without the defensive advantage of daylight, his men would have to be extra vigilant for craft approaching the harbor. But the admiral still had four technological advantages: the surface ship radar on each of his squadron's vessels, the patrol planes circling above, the new networked communications that had been installed on each of his ships, and advanced onboard computers. A small guerilla force seeking to enter and destroy the harbor simply could not overcome those modern advantages.

The admiral walked inside the pilothouse and checked the radar screen. The surface contacts outside the harbor continued to approach Trincomalee. Probably fishing boats and freighters expecting to unload and pick up cargo. A pattern emerged on the screen—two distinct lines of contacts, one ship behind the other, following the traditional shipping lanes and anticipating the course corrections at the first markers for the channel. On the bridge-to-bridge radio he heard the captain of his outermost ship calling to the merchant captains and advising them where to anchor. The dots that were the freighters separated and slowed. Other contacts approached the harbor more chaotically—fishermen avoiding the larger freighters as they returned home, as they and their fathers and their fathers' fathers had done for hundreds of years. Somewhere out there or beyond, the insurgents were preparing their attack.

Dozens of voices began crowding the radio waves. One belonged to the captain of SLNS *Nandimithra*. Freighter captains began to chatter. Then the fishermen chimed in. Too many voices. Music began to play over someone's open microphone. The cacophony continued to rise until individual voices were no longer recognizable. The admiral lifted the binoculars hanging around his neck and focused on the three smaller patrol craft to ensure their guns were manned, then turned to the sailor manning the onboard communications terminal. "Are we up on chat with the squadron?" he asked, referring to the instant messaging system in the combat information center.

"Yes, Admiral," the sailor quickly replied.

"Pull *Nandimithra* back to the harbor entrance and have her take up station one hundred yards to our starboard."

"Aye, sir." The sailor quickly typed the command.

The admiral turned down the volume on the radio. In the sudden quiet he heard a sound through the open hatch. He stepped onto the bridge wing to listen, his aide dutifully following. The harbor around him was as eerily silent as the radio channel was disturbingly dissonant. On land, he knew, the army was patrolling the streets and the citizens had been directed to remain in their homes. Then he heard it again. A bell tolled slowly into the silence, the sound echoing across the calm water of the harbor. The bell became louder, calling out a warning in the waning light. He lifted his binoculars again and scanned the shoreline, stopping at Konesar Malai, a hill overlooking the harbor. He knew only one structure with a bell in that vicinity—the Koneswaram Kovil Hindu temple, a two-thousand-year-old landmark dating back to the Pandyan Kingdom. A faint light appeared in the bell tower. He needed to contact his army counterpart now to tell him to investigate the tower, but as he was about to reenter the bridge his aide grabbed him by the arm, normally an inexcusable offense.

"Admiral, what is that?" the aide asked, pointing toward the moored sailboats.

The admiral let his binoculars fall as he squinted toward one of the boats. A tiny star appeared atop the mainmast of one of the sailboats and then shot up into the sky, followed by a thin plume of smoke. Seven more stars appeared on seven more masts. One after the other they exploded into blue-green fireworks that blinded the crew manning the .50-caliber weapons and sparkled as they drifted down toward the water. And then again silence. He raced back into the bridge towing his aide, who was still clinging to his arm in shock.

"Sailor," he said, approaching the communications terminal, "tell the squadron—" He stopped as he noticed the sailor furiously pounding keys, yelling something into his mike. "What is it?"

"Sir, I am sorry, but we're having difficulty. The chat room just went dead. I'm trying to reestablish contact, but nothing is working."

The admiral noticed something else. The radio was now silent as well. "Who turned off the radio?" he barked. No one responded. He turned up the volume, but there was nothing. He picked up the mike himself and called to one of his ships. Nothing.

Another sailor slammed his fist on the radar console.

"What now?" the admiral asked.

"Sir, it's not working. I can't see anything on the radar. We've lost all contacts."

And then the admiral realized that every technological advantage he had relied on to defend the harbor was gone and there was little he could do. The Sea Tigers were coming, just as they said they would.

Highland Maritime Defense Training Facility, Scotland

Connor Stark sucked air into his lungs, recognizing that he was at the point of exhaustion and unable to react in time to deflect the next blow. He had held off his opponent for nearly four minutes, an unheard of feat. Martial arts battles were usually over in less than a minute. The blows had to be quick, the counterblows even quicker. The slightest mistake could mean death. Stark had an inch in height over his opponent and a longer reach, but he was a few years older and an eternity slower. The man he faced had spent most of his life honing his skills as a fighter. Beads of sweat glistened on the man's dark, bald head as he himself began to strain from the effort. Onlookers formed a ring around them. Stark heard a few taking bets; most of the money was on his opponent.

Both men took a step backward to rest a moment and gain enough strength for one last melee that would determine the victor. Neither took his eyes off the other. A glance down or away or even an eye blink could determine who won. But Stark was tired, and his head drooped just long enough for the other man to seize the advantage.

The man rapidly took two steps forward and hit Stark with a left uppercut and a quick right jab. Blood poured from Stark's nose and a cut near his right eye. The man followed up by tackling Stark and taking him to the ground. He kneeled on Stark's chest, grabbed the neck of Stark's t-shirt with his left hand, and cocked his right arm for the final blow. He paused when Stark managed to open his left eye.

Stark summoned the strength to whisper up to his victorious opponent: "Had enough, Gunny?"

"Nah. I have a couple rounds left in me, Skipper," responded the recently retired Marine before releasing Stark's shirt and letting him slump back to the mat. "Four minutes, seventeen seconds," Gunny Willis said, looking at the clock in the training room. "Way too long. We'll work on your stamina more, but you have got to finish a fight a lot quicker than that, especially if you're fighting a young'un. I know you've been in a few scraps, but you've been lucky."

At this moment Stark didn't feel lucky. "So what's your recommendation of the day?" he asked.

"Get help."

"Thanks a lot, Gunny."

"I'm serious, Skipper. Nothing wrong with bringing a knife or a few other aids to a fight."

The team's medic approached Stark with a towel to wipe away the blood and then helped him stagger over to a chair so he could repair the damage to Stark's face. When he had finished, Stark slumped over, still breathing heavily, and waited for his heart rate to slow. The employees of Highland Maritime Defense who had watched the session exchanged a few pounds or euros to settle their bets and returned to their own workouts. The old man had heart, they knew, but heart alone wouldn't necessarily win a fight—especially against the gunny.

When Stark rose to leave, the men stopped what they were doing and in one voice began to recite Saint Barton's Ode. Stark had said it once after a particularly grueling training session, and Willis, the firm's training officer, had instituted it as their mantra. "I am hurt," they all said in unison, "but I am not slain. I will lay me down and bleed awhile, then I'll rise to fight again."

The medic checked Stark's eyes with a flashlight, found nothing alarming, and released him to return to town. A couple of the firm's employees—a former SEAL and a former Royal Marine—accepted Stark's invitation for a ride back from the island, which served as both Highland Maritime's headquarters and its training site. The only signs of habitation visible as they walked across the small, windswept island were the five piers and a shooting range, gymnasium, classroom, office, and dormitory compound. The three boarded Stark's 345 Conquest Whaler, and Stark took the helm as the others cast off.

Stark had founded Highland Maritime Defense a few years before as an arm of his friend Bill Maddox's firm to provide security for its construction teams in high-threat regions. Highland Maritime had since grown into one of the world's premier private security firms. Stark had modeled its operations on the French Foreign Legion, a multinational group with a rigid code of conduct, rather than the fly-by-night private security companies that had emerged from the Iraq and Afghanistan wars. The world was becoming a far more dangerous place as Western navies ceded their traditional roles on the high seas. Highland Maritime was there to stabilize situations where it could.

The three Mercury outboards roared as the Whaler passed two of Highland's training craft. His passengers took seats in the cabin and settled in with a deck of cards to pass the time. As the boat reached the last channel marker, Stark eased the throttles forward, keeping an eye out for other boats and bad weather, always a possibility in this part of the world despite the clear late-afternoon sky. Stark looked at his watch as the boat slowly gained speed through the calm seas. He had made this run enough times in various weather conditions to know that if boat traffic remained light he could cross the ten miles of ocean and be tied up in Ullapool within thirty minutes.

Stark squinted as he searched for potential hazards in the water, relying on his left eye because Doc had put a couple of stitches above his right eyebrow after the training session. Maggie was certain to notice, and he began to wish he had remained in the Highland dormitory for the next couple of nights.

Stark throttled back as the Whaler approached several sailboats moored in the harbor; the engines eased from a roar to a gentle hum. The men on the decks of the fishing boats stopped their work and waved as he passed. He made the final turn into the line of slips, reversing the engines as he passed his own slip and spinning the wheel just enough to get the boat lined up. His passengers came out of the cabin and positioned themselves on each side as Stark edged the boat forward and let momentum bring it in. The men grabbed the lines and tied them to the appropriate cleats, then took their overnight bags, thanked Stark, and made their way into town.

Stark secured the Whaler in its slip and grabbed his own backpack, then set it and himself down, suddenly exhausted as the day's training caught up with him. He was already sore. That would get worse, he knew. He tried to remember how effortless training had seemed back when he competed for the U.S. Olympic pentathlon team. But that was more than twenty-five years ago. He hated growing old, but the alternative wasn't exactly attractive. He took a deep breath and closed his eyes as he listened to the harbor. The gentle slap of water against hulls and the squeaking of wet lines were the only sounds he heard. Few tourists ventured to picturesque Ullapool in winter. The peace and the cold sea air rejuvenated him enough to stand and walk the hundred yards to the Friar John Cor pub across the road from the dock.

The door creaked as he opened it. The pub, as usual, was full of locals. Mack was behind the bar chatting with a couple of regulars as they watched a football game on the overhead television screen. Maggie was at a table taking an order from a customer. She turned her head toward the creaking door and smiled at Stark. The smile faded when her eyes drifted to his wounds. She turned back to the customer and then moved toward the kitchen, keeping her back to Stark. As she passed the bar she told the bartender sharply: "Mack, get 'im a Talisker and throw it in his face." Mack poured the Talisker and was about to dutifully comply when Stark shot him the look; Mack thought better of it and drank the whisky himself.

Stark turned away to hide his smile. In the two years he and Maggie had been together he had learned not to expect subtlety from her. She would make him suffer for this, but only because she cared for him.

Mullaitivu District, Sri Lanka

"Son of a bitch," Melanie Arden groaned as she slid to a stop on the jungle floor. Walking along the unstable ridgeline hadn't been the wisest thing to do after the recent rainfall. She had been trying to get a better view of the village, but five feet from the edge the dirt and mud gave way, taking her down thirty feet of hillside and sending her sliding and scraping against exposed roots. She lay there stunned for a few minutes. The birdcalls that usually filled the jungle had gone silent when she fell. After a brief interruption the birds picked up again, bringing Melanie back to her senses.

She stood up carefully and took stock. No pain in her ankles or legs, and both arms still worked. A few scrapes and cuts, but nothing serious, thank God. Her backpack was nearby, but one of the zippers had broken when she fell, releasing the pocket's contents all the way down the hillside. She sighed when she recalled what had been in that pocket. The first aid kit was likely to be close to the top of the hill because it had been the last item she stowed. Holding onto roots and tree trunks Melanie carefully made her way back up the hill, picking up her things as she went and stuffing them in her cargo pockets. The wet soil gave way frequently beneath her feet.

It took her nearly fifteen minutes of repeated attempts to reach the top. The white first aid kit was easy to find. She brushed away some leaves and found her Swiss Army knife. A few MREs—Meals Ready to Eat—were below it. She pocketed the knife and then collected the kit and food, stuffing them hastily into the backpack.

Still dizzy from her fall, she rose and leaned against a tree as she tried to recall what else had been in that backpack pocket. The soil beneath the tree gave way, and she crashed down the slope to the bottom again. Unable to slow her slide this time, she tumbled head over heels the last ten feet and came to rest with her sternum against a medium-sized rock. Gasping for air, Melanie slowly rolled to one side, wrapped her arms around her midsection, and threw up the cold soup she had eaten just before she started on the path. She gingerly rose. *You've been through worse,* she told herself. There was no thought of turning back. This was something she had to do.

In her brief view of the village from the ridge she had spotted several dozen houses and a narrow river, but no people. It was still midmorning, and she decided to take time to rest before moving on. When she finally caught her breath, she opened the first aid kit and applied Neosporin to her larger abrasions, then covered them with gauze and secured them with bandages. She felt around her chest and knew from past experience as a rugby player that she hadn't cracked any ribs. That was lucky. A couple of aspirin might help dull the pain of her injuries, but she knew it would be a couple of days before it went away.

Melanie started to reach around to the right side of her belt but stopped when pain lanced through her chest. Instead, she unbuckled her belt and pulled it around until one of her canteens was close enough to grab with minimal pain. She took a swig and then poured a little on her face and let it drip over her chin and chest. Moving as little as possible she checked the rest of the contents of the backpack. The camera and video recorder were still operational. The digital audio recorder also still worked; her extra set of clothes had cushioned them during the fall. Most of her batteries seemed to be secure. She repacked the backpack, redistributing the contents of the broken pocket.

A half hour later she felt rested enough to begin walking toward the village. Slipping her arms through the backpack straps, she again felt the sharp pain in her sternum but soldiered through it. She took a deep breath and began the march under clear skies and the midmorning sun.

She was still a few hundred yards away from the huts when she noticed the first sign that all was not well. This was a farming village. The sun was well above the mountain ridge to the east, and yet there were no animals in the pens and no people working in the fields. Even the skies were empty of birds.

Melanie approached the first home, a primitive shack, and knocked on the outer wall. "Hello?" she called out, coughing with the second syllable as her sternum demanded that she be more careful. She knocked again. Nothing. The door was ajar, so she pushed it inward and edged inside. She gagged when the stench hit her nostrils. Rotting food, unidentifiable now, sat on the table. To her left was an unmade bed. She pressed forward through the kitchen to a back room. This bedroom too was empty. There was nothing on the bed except old wrinkled sheets. She made her way back out and went to the next hut.

Melanie checked another dozen huts on her way to the center of the village. All were the same—empty houses, rotting food, dust, insects, and a few small rodents. But no people. This village of forty or so houses should have had about two hundred people. She took photographs of the empty homes and the ghost village.

One building—slightly larger and better kept—stood out among the others. It appeared to be some sort of community center, or as close to one as a village this size could muster. It had been ransacked, though she couldn't imagine anyone finding much of value here. She left the building and walked to the other side of the village, where she found a patch of loose dirt and mud about thirty yards long and ten yards wide. Her heart sank. She had seen patches like these in Rwanda and Bosnia. She knew where the villagers were.

Melanie shifted her backpack to the ground and pulled out binoculars, checking the entire perimeter. She was alone. She set the binoculars aside and looked around for something to use as a shovel. She had to make do with a broken wooden chair she found inside the central building. She didn't have to dig deep. She saw the maggots almost right away. The bodies weren't even wrapped. She continued moving the soil aside until she had exposed dozens—all adults—breathing through her mouth to avoid passing out from the disgusting odor of rotting flesh emanating from the ground. Then she set aside her makeshift shovel, adjusted the camera settings, and began to take pictures and video.

When she was done, she moved the mud and dirt back over the bodies, ignoring the pain in her chest. And then she sat back against the wall of the community building and did something she was sure no one had yet done or would do—she cried for them.

Trincomalee

Vanni had become accustomed to the throngs that followed him everywhere—supporters and those just curious to see him. They had never seen his photograph, but they all knew who he was. In each town, village, and hamlet they spoke his name. Some spoke it in awe, some in fondness, and some in fear; but they all spoke it.

No one spoke his name here, though. He was alone and away from his home region. He had chosen not to travel with a retinue of sycophants or guards. Alone and in the clothes of a common man he was free to walk the streets of Trincomalee, to speak with the street vendors about their problems with the corrupt government, to watch the poor mothers with their children in rags—people thrust into the background where they would not offend the city's more affluent residents. Here he was a ghost—transparent to the politicians and, more important, invisible to the military, who had no idea what he was about to unleash upon them. He was free to observe his plan, his people, and his ships.

He nodded as the bell atop the promontory began to toll. A few worshippers were inside the temple. Outside, tourists from China, Japan, and Europe took photographs of the temple's famous statues and other ornamentation or of each other. Vanni took care not to appear in any photo. He reflected that the tourists probably didn't know that this wasn't the original Koneswaram Kovil temple; that had been destroyed four centuries ago. They probably wouldn't have cared if they did. This was merely another place tourists went. He didn't care about them either. The Chinese, the Europeans, the Americans—none of them concerned him. At this moment only the Sri Lankan leadership mattered.

Vanni crouched in front of a large rock in front of the temple on the Konesar Malai overlook and rested his back against it as he pulled out his binoculars. Surveying Gokarna Bay, he identified his boats; the first ones to come had arrived weeks before and had been safely moored ever since. At first appearance the sailboats were no different from the other pleasure boats in the harbor. All were sloops or ketches with roller-furling jibs. Their mainsails were lashed to the booms with lazy jacks. Only an observant mariner would have noticed the absence of lines from the tack to the head—a key part of a sailboat's rigging. Even someone who took a closer look wouldn't have seen the rockets hidden inside the masts. They weren't complicated rockets capable of delivering warheads to another continent. These were simple devices with composite propellants from rockets modeled on those used by the Lebanese Hezbollah against Israel. All they had to do was carry a five-pound payload and reach an altitude of a few hundred yards.

Vanni watched the Sri Lankan navy ships at the entrance of the bay. All of them were facing out to sea. He had told them his fleet would attack, and they did as he expected. They secured the entrance to the harbor and prepared for an invasion from outside.

When the bell tolled again, the first rocket launched from one of the moored sailboats. Then a second launched and a third. After each launch, the boat's crew left their sailboat and got into a smaller boat. When the rockets reached a preset altitude, they exploded in blue-green sparkles, one after the other. Vanni looked down from the hilltop and noticed cars stopping in the middle of the road near the docks. Only a few did not stop—those were probably older vehicles or diesel trucks. He focused his binoculars on the Sri Lankan navy ships and the other ships approaching the harbor. Until a few minutes ago they had been operating in a well-coordinated pattern directed by electronic communications. The explosions blocked the communications and left the ships powerless and rudderless.

The boats of Vanni's second squadron, in contrast, were very well coordinated. Each of the small boats that had left the sailboats, under the command of a very loyal and committed man, rowed swiftly toward a Sri Lankan navy ship. The men on the ships finally recognized the threat and were trying to mount a defense, but they lacked even internal communications—even the Phalanx weapon system on their largest ship was unresponsive.

A composite turtle shell covered each small boat, so the few small arms that managed to hit the boats glanced off harmlessly. Slowly, relentlessly, they came on. The crews of the navy ships would only watch in helpless horror as they approached. The first small boat, with a wedge-shaped explosive charge in its prow, slammed against the largest ship. The resulting explosion split the ship in half. Within a minute the other suicide boats had destroyed the other Sri Lankan navy ships.

The Trincomalee waterfront was a chaotic scene of screaming people shocked by the explosions and the destruction in the harbor. Few seemed to realize yet that their cars, radios, and televisions had stopped working. The tourists tried using the cameras on their smart phones to no avail. Technology had been used to silence technology.

Vanni stood and took a last look at the harbor to admire his work. He recognized this was only the first round in the new war. But it was a promising start. He walked over to his bicycle and pedaled away through the pandemonium he had caused, an invisible man in a now very visible war.

Ullapool, Scotland

Stark returned to the pub just as the last guests were leaving. Mack was cleaning up the bar and tables for the next day.

"Maggie in the kitchen, Mack?"

"Yep. Watch yerself, Connor," Mack whispered. "She's been in a mood since she saw you earlier."

Stark wanted to tell him to go home, that he would help Maggie close, but he had tried that—once. When Maggie found out, she made it clear that she ran the pub, and Connor had lost his license to walk into the kitchen or go behind the bar. Maggie, he sometimes thought, would have been a hell of a chief petty officer. He took a seat on a stool at the middle of the bar and eyed the wall of heroes behind it. Above the mirror were photos of Ullapool men who had gone off to war and never returned, beginning with the Boer War a century before and continuing through the two world wars, the Falkland Islands War, and right up to the Iraq war. They were the fathers, brothers, sons, husbands, fiancés, and boyfriends of Ullapool. Would his photo have been placed there had things ended differently in Yemen? He didn't think it was likely. He had not been raised in Ullapool—and he had been on duty in the U.S. Navy, not the Royal Navy.

"The new boys seem good. They're well behaved when they're here," Mack said as he dried clean pilsner glasses.

"Glad to hear it, Mack," Stark replied. He hired the best for Highland Maritime, unlike some of his competitors. Each was well vetted. Plus, an applicant had to know at least one person with the security firm to even get an interview. No one was a complete stranger.

The television was still on but the audio was off. The late evening Sky News report was broadcasting a story about some attacks in Sri Lanka.

"Can you turn on the volume, Mack?"

Mack complied, but the announcer was already halfway through the story. The same images were used in a loop. As best Stark could tell, Tamil Sea Tigers had sunk most of Sri Lanka's navy in a single day in the ports of Colombo, Galle, and Trincomalee. The anchor interviewed an analyst from a London think tank who called it one of the most significant and successfully coordinated maritime attacks in history. It was also a surprise. Sri Lankan forces had defeated the Tamil Tigers several years before, marking the end of the Sri Lankan civil war. No one had seen this coming.

Maggie walked through the swinging doors from the kitchen and caught Connor's eye—the one that still bore the mark of Gunny's work earlier in the day. "Go home, Mack, and kiss the little ones for me," she said, then took the remote control and turned off the television.

"Aye, girl. See you in the morning. Connor." He nodded. Stark nodded back.

Maggie's long red ponytail swung as she came around the bar and sat down next to Stark. "When are you going to stop trying to be a hero and let the young lads do the work?" It was less a question than an order.

"I need to train with them. I need to work with them. And I always have to be ready. Remember that surprise a few months ago at the dock?"

She didn't need to be reminded. Three Somalis had been sent to Ullapool to kill Connor, and while he had managed to take out two of them, the third might have succeeded had Maggie not arrived and made good use of a handy oar.

"Are you still leaving the day after tomorrow?"

"I have to," he said. "I won't be gone long. The new boat has been fitting out in India, and I need to be there for the final work. The crew's been there for two months. I'll take Gunny and the new security team with me."

"Why you?"

"Because I'm the one who bought the ship. And I know her better than anyone. I'll take her for a shakedown cruise, make sure everything works, and as soon as we arrive in the Gulf of Aden I'll hand her off to our team there and come home. Three weeks at most."

Maggie rose. Even without her high-heeled boots she was an imposing figure. She was tall for a woman—only a few inches shorter than Stark's six feet—and well built, but it was just as much her attitude as her size. Honest and forthright, she rarely backed down from an argument. That was one of the reasons he respected her. That was one of the reasons he loved her.

She went behind the bar, ostensibly to throw a damp towel into the laundry basket, but he knew it was to put the physical barrier of the bar between them.

"I don't need this," she said. "Look at what happened last time—when those military people came and took you away to Yemen. You might have died."

Maggie still didn't know the full story of what had happened there. She had overheard some of the Highland Maritime personnel mention the loss of the firm's ship *Kirkwall* with nearly all hands. But Connor had never told her about the firefight in Old Mar'ib or the subsequent battle when he found himself in command of a Navy cruiser facing down the forces of the man who wanted to seize control of Yemen. She hadn't asked, and he thought it best not to volunteer the information. She must have had some idea, though, because the wounds on his body, including a deep scar on his leg, were impossible to keep hidden.

"It's just a simple cruise," he said patiently. "We leave India for Yemen. I'll have teams on board, including Gunny Willis, if anything comes up. And this is a really good ship. She's different from anything Highland Maritime has had so far."

"Still. You shouldn't be doing this anymore," she said, her gaze flicking up to the wall of dead heroes.

She had never told Stark about the photos. He had learned about them from Mack on his first night in Ullapool. One photo—that of a Royal Navy lieutenant killed when HMS *Coventry* sank at the Falklands—was of her father. Another photo—that of a Royal Marine killed in Iraq—was of her only brother. Like Maggie, they hadn't been people to back down from a fight. But they had died far from home. From now on she wanted to keep her family close. And Ullapool was where Connor should be if he wanted to be her family.

"I won't be gone long, Maggie. Really."

"If your picture goes up on that wall, I'll kill you myself."

Connor's lips quirked up in a half smile. He knew better than to point out that if his photo was on the wall, he was already dead.

Maggie took a long look at Connor, then bent over and unlocked a drawer. She pulled out a knife—more accurately, a *sgian dubh*, a traditional Scottish weapon. The antique scabbard was made of wood, leather, and silver. On the hilt was her family's clan crest, a thistle above a crossed sword and pen. The six-pronged ornament at the top of the hilt held a brownish-gray piece of quartz—a cairngorm.

"Then you'll take this," she said. "For luck. Just in case."

"Just in case what?"

"Just in case you face someone like Gunny Willis out there and you can't duck in time. And don't lose it," she snapped.

He admired the *sgian dubh* for a few seconds, then returned it to its scabbard and slipped it down inside his right boot. For luck.

Singapore

He cursed the minor State Department bureaucrat who had forced him to travel coach from Washington, D.C.—and at the back of the plane, no less. A full eighteen hours huddled with the masses—trapped next to the snoring seatmate, the stench emanating from the restroom a few feet away, the sleepless child who kept kicking the back of his seat, the bland airline food and the wine that tasted as if it had been fermented in a barn. He hadn't drunk more than a sip from the glass when the child behind him had kicked the seat, jogging his elbow and spilling cheap wine on his impeccable slacks. The flight attendant was too busy responding to other complaining passengers to see him trying to ask for towels to dry himself. Unable to waken his seatmate, he sat like a baby in damp diapers for another hour until they landed.

Damien Golzari was decidedly unhappy. He skulked at the baggage carousel until his black bag appeared. Then he removed himself to the closest restroom, changed his trousers, and made his way to the taxi stand. Fortunately the line was short and he waited only a minute for his turn.

"What hotel?" the cab driver asked.

"None. Take me to the United States embassy," Golzari replied without looking up as he texted his contact. It was only six-thirty in the morning, and the streets of Singapore were not yet crowded by rush hour traffic.

Golzari got out at the embassy gate and showed his badge to the Marine guard. As he was slipping the wallet back into his jacket pocket a stern-looking woman with fair skin and auburn hair came through the embassy entrance. "Agent Kelly, I presume?"

"You presume correctly, Agent Golzari. Welcome to Singapore. Follow me."

She took him inside and paused before a locked door, which she asked the secretary to unlock. Golzari set his bag down in the hallway and stepped into the nondescript office. Agent Kelly and the secretary followed him inside and waited silently as Golzari looked around.

"When was the last time he was in here?" Golzari asked.

"Two days ago. He left at ten a.m.," the secretary replied.

Golzari sat in the chair and examined the desktop for anything out of the ordinary. Nothing. A few pages of standard State Department bureaucratic forms were halfway completed. He ignored the stack in the man's in box. Those would have come in afterward. Golzari paused when his gaze landed on the family photos on the desk. One photo was of the man's wife and son. Golzari had never met the boy, but he remembered meeting the wife when she was pregnant.

"Did you know Special Agent Blake?" Agent Kelly asked.

Golzari reflected for a moment. "Yes. Yes, I did. We were classmates at Glynco."

Agent Kelly immediately understood. Glynco, Georgia, was the location of FLETC—the Federal Law Enforcement Training Center.

Bill Blake had been a former police officer, just like Golzari. He was also one of the few classmates not to mock Golzari's slight British accent, the result of his early education in England.

"Do you need to go to the morgue?" Kelly asked.

"Has the autopsy been performed?"

"Yes. I have the full report here," Kelly said, handing Golzari a packet. Golzari thumbed through the papers and the photos.

"Looks thorough," Golzari observed. "I see no reason to go there. Would you concur?"

"Yeah. He was killed with two shots in the chest and one in the head. All at close range."

"Anything found on the body?" Golzari asked. The young secretary gasped when Golzari coldly said "the body." Holding a hand over her mouth she darted down the hall.

"Sorry, Agent Golzari. She's had a tough time since we found him. It's her first overseas assignment for the State Department, and Blake was her first boss,"

Kelly explained. "And to answer your question, there was nothing on him. Literally. Not even a shred of clothing. He had been killed and dumped naked near the zoo. The embassies got a report that a Caucasian male was found yesterday morning. That's when we found out who it was. I identified him."

"Singapore has a lot of cameras. Did you check with the police?"

"Yes. He was dumped in a blind spot. No cameras."

"So it was premeditated. The killers picked the spot because they knew they wouldn't be seen." Golzari looked back down at the autopsy report. "And he was shot with a .45-caliber pistol. I presume no pistol was found nearby?"

"We did a sweep of the area. Nothing."

"So we know how he died and where he was found. Now I just have to find out where he was killed and why. Do you think the secretary could pull herself together long enough to help me get access to his computer files?"

"Sure, I'll get her."

Golzari wasn't expecting to find much. Bill Blake had expressed a distinct aversion to computers when they were at FLETC together, preferring telephone calls to e-mails and pens to keyboards. In that way Blake reminded him of another former associate of sorts, Connor Stark. The mercenary.

Golzari thumbed through a couple of small notepads filled with Blake's scribbles. The second to the last page had a few phone numbers—all from around Washington, D.C. On a whim he called the last number. It was late in the afternoon in the capital.

"HSI Fraud. Lowell."

Homeland Security Investigations, Fraud Division. Well, Golzari thought, *so I've reached someone in the bureaucracy.* "Yes, this is Diplomatic Security Special Agent Damien Golzari. I'm calling you from Singapore."

"Singapore? I thought Blake was working this."

"Not at the moment," Golzari replied. "I was just looking for the paperwork on this and can't find much to go on."

"Well," the HSI agent explained, "it's pretty simple. A few days ago we were asked by the Office of Export Control at the Department of Commerce to check into a license for a research lab in Singapore. I talked to our Diplomatic Security liaison here and he gave me the e-mail for the RSO there—Blake—to check with the lab."

"Why did Export Control want to know about it?"

"They said they approved the shipment of some lab equipment but they never got confirmation it arrived."

"OK. Look, we've had problems with some files. Could you resend whatever you have about this lab to the RSO secretary here?"

"Sure thing, but it'll have to wait until tomorrow morning. I gave it to my secretary to secure, and she's already gone home for the day."

"I understand." Actually, he didn't. Golzari had never understood that cases could be solved and wars won despite small bureaucratic delays and the eight-hour workday. Golzari's workday had no end. Morning, noon, and through the night he was always on call, always on the move. That was one of the many reasons why his two brief marriages had failed early in his career. "In the meantime, Howell, is there any information you can recall that might be helpful here?"

"Ah, not much. I processed it real quickly. The only thing I remember is the name of the lab. Academic Solutions."

"Excellent. I'll start with that. Thanks for your help."

"Yeah, no problem."

Kelly returned with the secretary, who was still wiping away tears with a wad of tissues.

"I need your help," Golzari said. "I know this is difficult for you, but we need to find out what happened to Special Agent Blake. I need a list of his cases, access to his computer, and anything you received for him from a lab called Academic Solutions. Can you do that?" Golzari spoke with as much sympathy as he could muster, which wasn't very much. He had a low tolerance for human weakness.

She nodded and went back to her desk.

"You look tired," Kelly said.

"I feel tired. Long flight."

"Let me guess. Because of the latest Capitol Hill budget battle your department downgraded you from business to coach?"

Golzari nodded once. "And yet they expect us to walk off the plane bright-eyed and ready to work."

"Tell you what," Kelly said. "It'll take a little time to get this stuff for you. Why don't you head to the hotel? You're at the Marriott downtown. Get a couple of hours of rest, clear your mind, and then I'll give you any help you need."

"Thank you. I'll do that." Golzari wasn't happy about any delay at all, but at least it would give him a chance to get his wine-soaked trousers cleaned.

DAY 2

Port of Chennai, India

The khakis, boat shoes, and white long-sleeved cotton shirt Stark wore were an adequate combination for the heat of southeastern Indian weather. The bustling daytime activity at the large port made him cautious. Cranes, vehicles, and people all trying to move cargo and ships as quickly as possible to maximize profit were a dangerous combination. Accidents and injuries—even deaths—were not uncommon in busy ports. Stark slung his large backpack over his shoulder and made his way to one of the smaller piers. Gunny Willis was by his side.

"What do you think, Gunny?"

"No offense, but give me terrain instead of the sea, Skipper. Never liked being on an amphib or in port."

The out-of-the-way pier was just as busy as the rest of the port and the nearby shipyard, though on a demonstrably smaller scale. Dockworkers were loading crates of food and supplies onto an unusually shaped ship that resembled a shoebox with a horizontally pointed bow. The ship's pilothouse sat forward and was offset to port, making her appear lopsided as well. Two men were on the deck watching a crane load pallets. One of them, a tall, burly redhead, caught sight of Stark and Willis and made his way down the ladder to the dock.

"She don't look like much," Willis remarked.

"It's all in how you look, Gunny," Stark said as he leaned across and put one hand on the familiar aluminum hull. "She's a very special ship." *It's good to see you again, old girl,* he thought.

"If she's so special, why did the U.S. Navy get rid of her?"

"Shortsighted flag officers and rice bowls, Gunny. If the Navy had built a whole class of these ships, things might be different. They're small, but they have a lot of potential."

"That's why Highland Maritime bought her? For her potential?" Gunny asked.

"Yeah, potential and more. I commanded her for a few months back in the day when she was first built. I know her. And she's got as much heart as *Kirkwall*," Stark said, referring, Gunny knew, to the Highland Maritime ship lost in the Gulf of Aden in a battle with pirates. "But in the end, it's not the ship but the crew that makes her special."

Stark checked the lines that secured the ship to the pier as the redheaded man reached the end of the gangplank. "Jay, what's the good word?" Stark said, shaking the outthrust hand of Jay Warren, Highland Maritime's utility infielder. Warren was one of the new hires in Highland Maritime—in the non–security operations wing.

"Boss, are we glad you're here!" Warren said, pulling Stark close and embracing him in a bear hug. Gunny Willis frowned at the informality and took a step backward to put himself out of reach. Stark didn't appear too comfortable with it either, but he had learned long ago to give Warren leeway. You had to do that when dealing with a genius.

"I got here as soon as I could, Jay," Stark said, gasping as Warren's giant arms finally released him.

"You have *got* to see the new engines," Warren said enthusiastically. "They work like a dream! She'll be the fastest ship in the Indian Ocean."

"Speed burns fuel fast, Jay."

"I know, I know, usually; but that's the beauty of the new system I installed. We'll get 30 percent more range at top speed," he said, happy as a child with his first bicycle. "I wish we'd thought of it back when we built her. Remember? We talked about it, but the technology just wasn't there yet."

"Thirty percent? This I have to see."

Gunny Willis touched Stark's arm. "Sir, we have company coming," he said as a black limousine approached.

"Jay, this is Gunny Willis," Stark said. "Would you take him on board while I do a meet and greet?"

The limousine stopped a few feet away from Stark, and two men exited from the rear door. One was a military officer; the other was a civilian holding a briefcase.

"It's good to see you again and with another ship," said the officer, extending his arm and clasping Stark's hand warmly.

"Captain Dasgupta, this is a pleasant surprise," Stark greeted the captain. "I hadn't thought to see you on this trip. I appreciate your recommendation that we refit the ship here. This yard completed the work six weeks ahead of schedule."

"We look forward to seeing how she performs," the Indian naval captain said with a smile, "although you understand that my government remains concerned about maritime security companies. Your adherence to our regulations has assured them that Highland Maritime remains on our approved list for now."

"Thank you, Captain. You have my personal assurance that we won't engage in some of the practices of some of our competitors."

"Yes. In fact, that is why I would like to introduce you to Ambassador Adikira of the Democratic Socialist Republic of Sri Lanka," Dasgupta said, gesturing toward his companion.

Stark nodded briefly in respect. "Mr. Ambassador."

"A pleasure, Captain Stark," the slender, swarthy man said politely. "On Captain Dasgupta's recommendation I have come to you with a proposal. You are aware of the recent terrorist attacks on the Sri Lankan navy?"

"I've seen a few news reports about it."

"Then you will know that the Tamil Sea Tigers have returned. They succeeded in destroying most of our fleet. That is no secret. We seek . . . assistance."

"What kind of assistance?" Stark asked warily.

Adikira pulled two sheets of paper from his briefcase and handed them to Stark. The first was in the ambassador's native Sinhalese. The other was formatted the same way but in English. Three words immediately stood out.

"A letter of marque?" Stark asked in disbelief as he read the document.

"We have no ships, Captain Stark, except a few that are in great need of repair. Two American Navy vessels are being temporarily transferred to our government. They will arrive in a few days. I believe the term your government used is 'capacity building.'"

Stark laughed. "Mr. Ambassador, letters of marque haven't been used since the nineteenth century. I'm not sure they're even still legal."

"I assure you they are, Captain Stark," the ambassador said with a smile. The smile faded quickly. "These are difficult times. We need ships and people and very quickly. Captain Dasgupta recommended your firm and you, based on your actions against the Somali pirates."

"I wasn't hunting anyone then. I was just providing security."

"This *is* security," the ambassador said, "the security of our ports and our livelihood. We need you to gather as much information as you can about the Sea Tigers and then provide that intelligence to the new American ships so they can take action."

"That's all?"

"We understand that you are experienced in conducting vessel searches, Captain Stark. We expect that your intelligence gathering will include stopping and searching any ship within our territorial waters."

"Does that include only Sri Lankan vessels?"

"No," he said firmly. "It means any ship."

Stark's face was grave as he thought about that for a moment, considering the implications. What if his men boarded a Russian or even an American-flagged ship? What were Highland Maritime's legal rights? What were the other ships' legal rights?

The ambassador must have noticed Stark's apprehension. "I think I understand your hesitation, Captain Stark. Your ship would operate under Sri Lanka's flag and would fall under our government's jurisdiction. You will also have a Sri Lankan liaison on board to provide additional legitimacy to your activities. He is a commander in our navy—one of the few who escaped the devastation."

"This does not fall within my plans. I am supposed to deliver this ship to the Gulf of Aden for security duty," Stark responded. "Nothing more."

"As you have just said, you are six weeks ahead of schedule."

"That's true, Mr. Ambassador," Stark said. "But I have to pay my men, and fuel isn't free."

"We are prepared to pay your firm very well for this service and will provide an advance. But you must begin as soon as possible. Time is of the essence."

Stark was not at all comfortable with the sudden change in mission, particularly in a region where he had never operated or even planned to be.

"Your military is willing to share information before we begin our search?" Stark asked.

"Of course. You will have access to every bit of knowledge my government has."

"Ambassador, my team would need some time to plan. We'll need supplies for the mission."

"Our naval station in Colombo will provide you with whatever food, fuel, and ammunition you need," Adikira said quickly.

Stark narrowed his eyes. The ambassador was fidgeting. Experienced diplomats didn't do that. And he appeared desperate to hire Stark and the company. *This isn't going to be as easy as he says. Still . . . it would make a good shakedown cruise.* Boardings, if done correctly, were simple procedures so long as the teams were vigilant. And for a little intelligence gathering he would get enough money to pay for the final upgrades on the ship with enough extra to give the crew and security team a bonus.

"I'll give you four weeks of my time, Mr. Ambassador. Perhaps you will join me here tomorrow so we can work out the details of this agreement?"

"Of course," the ambassador said, his relief showing. "Our navy's operations center will coordinate with you on the areas where you will work. Until tomorrow, Captain Stark."

Stark nodded. "Tomorrow."

"I wish you good luck," Captain Dasgupta said, to Stark.

"It won't be the same without you this time," Stark said, and received a knowing grin from the Indian captain.

"Perhaps," Dasgupta said. He turned to the ambassador and gestured toward the limousine, then took Stark's arm and walked out of hearing distance from the ambassador.

"Connor, we are pleased that you have taken this assignment."

"Why? I don't understand."

"Your ship. My navy is impressed with her, but they would like to see how she performs in Sri Lanka. I understand that Highland now owns the ship and the patents. My navy may be interested in building a number of these."

"I'm not in this to make a lot of money. We're just trying to do a job."

"Yes, of course. But we have maritime security concerns, and if we buy the plans from you instead of buying old Russian ships, we both benefit, my friend. The ship's name is not yet painted. How shall I hail you?"

"Don't worry," Stark grinned. "She'll call out to you. Her name is *Syren*."

Singapore

The captain of USS *LeFon*, one of the U.S. Navy's newest destroyers and only six months out of the shipyard, brushed back her wiry blond hair, quickly retied it in a regulation bun, and pulled on her ball cap bearing the ship's crest and motto: "For strength. For courage."

LeFon had been at sea forty-four days without a port visit. Every mariner on board—enlisted and officer—knew what that meant. By Navy tradition and regulations, a beer would be served to each person on the ship in one more day. That was little consolation for a crew within sight of a city famed for its nightlife. Nearly every crewmember had offered to man one of the small boats that went ashore or were conducting antiterrorism force protection duties. *LeFon's* task was a significant responsibility. Off one of the busiest ports in the world, the crew maintained high alert for possible threats. Just this morning the captain had noticed a couple of new gray strands in her blond hair.

Cdr. Jaime Johnson leaned back in the captain's chair on the starboard side of the bridge and held her binoculars tightly against her eyes. The wind had shifted from south to northeast and had slowly pushed the ten-thousand-ton warship like a great horizontal pendulum until her bow was directly facing the city. Johnson counted three dozen containerships under way, all steering well clear of *LeFon*. Johnson double-checked the gun crew below manning the port and starboard bow .50-caliber machine guns. The rising sun to starboard reflected off the water, and Johnson looked back at the starboard watch to make sure he had his sunglasses on so he wouldn't miss anything out there. She trusted her crew, but it never hurt to double-check. Her jaw muscles tightened. She wasn't going to lose another ship or crewmember.

"Ma'am," a baby-faced young ensign said behind her.

"What is it, Ensign?" she said with a smile. She had a soft spot for Bobby Fisk.

"Latest message from Seventh Fleet should be on your screen now," Ensign Fisk said. Johnson pulled the monitor and keyboard closer and typed in her password.

"One more day, ma'am," Fisk said. "Think Seventh Fleet will let us pull into port and grant us liberty instead?"

"I doubt it," she said, adding after a moment, "in fact, I'm sure that's not going to happen. Looks like we're leaving. We're escorting two littoral combat ships to Sri Lanka. We get under way first thing tomorrow morning."

"Ma'am, terrorists there just wiped out their navy. Does this mean we're going to war?" Bobby asked that only to clarify their mission. He had been in battle before. That action had tempered the young man's desire to go to war, but it had also left him far better prepared if he and his ship were to engage in combat.

"No, Mr. Fisk, I think we're staying out of this one," Johnson said with a laugh. "The Navy is giving the ships to Sri Lanka, and they have skeleton crews of Sri Lankan officers and sailors. A U.S. Navy flag officer is coming along to supervise the changeover. *LeFon* is just the shepherd. Looks like the admiral will be on board with us until we arrive in Sri Lanka. Huh, no name in the message."

"Is that unusual, Captain?"

"Not necessarily, but it would be nice to know so we can prepare. Flag officers all have their idiosyncrasies."

The radio crackled as she spoke. The radio operator lifted his headphones momentarily to say, "Captain, an admiral is inbound."

"Already? The message said they aren't supposed to be here for a few hours."

"Sorry, Captain, that's all we know. The RHIB just left the seawall and should be here in about twenty minutes," the operator replied.

"Damn it, is a little freaking common courtesy unreasonable?" she muttered under her breath. "Bobby, call down and have them make sure the VIP stateroom is ready." There was little reason it wouldn't be. The stateroom was never used unless there was a dignitary or senior officer on board.

Johnson made her way across the bridge to the 1MC—the shipwide radio. "Good morning, LeFon. I know you'll be disappointed, but we weigh anchor at 0700 tomorrow on a temporary assignment. The Supply Department will provide one beer per person to those who wish it at tomorrow evening's meal. You'll enjoy it. Before we left San Diego I replaced the bottom-shelf beer the Navy provides with Guinness—for strength. Now, attend to your duties. We have a flag officer arriving in a few minutes. Show the admiral what I already know—LeFon is the finest ship and crew in the fleet. Have a good day and live your profession. LeFon Actual, out." Even through the bulkheads she heard the crew explode in applause and cheers.

Johnson, Fisk, the navigator, and the quartermaster pored over the charts of the harbor and the Strait of Malacca as they sipped freshly brewed coffee. The starboard watch entered the bridge with her binoculars in hand.

"Captain, one of our small boats is arriving."

Johnson checked her watch. Had the RHIB been on full throttle the whole way? She grabbed her binoculars as Fisk followed her to the bridge wing. She saw the small boat only three hundred yards from their anchorage, and it was, as she suspected, on full throttle. What the hell was her small boat crew thinking? She brought the binoculars up and focused on the approaching boat. Something was odd about the crew. They weren't positioned as her boat crews were instructed to be, they were coming in too fast, and they hadn't notified the ship when they were at four hundred yards. There was one more person on board than normal—it had to be the arriving admiral. But why was the boat crew disobeying her instructions? Her mind flashed back briefly to the events on *Kirkwall*, when an incoming small boat had spelled doom to most of her crew.

"Bobby, hail them!" she ordered. Then she yelled to the bow gun crews: "Train weapons on that small boat." They immediately did as she directed.

"Nothing from the small boat, ma'am."

She took the hand-held radio. "This is Warship 125. Small boat, you are on a direct course with us. Veer off now or we will fire."

The boat slowed and veered to port. Through the binoculars she saw the passenger flailing his arms and yelling at her boat crew. The small boat's commander reached for the radio.

"Warship 125, this is *Tomcat*, requesting permission to come alongside with our passenger."

Johnson breathed a sigh of relief, then ordered Bobby to give permission and called to the gun crews to stand down.

Bobby stood close to Johnson on the bridge wing and pulled up his own binoculars. When the boat's occupants came into focus he gasped. "Oh, fuck," he said aloud.

Johnson was shocked. She had *never* heard Bobby curse, not even a "damn." The baby-faced ensign looked and acted like a choirboy. "What's the problem, Ensign Fisk?" The boat was now only fifty yards away.

"That admiral, ma'am. I mean . . . I didn't realize he made flag. I don't know how he could have. And he's coming here. And I'm here. Oh, fuck, ma'am. I'm screwed."

"You're not making any sense. What the hell's the matter?"

"It's him, ma'am. Daniel Rossberg. He was my CO on *Bennington* last year."

"Oh, my God," she said. "Maybe I shouldn't have stood down the gun crews."

Malacca Strait

The cargo ship *Nanjing Mazu* had just exited the north end of the Singapore Strait, a day out of port. The dockworkers and government inspectors in Singapore had been well paid to ignore the seventh forty-foot container unit loaded onto the ship. Gala had made sure it was positioned close to the aft superstructure, behind all the other containers. That had been easy to do with the ship's high-tech deck crane. A software program called Tetris, named after the old computer game in which the player had to fit various shapes into a compact pattern, controlled the crane and organized the placement of the containers based on their destination to facilitate speedier unloading. The transfer had appeared completely ordinary. Nevertheless, Gala wanted to make certain the container's contents were properly secured.

The wind had picked up by the time Gala was certain that no Singaporean coast guard craft had followed them. The sea was choppy now that the ship had left the lee of the land to the west and east. He pushed his 120-pound body against the heavy hatch, which refused to open. A passing sailor assisted him and told him to be careful on the deck. Gala immediately went to the container, unsealed it, and entered. He hadn't counted on the rolling sea. The door swung closed when he was halfway inside and struck him in the back, launching him head first into the crated equipment.

In the darkness, Gala tried to cry out for help, aware that no one would hear him above the drone of the engines and the wind. His hands shook as he struggled to find the flashlight in his pocket. The sea rolled again, opening the door and shedding light into the container. He grabbed the crate and held on as his attempted cry became a sob. At least the crate was here and safe. Gala had spent months trying to find this piece of equipment after the first had been damaged in an accident.

The door swung closed again, plunging him back into darkness. He found his flashlight and shone the light on the crate. The hydrostatic extrusion press was safe inside within several layers of shrink-wrap. Satisfied that all was as it should be, he turned to leave. The door creaked open and then slammed shut as the ship rolled, taunting him, beckoning him to exit as it opened and denying him just as quickly when it closed. He knew he wasn't fast enough or coordinated enough to judge the right time to jump through, so he decided to stay with the crate for a while. As he turned back toward the equipment, he noticed a red spot on the shrink-wrap. He instinctively brought his free hand to his head and felt the place where it had struck the crate. His head was wet. He shone the flashlight on his hand, now red with his own blood. He felt lightheaded, nervous, and fearful. Suddenly shaking, Gala dropped the flashlight, which broke into two pieces as it hit the floor. His legs gave out beneath him and he collapsed onto the floor. The door slammed shut and this time did not open again, even when he pounded on it.

The accidental loss of the first extrusion press had been a devastating setback. Even with the new replacement, though, he needed more people and more resources to extend his research. He had tried to explain that to Vanni, but his leader had said only that there were too few people to spare. His Chinese assistants would have to suffice until more people were inspired to join the cause. Once that happened Gala would have all the workers he needed. If only Vanni had given him just two strong men, he reflected bitterly, he would not be clinging to a crate inside a dark container while his blood pooled on the deck below. Would he have to hang on like this for two more days until they reached Sri Lanka?

Gala felt the great ship surge forward on a rolling wave and his stomach lurched. Life at sea was foreign to him, but not to Vanni, who saw the sea as the great liberator of his people. In fact, Gala had first met Vanni on a ship—a large freighter that had been intentionally beached, along with many others, at one of the largest breaking yards in the world. Gala had watched in awe as Vanni tore through the ship, savagely ripping away pipes, culling every piece of valuable metal for reclamation that would profit the rich of Sri Lanka while the local Tamils labored at the dangerous work for paltry pay. Gala had struggled to do the manual labor while his mind naturally gravitated toward ways to make their jobs easier.

Gala's time working in the Mullaitivu Breakers was short-lived. Vanni quickly recognized the young man's intelligence—a gift that would be wasted in hard physical labor. "Gala," Vanni had declared during a brief work break when they were given time to sip some water, "you came here from school. Now you must return to school and learn more. Much more. I will see to it."

A few days later a manager came to take him away. Vanni had nodded once at the manager and once at Gala, and with that Gala was sent to school in Trincomalee and then eventually to university in Beijing. And when Gala's scientific training was complete, Vanni had contacted him. Gala could not deny the man who was his benefactor.

Now Gala was alone and afraid; he could think of nothing to counter the forces of nature that held him in a prison as dark and dank as the ships in the Breakers yard. He turned back to the crate. Inside was his salvation—the means to get back into Vanni's good graces and to save his people from the powerful elite who ran Sri Lanka. He just needed to escort it safely until he could transfer it to its final destination.

DAY 3

Syren hummed along effortlessly toward Colombo at twenty-five knots. Stark left control of the bridge to his helmsman and began the underway inspection of the ship. He made his way down the ladder, through the galley, past the combat information center, and to the cargo bay. The sixity-foot-wide aft cargo bay doors were open, and some crewmembers were working on the RHIB launch platform. All were wearing the Highland Maritime uniform—light gray coveralls with yellow nametags and charcoal gray ball caps with the company logo.

Six twenty-foot containers lined each side of the cargo bay. The first on his right and left were extra crew quarters, each able to house eight personnel. The next container on the right was labeled "Weapons." Inside he found Gunny Willis cleaning pistols with two of the Highland Maritime guards. Willis acknowledged his captain's presence but kept on with his work; this wasn't the military. He had worked long enough with Stark to know that Stark preferred informality so that training and maintenance duties could proceed uninterrupted. The ship was well provisioned with weapons and ammunition, a necessity for ships operating in the Gulf of Aden. Other private security firms relied on the twenty-two floating armories stationed from the Red Sea to Sri Lanka for their weapons, but many of these facilities were operated by questionable Ukrainian or Russian companies. With *Syren*'s storage capacity and port agreements Stark had no need to deal with ships and personnel who looked more like the depraved misfits in the post-apocalyptic movie *Waterworld* than legitimate twenty-first-century businessmen.

Next on Stark's right—which was actually the port side of the ship because he was walking from bow to stern—were three containers with food, uniforms, and ammunition. One container was a reefer—a refrigeration unit—that held enough to feed the crew for a couple of months if necessary. The last container on Stark's right held two commercial UAVs, unmanned aerial vehicles more popularly known as drones. Though Stark preferred manned airborne craft like helicopters for multimission roles, he recognized the cost savings and low maintenance the UAVs afforded.

Each of the five remaining starboard containers was devoted to a particular crew component—gear for the boatswains, repair equipment and extra parts for the engineering department, a medical bay, and a sealed container that only one man was allowed to open.

As if on cue, the big redhead strolled past Stark humming. "Hiya, boss," he said as he reached out to type in the code for the door lock. He waited until Stark looked away to enter the numbers.

"Jay, what kind of toys are you playing with in there?" Stark asked.

"No, no, no, boss. No way do people see my stuff until it's ready. You agreed to that. And don't forget, we have yoga in thirty minutes."

How could Stark forget? It was one of the conditions he had reluctantly agreed to when he hired Jay. But to his surprise, Jay's yoga sessions had proved as beneficial as the more strenuous routines that Gunny Willis had instituted. And Willis admitted that the flexibility the crew gained from yoga was a good complement to their other physical training. Even Stark had embraced the discipline.

With that the mad scientist, still humming, entered the darkened container and secured the door behind him.

Stark had a penchant for hiring misfits—at least the right ones. When he first met Jay on *Syren*—back when the U.S. Navy was still calling her *Sea Fighter*—Warren already had a reputation for being a nonconformist. And then he lost his job with the federal government after some minor indiscretions. When Stark purchased the discarded experimental SWATH (small waterplane-area twin-hull) ship, Warren was the first person he hired. Stark tracked him down in the Upper Peninsula of Michigan, where he was living in a doublewide with no furniture except a bed and working in a barn full of unrecognizable equipment.

Stark made his way further aft and observed the deck crew working on the stern boat ramp. Of all the legacy systems on the ship, this was the one that never seemed to work properly. They'd have to completely redesign it after this assignment. In the meantime, one of the crew was trying to jury-rig the small-boat recovery system.

A few minutes later Stark made his way topside. *Syren* rode smoothly at twenty knots in the calm seas between India and Sri Lanka. Dozens of local fishing boats peppered the waters, but the helm deftly guided the ship and steered well clear of them. A large long-line trawler from China was the only foreign ship present. Stark recognized the construction. Chinese trawlers were quickly depleting the world's few remaining untouched fisheries. The world had no interest in stopping them because many other nations did it themselves.

Stark had never been to Sri Lanka, but he didn't expect to spend much time there on this mission. After resupplying in Colombo, their assignment was to head to the northeast coast where the Tamil Tigers were thought to be based, as they had been in the recent civil war. If he could find the Sea Tigers' base of operations, he might be able to prevent another civil war and needless deaths. If not, then Stark and *Syren* would simply leave and head to the Gulf of Aden. And then he could return to Ullapool and Maggie.

"Four weeks," he said aloud, though no one was topside to hear him. Four weeks of patrolling waters he didn't know. There was always an element of risk in Highland Maritime's operations. Stark had faced such a risk—and paid a high cost—when he had intervened in the Quebec separatist affair. People had died, including someone close to him. It had cost him his career in the Navy and had made him an expatriate, a man without a country. Then there was the incident in Yemen he had been drawn into just months before. More people had died, some by Stark's own hand, but he had averted a wider conflict. Now Sri Lanka. He vowed to himself that there would be no more deaths if he could help it.

Mullaitivu District

Melanie pulled herself together and started out again, desperately trying not to think about what she had just seen and the evil men could do left unchecked, unaccountable, unexposed. She had vowed to expose the evildoers and make them accountable through her work.

Only weeks before, while she was on a retreat in Thailand, a Buddhist monk had told her that he had lost contact with some members of his order in Sri Lanka. Neither he nor anyone he knew had heard from them in months. The Sri Lankan government would not help, and even the local Tamils refused to investigate. The monastery had stood for nearly sixteen hundred years on Mount Iranamadu in the Mullaitivu District, the highest point in northeastern Sri Lanka. Would she help, he asked?

How could she say no? She and the monk shared the same dojo in Phuket, where she had been based as a freelance journalist for the better part of two years learning the martial art of *muay thai*. The monk had been her spiritual guide in the aftermath of her last assignment in the jungles of South America, where her life had shattered into tiny pieces. She was still trying to put it back together.

Her boss at the newspaper had told her it would be a simple but dangerous short-term assignment. And she would need to take a photographer. Her sister Callie had recently graduated from journalism school and was ready—begging—for her first assignment. Melanie put her off, but the boss had other plans. The paper wanted a sister act—journalist and photographer. The storytellers would become a story themselves. And so the paper hired Melanie and Callie and sent them to the tri-border region of South America known as Ciudad del Este to investigate the ties between the drug trade and a terrorist organization.

Things went wrong when Melanie began checking sources with local law enforcement. The next day three men dragged the young women from their hotel room, threw them into a van, and took them to an encampment a few miles from town. They gagged and bound the two to stakes facing one another, the older protective sister in no position to help the baby of the family. Melanie was forced to watch for two days as the cartel brutes beat her sister—forced to look into Callie's pleading eyes. Whenever the gag was removed she cried out to Melanie, who fought wildly against the rope binding her to the stake. By the end, Callie could no longer cry out. When she was nearly dead from the pain and exhaustion, they threw water on her face to wake her just long enough to look at Melanie one more time as one of the thugs took a knife and slit her throat. Melanie watched the blood pour out of her sister's body as it slumped limply against the stake. Never, if she lived to be a hundred, would she forget Callie's eyes as the life drained from her body.

The cartel men focused on Melanie the next day. She said nothing, refused to cry out, only stared at each attacker's face, memorizing every feature. She was barely conscious when she heard gunfire and saw the cartel members running around haphazardly. She fought to stay awake, to record everything in her memory. She suspected the men were special forces because they killed each of the dozen men swiftly and mercilessly. They unbound Melanie and then untied her sister, respectfully covering her body.

She wrote the story—all of it—for the paper and promptly resigned. Every assignment from now on would be of her choosing, and she chose to shine light into the shadows cast by drugs and terrorism. She vowed never to allow any photographer to work with her again. And, she decided, she needed to know how to defend herself. That was what had brought her to Thailand and the dojo, and the Buddhist monk.

She had seen many signs of violence since coming to Sri Lanka, though it wasn't clear who was responsible. She intended to find out. She turned her back on the mass grave, repacked her bag, drank some water, and started once more toward Mount Iranamadu.

By midafternoon she was within a few miles of the mountain and monastery. When she heard voices she stopped and took cover beneath some tall ferns. Five men in tiger-striped fatigues and ball caps with weapons slung on their shoulders walked by thirty yards to her left. One was talking, another was laughing. She carefully brought out her camera and took some quick shots just after they passed her, taking care to stay low.

Even that slight movement was enough to alarm a bird sitting on a branch above her. The sound of its flapping startled the soldiers. Two of the men immediately swung around and took their weapons off their shoulders. A few more birds took off, and one of the men laughed and motioned the others forward. One man, however, remained behind to take a closer look. He had walked ten yards in her direction when he saw her. Fortunately, he wasn't one of the soldiers who had unslung his weapon.

Melanie had no choice. She shoved the camera inside her backpack and ran as fast as she could, jumping over a fallen tree and ducking branches as deftly as if she were on the rugby pitch back at school. She heard shouting behind her as the soldiers took up the chase. She had a full hundred-yard lead on them, but she didn't know the area. She heard some shots and darted to the left. The telltale sign of birds flying from their perches as she passed suggested the soldiers would have no difficulty following her.

Melanie eyed a grove of trees ahead and summoned another sprint. When she was out of sight, she stopped briefly behind a clump of three trees with thick ferns growing at the base. She reached into her backpack and turned on the voice recorder and her mobile phone's recorder, and then tucked the backpack under a fern. Another shot was fired. She couldn't see her pursuers yet, but she knew they were closing in. She rose to her feet and ran again, this time away from the backpack at an angle perpendicular to the approaching soldiers. In less than a minute she had crossed the grove and reached an open field half the size of a rugby pitch two hundred yards away. She looked back and saw the way was clear, then darted across the field. Her rugby days were years behind her, but she had never run faster.

She made it to the far side of the field and ran north along its perimeter before entering the jungle again. Someone was shooting behind her, but that was no longer important. Far more pressing were the five soldiers standing ahead of her, weapons raised. She had been so concerned with escaping the ones she saw that she hadn't considered that other teams would be nearby.

At least this time they didn't get my equipment, she thought. *And this time they won't get my baby sister.*

Singapore

The white complex of buildings where Golzari awaited his contact took up an entire city block between North Bridge Road and Beach Road in the heart of Singapore. It had been the colonial house for the British government prior to World War II; after Japan's successful invasion in 1941 it became Japanese headquarters. Today the complex included a luxury hotel and several bars. A bar seemed an unlikely place for a meeting, but Golzari's contact had insisted on it—and had insisted as well that the Diplomatic Security agent pay for the meal. Golzari had been to Raffles several times, but he preferred the hotel's formal dining room to the historic bar, which fell short of his standards of cleanliness. He shuddered when he shifted in his chair and the discarded peanut shells on the floor crunched beneath his elegant Ferragamo shoes.

Mallosia imperatrix is a beetle found in the Middle East. One of Golzari's few memories of his childhood in Iran, before his family fled after the Ayatollah rose to power, was crushing one of those beetles. Its tan-and-yellow body had a honeycomb pattern not unlike that of the roasted peanut shells he was now stepping on. The beetle had made a distinctive crunch when young Damien pressed his sandal onto it. The peanut shells on the floor made the same sort of sound when stepped on, but much louder, like the crushing of dozens of beetles. He imagined the peanuts as bugs, their exoskeletons breaking from the weight of his shoe as their guts spilled out.

Agent Blake's secretary had given Golzari the file on Academic Solutions earlier in the day. There was little in it, just one letter from the government of Singapore stating that no articles of incorporation or any other record on the company existed. Golzari thought that curious. The Singaporean government was rather obsessive when it came to such details. Surely someone would have known about a company operating in this small state. The only other piece of paper in the folder had a local phone number. He called it from Blake's phone.

"Why did you not call sooner?"

"I was unavailable," Golzari replied.

"You are not Blake."

"No. He is dead."

There was a pause at the other end of the line. Golzari's previous investigations had taught him to say nothing, just wait. The man would either hang up if he was scared and guilty or would say something if he was scared and an informant. Fortunately for Golzari, it was the latter.

"Why do you call me?"

"For the same reason Blake did," Golzari responded.

"Information."

"Yes."

"Meet me today at three o'clock in the bar at Raffles. You know this place?"

"Yes. I assume you mean the Long Bar?"

"Yes. And bring money."

"How much?" Golzari asked.

"Enough." With that the call ended.

Enough. Golzari also knew from experience that someone willing to meet him on very short notice with few details needed cash, not a ticket to another country. That meant a few thousand dollars, which he didn't have.

Golzari had selected a corner table in the nearly empty Long Bar. The last time he had been here was with Robert, when they were young agents. Robert had insisted that he have a Singapore Sling because the cocktail had been created at this very bar. Golzari now wondered if the bartenders continued to make Singapore Slings after the Japanese army captured the city.

A couple of young Americans sat at the bar, easily recognizable by their blue jeans, flip-flops, and Polo shirts. A Singaporean man and two young women sat at a table on the other side of the bar from Golzari. They appeared to be immersed in themselves and turned their heads from the table only long enough to call to the bartender for more drinks.

Golzari stared at his ginger ale and waited. The rows of palm fans suspended from the ceiling swished the air back and forth. Out of the corner of his eye he saw a short man peer into the bar, looking first at the Americans, then at the table of three, and finally at Golzari. Like a hunter not wanting to spook his prey Golzari kept his eyes on his drink as the man entered the bar and walked slowly toward him. The steady crunch of peanut shells betrayed his approach.

"Are you the person I spoke with earlier?"

Golzari raised his head and looked the man in the eyes. "Yes. Have a seat."

The man complied hesitantly. "Where is my money?"

"Where is my information?" Golzari responded.

"The company Blake asked about does exist."

"How do you know that?"

"I know through my work."

"Why did the government write to Blake that they had no record of Academic Solutions?"

The man paused when the three people at the table on the other side of the bar laughed loudly. The Americans paid their bill and left just as three well-dressed Asian men took stools nearby. Golzari's informant grew even more visibly nervous.

"Relax," Golzari said. "This is a very safe place." As a precaution, though, he reached under his single-breasted suit jacket and undid the strap on his holster. His very discreet tailor at Gieves & Hawkes in London modified every one of his suits so that the cut hid his pistol.

The man said softly, "The government official Blake contacted was being paid by another company to protect the information."

"You have proof?"

"I am the man being paid."

Golzari hid his distaste. He had seen this before. A corrupt official being paid for information—or in this case to hide it—gets greedy and wants money from the other side as well. "What's the name of the company?"

"The money first. Give me the money."

"I don't have it here. You'll have to come to the embassy for it."

"No," the man said, slamming his fist on the table. The others in the bar looked in their direction briefly and then went back to their drinks. The two young women seated at the table stood up.

"You will have money. Two thousand," Golzari offered.

"No, ten thousand."

"Five thousand," Golzari countered. "But first you must give me the name so I can confirm that the company exists."

The two ladies were not walking toward the restroom. They were walking toward him. *My God,* he thought. *Are those hookers coming over to proposition us?*

"Very well. It's Zheng Research and—"

At that moment each of the women reached into her purse. Golzari's reflexes and training took over as he grabbed his Glock 19 with one hand and threw the table aside with the other. His response distracted them for just a second, long enough to delay them from raising their pistols. Golzari had no time to order them to drop their weapons even if he had known what language to use. He fired two shots, one at each of the women. Both fell. The three men at the bar turned toward the commotion, jumped off their stools, and pulled out their own weapons. Golzari reacted with two more shots. The first dropped the closest man, the second hit but only delayed the next man. The third man ran toward Golzari's contact, firing all the while and hitting the corrupt government employee with each shot before the Diplomatic Security agent could train his weapon on him. Two shots ended the third man's assault and Golzari turned back to the second man, who was doubled over and holding his leg. He still had the strength to raise his weapon, but Golzari was too quick. Three more shots and the man was as dead as the other four.

Golzari crouched, anticipating more shots from somewhere. The bartender was yelling something from his hiding place behind the bar. Golzari turned to the table where the women had been sitting, but the man who had been with them was gone. Golzari had no way to determine if he had been part of the attack or simply their unwitting pawn.

Golzari bent over his contact, who clearly was dead. His eyes and mouth were wide open, and the blood leaking from the bullet wounds that peppered his chest soaked the peanut shells that littered the floor. Golzari thought once more of *Mallosia imperatrix* as he holstered his gun and crunched across the floor toward the inevitable conversation with the police.

USS *LeFon*, Southern Bay of Bengal

Rear Adm. Daniel Rossberg, who owed his Navy career to connections rather than accomplishments, had been on *LeFon* for a day. During that time he had chewed out the captain, insulted every sailor he encountered, dressed down every chief petty officer, and threatened with court-martial nearly every officer. Only Ens. Bobby Fisk escaped Rossberg's displeasure, and only because Commander Johnson had ordered Fisk to remain in his stateroom until they reached Sri Lanka.

Jaime Johnson had been on Rossberg's last ship briefly, but it was as an unconscious patient awaiting transport to a medical facility, so she had never met him. Nevertheless, his reputation preceded him. The nephew of an influential senator who sat on the Armed Services Committee and the brother of the admiral in charge of OLA, the Navy's Office of Legislative Affairs, Rossberg had proceeded smoothly up the promotion ladder, every assignment cherry-picked for him, even after losing his last command. Jaime had not been on USS *Bennington* during the Battle of Socotra, but she knew directly from a few of those present—Bobby Fisk, Connor Stark, and her helicopter detachment—what had really happened. Rossberg's arrogance and intransigence had cost the lives of most of the ship's officers and chief petty officers.

His connections in Washington, however, saw it differently. They made a hero of him and ignored the role Bobby, Connor, and the rest of the crew had played in defeating the terrorist attack. At the direction of OLA, the Chief of Naval Information released a carefully crafted—and almost completely fictitious—description of the events on *Bennington*. The press release lauded Rossberg's heroic leadership in rallying his surviving crewmembers and launching a counterattack. There had been no reporters present on *Bennington* who could contradict that. No one who could inform the public that Connor Stark and Bobby Fisk had taken control of the ship and led the counterattack. No one who could say that during that entire time, Captain Rossberg was unconscious in sick bay, coincidentally on the same bed on which Jaime had lain only days before. Only the U.S. ambassador to Yemen, the Yemeni leadership, and the crew of *Bennington* knew the truth. Captain Rossberg was awarded the Navy Cross and promoted to rear admiral. And now he was on his way to Sri Lanka to deliver two U.S. Navy ships to the Sri Lankan navy.

The clash was inevitable. Jaime Johnson was not one to suffer fools when it came to her ship and crew—a crew she had groomed since taking command five months ago. Jaime lacked experience in the ship's tactical systems, given her absence from the Navy for several years, but she made up for that in her crew's morale and efficiency. Like every member of her crew—enlisted and officers alike—she spent the first hour of every workday cleaning compartments. Every day she joined a different division cleaning passageways and heads. She got to know her crew, and they her.

Rossberg had been on board less than twenty-four hours when he passed Johnson in a passageway on her hands and knees scrubbing the deck alongside a chief and three sailors, all clad in blue work overalls. "Commander," he gasped. "*What* are you doing?"

"Cleaning, Admiral. Standard operating procedure for this time of day."

"That's not Navy regulation. Get up this instant. Sailors clean. Officers command at their stations."

"Not on my ship, sir," she said evenly. "Everyone cleans. It's part of everyone's assigned duties."

Rossberg pulled himself up to his full five and a half feet and pointed a short, stubby finger at her. "You listen, missy, I am the senior officer on this ship and you will do what I tell you. You will stop cleaning this instant and go to the bridge. We have important work escorting those two ships to Sri Lanka. Now!"

Commander Johnson rose from the deck and met his eyes squarely, then walked over to the 1MC and picked up the handset. "Good morning, *LeFon*, this is the captain," she said calmly. "Secure from cleaning and proceed with the plan of the day. You know what day this is and how long we've been at sea. Each of you who wants one will be given one beer at noon. Captain out."

"*What*?!" the admiral huffed. "No, no, no. Give me that." He took the mike and made his own announcement to the crew. "This is Admiral Rossberg. Belay the captain's direction. This is a United States Navy ship, and there will be no drinking."

Johnson was beginning to understand what had happened on *Bennington*. It sure as hell was not going to happen on her ship. "Admiral, Navy regulations clearly state that after sufficient days at sea, the crew will be given one beer."

"Did you hear me, Commander? No drinking. Now you get to the bridge."

"Aye, sir."

Jaime remained on the bridge the entire day and evening as *LeFon* led the two surplus warships toward Sri Lanka. She left only to personally deliver a sandwich to the imprisoned Bobby Fisk. Neither mentioned Rossberg's name. It wasn't necessary. Bobby knew what she was facing without having to leave the confines of his stateroom.

While the admiral was eating a salad in the wardroom that evening, Jaime called the SUPPO—the supply officer—to her stateroom. She gave him clear verbal directions. Then she pointed to a box of bottles and presented him with two cards to be placed on a monitored table in the galley. The SUPPO understood. After that she approached the admiral and advised him that once he was in his stateroom for the evening she planned to post the master-at-arms outside his door so that he was assured of a quiet sleep. A better officer would have thanked her for the thoughtful gesture. Rossberg merely acknowledged it as his due. What Jaime didn't tell him was that the master-at-arms was under orders to call her immediately if Rossberg left the stateroom.

Later that night, when the admiral was asleep, the word went out verbally to every sailor. One by one they filed up to a table on the mess deck where a glass of Guinness awaited each crewmember, accompanied by a card that read "For strength." Also waiting, courtesy of their captain, was a shot of Jameson with a card that read "For courage."

DAY 4

Colombo, Sri Lanka

When *Syren* reached a point ten nautical miles from Colombo off the southwest coast of Sri Lanka, Connor ordered the security teams to man the guns mounted at four stations topside. He set his coffee mug on the counter in front of him as he settled back in the captain's chair. The laptop mounted on the right arm of his chair showed photos of the twisted hulks that were all that remained of the Sri Lankan navy. In the past few hours he had read everything that was publicly known about the attacks, but he knew from experience that first reports were usually wrong. The only undisputable fact was that Sri Lanka's warships were now either at the bottom of the harbors and channels of the three major port cities or drifting helplessly on the surface.

"Slow to one-third," he said.

"One-third, aye," the helm responded, gently pulling back on the joystick and adjusting the controls. The era of turning the ship's wheel to set a course was passing. The seven-hundred-ton *Syren* responded not with the pronounced shudder that shakes most Navy ships when their huge propellers slow, but with a calm sigh as the water-propelled jets relaxed their intake.

The high-resolution navigation monitor next to the helm showed the contour of the coastline ahead of him and the depth of the water around it. Stark checked the time on the digital clock on the bulkhead above. The Sri Lankan liaison would be here soon. Stark had advised the Sri Lankans that he would await the liaison at this location rather than enter the harbor so soon after the attack, but communications with them were still spotty.

Even from this distance Stark could see with his naked eyes the high-rises that dotted the city behind the harbor. The city was home to four and a half million people. The harbor itself, though, was oddly empty. Small fishing boats were going about their business, but no large ships were entering or leaving port. He took out the binoculars to confirm what he was reading on one of the radar displays. Several large container ships were indeed out there, but all were anchored well away from the harbor. One signal mystified him because it coincided directly with the coastline.

"Helm, all stop."

"All stop, aye."

"When was the last time you did maintenance on the radar, Stephanie?" he asked the technician to his right.

"Last night at 2130. It's all good, sir."

If the radar and navigational display were both working correctly, then a containership had run aground outside the port.

"Small boat approaching, sir, coming in dead ahead," one of the watchmen called over the ship's communications system.

Stark picked up the radio mike and spoke. "Small boat approaching, this is the security vessel *Syren*. State your intent, over."

"*Syren*, this is a Sri Lanka navy boat delivering an officer for assignment to your ship," the voice crackled over channel 16. "Request direction, over."

"Sri Lanka navy boat, you are at—" he checked the radar quickly—"three hundred yards from our ship. Stop immediately, over."

The small boat responded.

"Navy boat, remain where you are. We will meet you for transfer, over."

"Understood. Out."

The memory of the attack on *Kirkwall* in the Gulf of Aden by several suicide boats was still fresh in his mind, as was the additional loss of life that had occurred on *Bennington* when an armed terrorist was allowed on board. Stark picked up the shipboard mike. "This is the captain. Launch small boat *Somers*. Gunny, have the team check any backpack or gear the liaison is bringing aboard—and frisk him."

"Understood, Skipper," the security team leader replied.

Stark took another sip of coffee as he watched the launch of *Somers* on the live-feed monitor. The left side of the monitor showed feed from the camera in the well deck. Another camera showed the view from just above the stern launch platform. The coxswain swung the small boat around and prepared to leave. Connor couldn't distinguish the security team members from one another in their identical gray uniforms and black protective gear, but he knew from previous training that Gunny Willis was on the bow. Willis rested his weapon on his thigh momentarily as he turned back to direct the spacing of the other four security personnel, then he faced forward and the boat disappeared off to port.

Stark typed in a number on his console, and the monitor showed the feed from the camera mounted one deck above the bridge atop the rarely used landing signals officer's shack. The LSO shack was originally designed for helicopter operations, but Highland Maritime had modified it slightly for other air component requirements. Stark typed in new orders for the camera, and it faced forward and zoomed in on the Sri Lankan navy boat.

The boat had only three seated men on board, including the liaison assigned to *Syren*. *Somers* circled the Sri Lankan boat twice to give Willis enough time to look for anything out of the ordinary, then the gunny waved his arm and the coxswain guided *Somers* alongside as one of the Sri Lankans rose. Gunny and one of the team boarded the other small boat and checked the contents of a sea bag as Stark had directed. A few minutes later the officer and his bag were transferred to *Somers,* which sped back to *Syren* while the other boat went in the opposite direction, back to shore.

"This is the captain," Stark called on the shipboard mike. "When *Somers* is recovered have Gunny Willis escort our guest to the CIC. Jay, meet us there."

Stark turned to his left and looked at the ship's English-born executive officer, Olivia Harrison. "XO, let's head down," he told her. "Helm, you have the conn. Hold us here for now. Standard security measures apply."

"Aye, sir," the helm responded.

M/V *Nanjing Mazu*, Northeast of Sri Lanka

Gala was bloody and clinging to one of the shrink-wrapped pallets in the container when they found him. The Chinese sailors kicked him awake.

Gala didn't know how long he had been in here, only that the container door had finally closed on him for good and locked, trapping him here in the dark. He let go of the pallet and stretched out his stiff fingers, and suddenly realized that he no longer heard the ship's engines or felt the vibrations that had lulled him to sleep. The ship was still. "Have we arrived?" he asked.

"Yes. We are pulling alongside the ship for the transfer. We thought you had fallen overboard," added one of the crew.

Gala rose and limped out of the container as the crew secured it for transfer. Before he went through the hatch of the after superstructure, he noticed the other ship at anchor alongside. It was not as large as the freighter he was on, and it was rusty from age and the elements. It was home. He returned to his stateroom, took a shower, dressed, and grabbed his belongings—extra clothes, eyeglasses, some papers, and a tablet that had most of the information he needed to operate and modify the equipment.

The captain entered. He was, like the crew, Chinese. His clothes hung loosely on his lanky frame.

"You should knock," Gala said in imperfect Mandarin.

"It is my ship, Gala," the captain said dryly. "The company was concerned when I told them you were missing."

"It was an accident. The heavy seas . . ."

The captain laughed. "We had no heavy seas. You should stay on board with us. Perhaps you will really experience a storm." He sat at the table and picked up the tablet.

Gala seized it back. "I have had enough of your ship, Captain. Tell the company you found me and that I have arrived with the equipment."

"What is so valuable in that container?"

"You know better than to ask that," Gala responded. "It is of concern only to me and the company."

"Very well," the captain said thumbing through the papers, "but I will remind you that this ship and its missions are my concern. You will never speak of this ship. Ever. Do you understand?"

"Of course, of course," Gala said dismissively.

The captain rose swiftly and seized Gala by the throat with both hands. He threw the slender scientist against the bulkhead and dug his bony fingers deeper into Gala's throat until the Sri Lankan could no longer breathe. "Do you understand?" he hissed. "Do you understand that we can find you anywhere and do anything we wish to you or anyone you know?"

Gala could only nod in response, unable even to gasp for air in the stronger man's grip. The captain let him go, and Gala instinctively grabbed his own throat in a futile effort to sooth the damage already done.

"Do you understand? Say it."

Gala rasped out a weak, "Yes."

"Good. Now get off my ship," he said as he left Gala's stateroom.

Gala waited a few moments then grabbed his belongings and made his way to the deck. A crewman waved him over, pointing to the rickety wooden planks that served as the only bridge between the two ships. Gala peered over the side at the forty-foot drop to the water and then at the ten-foot gulf between the two ships. Other crewmen approached and began betting on whether Gala would make it across. The two planks shifted as the tide pushed one ship away from the other and then back again after the super-sized fenders bounced them apart.

Gala looked back at his container and the two crewmen atop it securing it to the chain of the unloading crane. He ran over to it, opened the door, and then slammed it shut behind him, blocking out the sound of the laughing crewmen exchanging money from the already won or lost bets.

Gala lay flat and grabbed the wooden pallet as he felt the container lifted from the deck. The ten-minute transfer seemed to take an hour as the crane swung the container carefully around and then slowly placed it on the deck of the waiting ship. The Chinese crew took care in lowering it, following the strict directions of the company.

Gala heard men above unlatch the container. He rose and pounded on the side of the container until they opened it.

"Welcome back, Gala!" a fellow Tamil Tiger said.

"Yes, yes," he said impatiently. "Please get that pallet below to my laboratory."

"We will. Did you hear the news? Great success with your weapon!"

"What?" Gala asked. "What do you mean?"

"You are a hero! While you were away Vanni ordered the attack. You did not hear?"

"No. I heard nothing on that stupid ship. But he used it too early. It wasn't ready."

"Gala, did you not hear me? We used it. At Trincomalee, Colombo, and Galle. It worked. The Sri Lankan navy is no more. We destroyed all of the ships," the Tamil Tiger said with a broad smile.

"But it wasn't ready," Gala protested. "It needed more work."

"Ha! Tell Vanni that when you see him. Tell *him* that the weapon didn't work."

Gala headed below toward his laboratory, considering the news. Vanni was not impetuous. He would not have used the weapon if the time were not right for it. Vanni was a great leader—the reincarnation of the great liberators of old. Gala would ask him. But he would ask carefully. In many ways Vanni was like the Chinese captain. Then he put the matter out of his mind and began rethinking the calculations for the next version of the weapon. He already had the basic material below, and now he had the right equipment to make it. And since the Sri Lankan navy was no longer a threat he had plenty of time to work on it.

M/V *Syren*, off Sri Lanka

The Sri Lankan naval officer was in his late forties, thin, and a bit gaunt—likely as a result of the shock and sorrow of the past few days. Stark wondered how he would look if his navy, his sailors, and his friends had just been wiped out in one fell swoop. The officer wore black coveralls with his rank on his lapels. Stark, who had been leaning against a table laden with fruit and drinks that he had ordered earlier from the mess, extended his hand in welcome.

The officer stood at attention and clicked the heels of his boots. "Commander Sampath Ranasinghe at your service, Captain," he said, shaking Stark's hand.

"A pleasure, Commander. You have already met Gunny Willis, head of my security team. Let me introduce my executive officer, Olivia Harrison, and our chief scientist and engineer, Dr. Jay Warren." Ranasinghe nodded at each in turn, and Stark motioned for all to be seated.

"We'll be working together closely for the next month, Commander Ranasinghe. As you know, I have a letter of marque from your government directing me to gather intelligence and attempt to locate Sea Tiger bases. We know about the attack, of course, but we are hoping you can give us more details."

Ranasinghe took a deep but measured breath. "Certainly, Captain. Little information has been released. My government has been criticized for not providing more to the international media, but we have not yet gathered all the facts. You see, we had very little warning—less than one day before the attacks came. We didn't know the Tamil Tigers—actually the Sea Tigers—had re-formed. We thought their defeat in 2009 had ended the insurrection. Our intelligence service had no indication of their plans. We received a warning that they would attack our harbors, so we closed them to traffic. We set our quarantine area, and our warships were on alert. I was not at sea," he explained. "I was assigned to headquarters as an aide to the admiral coordinating the defense."

Stark offered him a cup of coffee and a bottle of water, both of which the officer took. He set the coffee down and took a sip of the water before continuing. "One of our warships reported increased chatter on the radio—far above normal. Then everything cut out. *Everything*, Captain," he emphasized. "We lost communication with our entire fleet. Then we lost communication with our offices in Colombo, Galle, and Trincomalee. We don't know much about what happened next other than eyewitness accounts from civilians. People in each city reported small fireworks in the harbors and then everything went dead. Cars, phones, radios. Anything with electronics."

"Ah, yeah, uh-huh," Jay said, nodding.

"The portions of the cities closest to the port were in chaos," the Sri Lankan continued. "Our ships were dead in the water. And then the small boats came. Some were suicide boats, armed with some sort of high-explosive device. They simply rammed our dead warships and destroyed them. There were very few survivors in our fleet." Ranasinghe paused again to drink some water.

"The situation is far worse than the media know, Captain Stark. Some of our military aircraft crashed as well. We suspect that the Tigers are still based somewhere in the northeast, but after the attacks they warned us that they could down any plane, stop any tank, and sink any ship we sent to the area. Our army and air force would normally go after them, but the Tigers proved so capable in striking our navy that my government is being cautious in deciding how best to move against them."

"Jay," Stark said, turning to the misfit technology expert, "you have an idea about this?"

"Yeah, boss, and it's not good. Sounds like EMPs—a lot of them."

The Sri Lankan officer shook his head at the acronym.

"Electromagnetic pulses," Warren enumerated. "Bad shit, man. Fries fucking everything electronic."

The officer seemed to understand the scientist's colloquialisms.

"Jay, I've never heard of an EMP actually being used as a weapon," Stark commented.

"Neither have I, but a lot of folks have been thinking it was just a matter of time. And here it is. But we need to find out what kind of pulses they used. There are a few options, but it takes a lot of knowledge. Not just anyone could come up with this sort of thing. And how an insurgent group—"

"Terrorists, Dr. Warren," Ranasinghe interrupted. "The Tamil Tigers are terrorists, not insurgents. What they did to my navy—that was terrorism."

"Yeah, okay, sorry." Warren raised his hands in surrender. "What I'm saying is that this takes a very high level of sophistication—something most home-grown terrorist groups don't have."

"So you think they had outside help, Jay?" Stark asked.

"Most likely. They'd need knowledge, sophisticated equipment, and a way to experiment and test it. And they'd need the raw materials."

"What kind of raw materials?" asked Olivia Harrison.

Warren shrugged. "Depends. I need to do some testing. If we can get to Trincomalee just for a few hours I can run some tests with my equipment."

"Commander, what was the effective range of those EMPs?" Stark asked.

"We believe it was between three quarters of a mile to a mile in diameter."

"What did they use for a launching platform?" Warren asked.

"We don't know. All of the security cameras in the harbor were, as Dr. Warren noted, fried."

"Did you search any of the ships that had entered the ports before the warning was issued?" Stark asked.

"Unfortunately, we were not looking inward before the attacks, Captain. We closed off the ports and looked outward for the attackers. Once the attack was over, of course, we no longer had ships to conduct an investigation."

"Okay," Stark said. "At least we have something. We'll proceed to Trincomalee so Dr. Warren can conduct some tests in the harbor, and then we'll begin our search.

"Yes, Captain. There is one issue before we begin."

"What's that, Commander?"

"Your papers, sir, registering this vessel under the flag of the nation of Sri Lanka." Ranasinghe pulled the papers from his bag and handed them to Stark, who browsed through them quickly.

"Thank you. The XO will show you to your stateroom. Why don't you get some rest now? I have a feeling we have a lot of long days ahead."

"Thank you, Captain, but there is one other thing." From a pocket in his coverall Ranasinghe pulled out the ensign of his nation. "Now that you are registered under our nation, you are to fly this ensign instead of yours."

Stark was taken aback. But it was true. *Syren* was no longer operating under the flag of Saint Andrew. For the next month she would be a Sri Lankan vessel. That fact made him even more uncomfortable than he had been when he accepted the assignment in India.

Singapore

They had disarmed him, handcuffed him, and thrown a bag over his head when they put him in the car. The detention facility was a short ride away, though it didn't take long to get anywhere in Singapore, particularly if you were riding in a police car. The proximity of large-body jets as they slowed at their destination told Golzari that he was in the new Changi prison complex run by the Singapore Prison Service. The last time he had visited a Singapore prison it was to question an inmate who was hanging nude over a medieval-looking rack while the police completed caning him. Americans didn't realize that caning strips the skin and flesh off the person's buttocks. Golzari was hoping for a luxury suite in the prison instead of the rack. But he had just killed five people in a public place.

The police guided him down a corridor and into a room before they removed the sack from his head. He looked around as an officer patted him down to make sure they hadn't missed anything when they seized him at Raffles. He was clearly in an interrogation room. The table and two chairs made that clear. A policeman pulled him toward one of the chairs.

"Easy," Golzari said defiantly as the man tugged on his jacket. "I don't have time to see one of your city's excellent tailors this trip."

The police officer ignored him and pushed him into a seat opposite a well-dressed Asian man just as two other men in suits walked in. Each of the two wore an earpiece and had a PR-21 side-handle baton at his side and a holstered .38-caliber revolver. The man at the table had only an earpiece and was better dressed. *The homicide detective,* Golzari thought. The room was several degrees warmer than the outside temperature. He recognized the old trick: make the interrogation room uncomfortable for the detainee. It wouldn't work.

Golzari spoke quickly, as if he were in charge. "Good afternoon, gentlemen. I would like my weapon and credentials returned to me."

"First, we ask questions, Agent Golzari," said the detective as the other two men took up places in front of the door.

"Of course. I'm happy to cooperate."

"You killed five people at Raffles. It is a very popular tourist destination. That will cost us money."

"Screw the money," Golzari said sitting ramrod straight. "You are detaining a federal agent."

"Yes . . . of the United States. You have no rights here, Agent Golzari," the detective said coldly. Golzari wondered how it would feel when the cane sheared off his skin. Would he be able to contain his screams?

"You shot and killed five people and nearly killed six," the detective said as he locked his fingers together on the table.

"I had no choice," Golzari responded. "They had drawn their weapons."

"Not the sixth person."

"He left during the exchange." Golzari realized that he had not mentioned the mystery man who had been sitting with the two women. How did the detective know about him?

"It doesn't matter. You were also responsible for a sixth death—the man you met in the bar, who was killed in the firefight. Why were you meeting with him?"

"It's part of an investigation. Who was he?"

The detective shifted and turned his head very slightly—the telltale sign of someone receiving orders through an earpiece. Most people would not have noticed the officer's barely perceptible nod, but Golzari did. The detective had received orders and was confirming receipt.

"We have agreements with your country in that regard, Agent Golzari. Tell us why you were meeting with him."

"Very well. I'm investigating the death of Special Agent William Blake of U.S. Diplomatic Security. Your office was unable to provide—useful—information, so I investigated on my own and learned this man was involved. He was an informant who apparently was told to suppress certain information."

"What else did you learn?"

"That depends. Will you help in my investigation?" asked Golzari.

The detective thought for a moment, then dismissed the two men at the door and looked in the corner at a camera and motioned with his hand to stop recording.

"It was an unpleasant episode, Agent Golzari. My government does not condone the level of violence you displayed."

"The alternative was unacceptable to me. Self-defense is an inherent right for an individual or a country, wouldn't you agree?" Golzari said, lifting his chin.

"It is not my role to comment on political issues."

"One of my fellow agents was killed. *Here*," Golzari emphasized. "He was tracking down stolen equipment that went to a firm *here* that your government's records say does not exist."

"The name of the firm?" the detective asked.

"Academic Solutions," Golzari said.

"I have never heard of it."

"The informant said another company was covering its trail. The name was Zheng Research," Golzari answered.

The detective tilted his head to listen again but kept his eyes on the American. "Agent Golzari, you and I are both officers of the law. Because of that, I will give you this advice: drop your investigation."

"Why?"

"Because Zheng Research and Development is not a Singaporean firm. It is from elsewhere."

"Elsewhere as in China?" Golzari asked.

The detective shook his head. "Leave this matter alone. That firm is an octopus with many tentacles. Leave it alone and it will not harm you. Provoke it and it will reach out, grab you, and squeeze you until your bones are crushed."

Golzari thought about that for a moment. A Chinese firm powerful enough to deter a nation-state like Singapore was a firm that posed a danger elsewhere as well. They had killed Blake, and that was reason enough for Golzari to proceed. *What kind of R&D firm sends assassins to kill informants?* he asked himself. A firm that had the reach of an octopus and could crush his bones—or Blake's, or the informant's whose name he had never learned. He slowly leaned toward the detective. "I need a lead. Something. Anything to help me find out what happened to our agent and why."

The detective thought about it. "Agent Golzari," he said quietly, "your informant did give us some information."

"I'm listening," Golzari said.

"He told us of a shipment that was covered up by Zheng's money and people. He didn't tell us what the cargo was or the name of the ship, but he told us its destination."

"Where?"

"Sri Lanka."

DAY 6

USS *LeFon*, off Sri Lanka

ear Admiral Rossberg strutted around the bridge as he watched the two littoral combat ships keeping company with *LeFon*. Commander Johnson sat quietly in her captain's chair on the starboard side and sipped her coffee, the calm amid the storm. Jaime hid her emotions well during crises. She had taken to heart advice she heard in a lecture given by the former COs of USS *Cole* and USS *Samuel B. Roberts*, men who had led their ships during major incidents. Never let the crew see you sweat, they said. Crews have no confidence in an uncertain captain, and they will perform poorly as a result. On the day she graduated from the Naval Academy her father had given her a book of Rudyard Kipling's poems. He had put a bookmark at "If," Kipling's advice to his own son: "If you can keep your head when all about you are losing theirs . . ." At the line where Kipling had written "you'll be a Man, my son" her father had penciled in "you'll be a Woman, my daughter."

"These LCSs are the fastest and most capable ships ever built," the admiral said proudly.

Jaime said nothing. She suspected the admiral hadn't read much naval history, and he clearly hadn't read the recent GAO report on the shortcomings of the LCS. The Pentagon had been making herculean efforts to hide the ship's deficiencies, even trying to reclassify it as a frigate.

"Admiral," she finally said, tucking her wiry blonde hair under her ball cap, "why LCSs?"

"What?" he asked, spinning around and nearly tripping as the rubber sole of his boot caught on the linoleum deck.

"I understand these ships are being transferred to the Sri Lankan navy because of the recent terrorist attack," Jaime said, "but why LCSs? Why not the rest of our *Perry*-class frigates or some of the older cruisers?"

"Clearly you know very little about the ships in your own navy, Commander." He gestured at the two ships that had taken up station to port and starboard of *LeFon*. "That ship class is the future of the U.S. Navy! I helped design that class. The vice chief of naval operations himself commended me for my work. I know everything about it. I was the personal assistant to Admiral Fall when he conceived it," he boasted. "The LCS is the perfect ship. And all the critics who sit around eating cheese doodles and writing blogs in their parents' basements are being proven wrong."

"Weren't they even a little right?" she asked innocently. "I thought there were other new ship designs in the works."

"No, absolutely not! Oh, there were other ships in development—like this one boxy ship some people claimed was innovative. But we killed that plan and I made sure we sold that ship for scrap!" The admiral was in full stride now, doing what he did best—patting himself on the back.

Out of the corner of her eye Jaime saw the junior officer of the deck and the helmsman roll their eyes. She'd talk to them later about that. She didn't like the admiral either, but open dissension among the ranks could be dangerous.

"Where's the navigator?" Rossberg asked. "He should be here. Get the navigator up here now."

"Admiral, I'm sorry, but he's ill and I've confined him to his stateroom," she said.

"No one is sick when they have work to do. I'm not giving that order again, Commander. Now."

She nodded to the OOD, who called for the navigator. A few minutes later Ensign Fisk, his ball cap pulled low on his face, opened the hatch and stepped onto the bridge. He hadn't made three steps when the admiral stopped him. Bobby had covered his face, but he hadn't covered the name on his blue coveralls.

"You. Pull that cover off, mister!"

Bobby stopped in his tracks and did as he was ordered.

"Fisk. Ensign Fisk. You," he said pointing a stubby forefinger at Bobby, his voice rising. "You were one of the mutineers."

The other officers and sailors on the bridge froze at that word.

Admiral Rossberg turned back to Johnson. "Do you know who this . . . this . . . officer is? He's a traitor, that's who he is. He disobeyed my orders on *Bennington*. He and the others took my ship from me."

"No, sir," Bobby corrected.

"What did you say? Are you contradicting me?"

"Yes, sir. It was not a mutiny," said Bobby firmly, now standing straight and ready to face his fate. "I warned you about those visitors. I told you to check with the regional security officer. You didn't listen, and most of my friends—my shipmates—died on *Bennington*. And if Commander Stark hadn't been there . . ."

"Don't you dare mention that name, Fisk. You and Stark should have been court-martialed, and I—"

A British woman's voice on the ship-to-ship radio interrupted the admiral's rant. "U.S. Navy ships, this is the vessel three miles off your port quarter. We'll be overtaking you on your port side, over."

"What? Conning officer, what's our speed?" the admiral asked, his finger still pointing at Fisk.

"Speed is two-seven knots," came the reply.

"Two-seven? No ships out there can pass us except an ocean liner. All ahead full, increase speed to thirty-five knots and pass the word to the other ships."

"Admiral, there's no reason to put that much stress on the ships," Jaime noted.

"Is this another ship full of mutineers, Commander? You do as you're told."

Jaime obeyed. She had no choice. Then she sat back in her chair and pulled a pen and small notebook from her pocket to record the time and orders. She picked up the phone to the CIC and quietly told the tactical action officer to record every movement of the ships.

"All ahead full," responded the helm.

"Three-five knots, Captain," the CONN said to Jaime.

"Understood," she said firmly. The ship began to vibrate as the massive GM-2500 engines reached full speed. The two LCSs kept pace with the destroyer.

"I'll deal with you in Sri Lanka, mister," the admiral said to Bobby, then turned forward to watch his ships demonstrate their superiority to the unwitting commercial vessel on his port quarter. The port watch called Bobby and the OOD onto the bridge wing.

A minute later a different voice came over the radio—this time a man's voice. It sounded American, but some intonations suggested another influence, perhaps Welsh or Scottish. "U.S. Navy ships, this is the vessel off your port quarter. We'll be passing you on your port side. Acknowledge, over."

"What? Helm are you sure we're at three-five knots?" the admiral barked.

"Yes, sir."

Jaime grabbed her binoculars and hurried to join the crew on the port bridge wing, leaving the admiral mumbling impotently on the bridge.

The admiral followed her just as the boxy ship began to pass on the port side of the outer LCS. The admiral did a double-take as the ship glided smoothly past. "No, that can't be. More speed, more speed."

"Admiral, it's beyond inadvisable. We won't catch her," Jaime said.

The admiral ordered both littoral combat ships to match the speed of the other ship, then took the ship-to-ship mike. "This is the U.S. Navy warship. Who is that passing to port?" he asked, looking at the ship he had forced from the Navy's development program.

"USS *LeFon*, this is the private security vessel *Syren*, Captain Connor Stark in command. Have a good day."

"No, no, no! Not that ship. Not him," the admiral sputtered in disbelief.

"CONN, all ahead two-thirds," Johnson ordered.

The admiral had turned to say something to her when Bobby called out, pointing at the LCS to port. "Smoke!"

The call came from the CIC a moment later conveying a message from a Sri Lankan officer. The LCS was experiencing a mishap and was required to shut down one of her engines. The warship quickly fell back as *Syren* sailed on ahead.

Jaime returned to the captain's chair and picked up the mike to ask the LCS if *LeFon* could render assistance just as she noticed a new email on her monitor: "Regards, Jaime. The ship looks good but you need to work on those two barges in company with you. If you're en route Trin, hail us when you arrive. We have a good chef and scotch is permitted on my ship. Connor."

"I want off," the admiral said to Johnson. "Get me a small boat immediately. I'm going aboard that LCS to take command of the squadron from there."

M/V *Nanjing Mazu*, off Northeast Sri Lanka

Gala took a deep drag on his cigarette before leaving the deck and returning to the bowels of the ship. The smoke going down his windpipe was a harsh reminder of the Chinese captain's bony fingers around his neck. He tenderly stroked his throat again at the memory. The cool ocean evening air felt good against his body, which was drenched with sweat from hours belowdecks assembling the equipment. The laboratory had a cooling unit, but it couldn't keep up with the feverish activities going on in there. In a few moments he had to return to supervise the workers in the weapons lab using the 3D printers he had ordered through the ghost firm of Academic Solutions. Those had arrived on a previous voyage and were already serving their purpose.

He ignored the darkened fleet of ships that surrounded him and stared up at the stars in the cloudless sky. The power he was developing was miniscule compared with the forces at work inside those stars. It was insignificant even against the great arsenals of the world's superpowers. But it offered a way forward to the Tamils. Had the weapon been available during the civil war, the Tigers would now have their independent state and the thousands slaughtered after the war at the hands of the Sri Lankan government while the world stood idly by might still be alive.

The sound of a small motorboat broke the silence of the night. A few deckhands muttered something beyond his hearing, and a light came on amidships that focused on a small boat pulling alongside the anchored freighter.

Gala moved back from the railing and sat down on one of the boxes stacked on the deck, burying his head in his hands as he thought about the calculations for the next step in the experiment. The light amidships went off, and Gala heard the slow, light pace of a man walking on the deck toward him in the darkness. Gala sighed in frustration. All he wanted was to be left alone to his calculations. He couldn't think below because the people in the processing area made so much noise. He had thought to have peace and quiet here.

"Here, have some water, Gala," the man said.

"You used the weapon," Gala replied without looking up.

Vanni sat beside him, put his thin arm around Gala's back, and sighed. "I couldn't wait for you."

"It needed more testing, Vanni," Gala said.

"No. It works. But we used most of what we had against their navy and aircraft. We have only enough left for a few small rockets. You have returned just in time. We have much work to do. We have more people extracting the ore now. Another shipment will arrive in two days. You have seen the people working below."

"Yes, Vanni. They are working and sweating. Just as you and I did at the Breakers."

"Gala, Gala," Vanni said rubbing his back, "this is different. This is for a cause, and those are not our people."

"But they *are* people. Not the soldiers who fought against us."

"They are people who supported the soldiers who fought against us, Gala," he said coldly, removing his arm.

Gala straightened. "I will have more short-range rockets for you soon. The material for larger weapons will take longer, but now I have the equipment."

"Good, my friend," Vanni said. "Because now we have to worry about the American ships."

"What American ships? Why are Americans here?" Gala asked.

"Not Americans, but they have given two warships to Sri Lanka to attack us, according to my sources in Singapore."

"Then no Americans?"

"No. Only Sri Lankan navy personnel. So when we destroy the ships the Americans will have no reason to interfere. You will have one of the new weapons ready?"

"You are certain of this?" Gala asked.

"I am certain," Vanni said firmly. "Two ships, no Americans except in an escort ship that will depart as soon as the formal transfer is complete in Trincomalee." Vanni knew Gala. He understood his past, sensed his hesitancy about killing. But Vanni also understood Gala's weaknesses and knew how to exploit them, as he exploited the weaknesses of everyone he met. Gala was a scientist who wanted perfection in his work and a future for the Tamils. "Gala, you are working for our people, and you are achieving something that not even the Americans could accomplish. Did you not tell me of a group of scientists working for their military who were unable to unlock the secret that you have unlocked for our weapon? "

"It's true," the young scientist said with a smile. "I read their report about this technology. But," he added, "that report was from many years ago, and they did not have a pure lode to work with as we do."

"The Americans must never know of it."

"And the Chinese?" Gala asked fearfully. That was another of Gala's traits that Vanni knew how to exploit—his fear that his history of being bullied, beaten, and belittled would be repeated.

"Gala, Gala, you are now here among my forces—our forces. You are honored among our fighters for giving them a chance against the Sri Lankans. We have destroyed their navy. We have held off their air force and army. What do you think will happen when we launch the attack that will end this for good? The Chinese have already told me that they will be the first to recognize our government. A friend like that will give us leverage in the world."

"At what cost, Vanni? What do they want in return? They always want something."

Vanni gave Gala's shoulders a quick squeeze. "Do not think that way, Gala. You will be a hero of our liberation with your weapon, and you will make us rich when we sell it to the Chinese. We will have everything we need—security, friends, and money."

Gala merely nodded and went back to gazing at the stars while the sky was still clear.

DAY 7

Trincomalee

Syren held off three miles from the port of Trincomalee. It wasn't safe to come much closer. Just as it had been in Colombo, boats that had been under way during the EMP attack were now grounded on sandbars or hugging the shore. Four teams manned the topside guns while Stark ordered the aviation component to launch the unmanned aerial vehicles that would provide a bird's-eye view of the area. Specialists in the CIC would monitor the cameras, searching for anything out of the ordinary.

"Olivia, you have the conn. Standard operating procedure—keep the engines warm, warn off any ship, and if anything comes within a mile make best speed in the opposite direction."

"Lovely, Captain. Full retreat, then, is it?" she said with a wink.

"Best to live to fight another day until we can figure out this EMP thing," he retorted. "The executive officer has the conn," he said over the shipwide speakers.

Gunny Willis and another security guard joined Stark, Ranasinghe, and Warren on *Syren*'s RHIB *Somers*. Warren was still tightening the straps to secure his equipment when Stark gave the command to the boatswain's mate to lower the boat astern. He quickly found a seat. Each member of the team wore body armor and, except for Warren, held an FN FAL-308 select-fire rifle. The second security officer held onto the pedestal-mounted FN MAG-58.

The boat was halfway down the ramp when it jerked to a stop, almost throwing Warren into the water. The boatswain's mate gestured to two of the crew, who manually released the boat. "Don't worry, Captain, we'll fix it eventually."

Stark and the rest put on their sunglasses to block the midday sun as they sped into Trincomalee harbor. Stark surreptitiously slid his hand down his right pant leg to the spot where it was tucked neatly into his boot. Once he felt the bejeweled hilt of the *sgian dubh*, something he had done often since Maggie had given him the good luck charm, he was comforted. He removed the knife and took a closer look at the family crest on the hilt. When Warren noticed the weapon, Stark handed it to him and explained its significance in Scottish history.

Warren looked at it appreciatively. "Nice piece. Well balanced. I like the quartz on the hilt. Cairngorm, isn't it? And I like how they worked the iron into a crest. Great craftsmanship," he said as he carefully returned it to Stark.

Ranasinghe seemed to have no good luck charm to bring him comfort. He was visibly distraught, particularly when they reached the entrance of the harbor. Wrecks and flotsam still littered the water and shoreline because the local port authorities were skittish about proceeding with salvage efforts. The Sri Lankan commander pointed to the mast and partially submerged superstructure of one ship. "That, Captain, is—or rather was—*Sayura*. I had orders to report to her as my next ship. I knew her and her officers well."

There was little Stark could say. He too had experienced the loss of a ship and crew. A simple knowing nod was more meaningful than any words.

The fishing boats that had not been in port during the attack were now going about their normal business, casually laying lines miles outside the harbor. One sailboat—a catamaran—was slowly making its way to the port under power.

Stark missed his own sailing days. A cutter-rigged sloop berthed on the Potomac River had been his home during the year he spent as an aide on Capitol Hill. On long weekends he would sail down the river and out into the Chesapeake, especially on sun-filled, windy days like this. He smiled remembering full-bellied sails and a fifteen-degree heel as the boat dug steadily into the water. Something about the catamaran didn't seem quite right to him, though. On its current course the boat should be sailing close-hauled to windward, not putt-putting along under power. He couldn't imagine a sailor not taking advantage of prime sailing conditions like these.

He carefully set his rifle down and pulled binoculars out of the equipment case. The catamaran was an older design without the roller-furling jib, but it carried no headsail at all. The mainsail hung loosely from the boom, though he couldn't see a halyard attached to it. Stark's RHIB was nearly fifteen hundred yards from the sailboat, and even with the best binoculars he couldn't see every detail. He could see three men in the cockpit. One was standing and steering the boat. The other two were looking in Stark's direction.

"Commander," Stark said to Ranasinghe, "you wanted us to investigate ships. How about we get in a little practice here?"

"That sailboat?" the Sri Lankan officer asked.

Stark nodded and said, "Something's not right. Might be nothing. Coxswain, make for that sailboat. Gunny, stand by to cover." Willis motioned for the guard standing with the MAG-58 to focus on the sailboat while Stark kept the binoculars trained on it. He couldn't make out a name.

"Jay," he said to the scientist, "what's the distance between that sailboat and *Syren*?"

Warren redirected his attention from his instruments to take a look. "I'd guess about three thousand yards."

Stark did some math in his head. The men in the boat scrambled as the RHIB closed to two thousand yards from a different vector than *Syren*. Stark was about to hail them on ship-to-ship when he saw them scurrying around. The question remained: was something wrong, or was this merely a damaged sailboat seeking safe harbor whose crew took alarm at seeing an armed RHIB heading toward them?

"Hey, boss," Warren shouted. "More ships over there."

Warren was right. There *were* more ships—the two littoral combat ships and the *Arleigh Burke*–class destroyer *Syren* had passed earlier. Stark grabbed the radio and handed it to Ranasinghe with some directions.

"Catamaran, catamaran," the Sri Lankan commander said in Sinhalese, "this is the government boat approaching you. Do you require assistance?"

There was no response from the other boat.

"They just went below," Stark said.

Ranasinghe repeated his message, then said it in English in case the men were not locals. Still nothing.

The three Navy ships continued to approach, and Stark hailed them.

"This is Coalition Warship Twelve," came the reply, obviously from one of the littoral combat ships. "We are passing astern of you."

The high-pitched voice sounded familiar to Stark. "Coalition warship, this is *Syren* Actual. Recommend you stand off at least three nautical miles, over."

"This is a U.S. Navy warship! We do not take orders from you. We are coming through."

"Coalition warship, we are about to conduct a VBSS," Stark countered as Warren explained the acronym for visit, board, search, and seizure to a confused-looking Ranasinghe. Stark continued, "On behalf of the Sri Lankan government. I repeat: request you stand off at least three nautical miles, over."

"Captain," Gunny said calmly, "the catamaran's turning."

The catamaran had picked up speed and turned 180 degrees—right toward the two LCSs and destroyer. Stark saw two fishing boats in the distance also change course. He suspected that they would cut across the bows of the warships, although well ahead of them. But they were too far away for him to see what was happening.

"Coxswain, get us on the other side of the sailboat toward those two fishing boats. And crank it." The crewman complied, and in a few seconds the RHIB was bumping over the water at sixty knots. The passengers ducked down and held on. The RHIB was between the sailboat and the fishing boats when Stark motioned the coxswain to slow down.

When the boat eased to ten knots, he looked through the binoculars again. The two fishing boats were still on a line to cross ahead of the warships, and they were both towing long fishing lines. He couldn't actually see the lines, but he could make out translucent buoys, about the size of the lobster buoys he remembered as a kid in New England, spaced about twenty feet apart. The warships were still bearing down. They hadn't listened to him.

It suddenly occurred to Stark that no fisherman or lobsterman in his right mind would use translucent buoys. They should have been colored, identifiable to the waterman who owned them.

The catamaran was clearly not in distress, because it had turned away from the harbor and directly toward the warships, still refusing to respond to the continuing hails from Ranasinghe.

Stark looked back in time to see the sailboat raise a flag on one of the halyards—lions on an aquamarine background. Peering back at the two fishing boats he saw the same flag. "Do you recognize those signals?" he asked Ranasinghe.

The Sri Lankan didn't hesitate to respond. "Those are banned in my country. They are the flags of the Sea Tigers."

"Son of a . . . that's it." Stark grabbed the mike. "Coalition warships, these are Sea Tiger boats. Recommend you veer to port at best speed to avoid them."

USS *LeFon*, off Trincomalee

Cdr. Jaime Johnson was on the starboard bridge wing looking through the Big Eyes—the powerful, pedestal-mounted ship's binoculars—observing the movements of the boats ahead and off their starboard bow.

"Standing by, ma'am," Ensign Fisk said as he handed the ship-to-ship mike to her.

"Admiral, we need to do as *Syren's* captain suggests," she said to Rossberg on the ship-to-ship radio. "Something's not right and he has better situational awareness where he is."

"Commander, you will remain in formation. These boats will make way for us. We need to transfer these ships in Trincomalee, and I'm not going to let a bunch of fishermen delay us."

"Sir, we are being placed at risk."

"I am ordering you to remain in formation," the admiral barked.

Jaime took a deep breath and bowed her head for a moment of reflection, thinking of *Kirkwall* when she was attacked. If she had responded more quickly then . . . She looked through the Big Eyes again and saw the fishing boats trailing what appeared to be fishing nets. Clearly they would be towing the nets across the bows of the three American ships. And she still didn't understand why that catamaran had turned toward them. Was it carrying explosives? If she trained the 5-inch guns on the small boats, though, she would endanger Stark's RHIB. *I have to do something now!* "Admiral," she radioed, "nets. They've got nets. Recommend we change course to avoid entanglement."

"Don't be ridiculous. We'll cut right through them. Really, those stupid fishermen should know better."

Damn it, she thought, then made her decision. "Bobby, all ahead full, left full rudder," she said as she opened up the distance to the LCSs.

"What are you doing? Get back here now, you," the admiral shouted into the radio.

"This is USS *LeFon* to littoral combat ships. There is something wrong. Turn away from those small boats immediately." *LeFon's* powerful engines took her past the fishing boats before they could cross her bow as she distanced herself nearly two nautical miles from the catamaran.

RHIB *Somers*

"Good job, *LeFon*, but why the hell are those two other ships still on course?" Connor demanded.

"Captain, what do we do?" Gunny Willis asked.

"Fire shots across the sailboat's bow," Stark said to the guard at the pedestal gun. Immediately the MAG-58 let loose a short, staccato burst of fire. The catamaran continued toward the ships undeterred.

"Commander," Stark said turning to Ranasinghe. "You said the Sri Lankan navy didn't know how the EMP hit the harbors and you never caught the Tigers who did it."

"Correct."

"Jay, that catamaran isn't making use of its sails. Do you remember when we were building *Syren* and we got that brief on those Hamas rockets?"

"Yeah, boss," Warren nodded. "The Qassams they were using against Israel."

"Remember their diameter?"

"About five inches."

"Small enough to use a mast as the launcher?" Stark asked, already knowing the answer. "Gunny, open up on that catamaran now."

Stark got back on the radio and warned the LCSs again but in response only got an admonition from their commander to stand down from firing on an unarmed vessel. The fishing boats with their long lines had already crossed the bows of both LCSs.

Hundreds of bullets from the RHIB peppered the composite hull of the catamaran, and smoke emerged from its engines. The man in the cockpit was down, but there was no sign of the two men who had gone below. Suddenly, fiery smoke blew out of the top of the mast like dragon's breath. And then a small rocket emerged.

Singapore

All Special Agent Damien Golzari knew for certain was that lab equipment from the United States had been passed to a nonexistent company in Singapore, a dead informant knew of a shipment to Sri Lanka, that shipment had ties to a Chinese firm called Zheng Research & Development, and Bill Blake had been killed because he was asking questions. Nothing else he found in Blake's office had proved to be of any use in the investigation, and there was no other source of information in Singapore. He looked at the files spread out on Blake's desk.

The file from Homeland Security Investigations had been faxed to him a few hours earlier. The agent he spoke to was correct about Academy Solutions. A modern hydrostatic extrusion press had been sent to the ghost firm from the Argonne National Laboratory in Illinois. A quick search on the Internet told Golzari that an extrusion press was used to shape metal into tubes, rods, and wires. The HSI file also showed another shipment from a company in the United States two months before to Academic Solutions—four large 3D printers.

After Golzari completed the paperwork for the State Department on the deaths at Raffles, he made two calls. The first was to Argonne National Laboratory to find the person involved with the extrusion press. After being transferred several times, he reached someone familiar with it.

"Dr. Paddock," the man said abruptly.

"This is Special Agent Damien Golzari with the Diplomatic Security Service."

"What do you want?"

"Information. About a hydrostatic extrusion press," Golzari said.

"Any press in particular?"

"Yes, one that was shipped several weeks ago by Argonne to Academic Solutions in Singapore."

"My colleague, Dr. Sims, ordered it. Why?"

"Well, sir, we're following up on paperwork here in Singapore. Can I speak with Dr. Sims?"

"No, you can't. Unfortunately he passed away last week."

"Oh? Had he been ill?"

"No," Paddock said. "There was an accident at the lab. He was working alone at night and there was a fire. Apparently the sprinkler system was faulty."

"My condolences," Golzari said trying to sound sincere. "But I do need more information. Can you help me?" Golzari made a note to check the fire department's report on the incident.

"All right, I guess so," Paddock responded. "What do you want to know?" Golzari heard the distinctive sound of mastication. It was morning in Chicago, and judging by the chewing sounds on the line followed by slurps the scientist was eating breakfast and washing it down with coffee.

"Can you tell me who ordered the press?" Golzari asked.

"Not specifically. Any paperwork on it was in Sims' office, and that was destroyed in the fire, although I did ask him about it when they were putting it on the pallet for shipment to Singapore."

"What did he say?"

"He said he met a very smart young scientist at a conference earlier this year in San Francisco," Paddock responded. "He discussed his work with Sims and asked if his lab might borrow a hydrostatic press."

"Did he give a name?"

"It was short. Gama? Galu? No, Gala. That was it."

"And what was the focus of his research?" Golzari pressed.

"He was working on new applications for zirconium."

"And the press would help how?"

"I don't know. I believe he told Dr. Sims that he needed one for testing."

Golzari was beginning to get a bad feeling about this. "Do you have a *guess* on how the press might be used with zirconium?"

"Nothing specific, Agent Mozilla," the scientist responded.

"Golzari."

"Yeah, right. Look, it could be used for a lot of different things. Without seeing the proposal, I can't give you more information. But this is the latest model, so it would work with metals with potentially volatile characteristics."

"Is zirconium volatile?"

"Not that I know of. And it's pretty common. It *is* kind of strange though," he said almost as an afterthought.

Well, at least I have a name. Golzari thanked Dr. Paddock and hung up the phone. Then he picked it up again and placed a call to the field office in San Francisco to get the name of the conference and a list of attendees and anything they could find on this scientist Gala.

Among Blake's files was a list from the naval attaché of all the ships that had left Singapore for Sri Lanka during the past month. Unfortunately for his investigation, Singapore was one of the busiest ports in the world. In the past month alone more than one hundred ships had followed that itinerary, and Golzari doubted that any of the reported manifests would include stolen lab equipment.

As Golzari worked through his dilemma Agent Kelly poked her head in the door. "How are you making out?"

"Nothing but dead ends here. I need a flight to Sri Lanka."

Kelly shook her head. "That'll be tough right now. Haven't you seen the news from there over the past few days?"

"A few reports. Some cities experienced power failures and there were attacks on the navy."

"It was much more than that. Looks like the Tamil Tigers are back in force," Kelly said. "No advance intel that we were aware of, but they took out the Sri Lankan fleets at Galle, Colombo, and Trincomalee. All flights to and from Sri Lanka have been suspended."

"Great. What about a flight to India and a ship to Sri Lanka?"

"Possible. Let me see what I can do."

An hour later Golzari had his itinerary. He was boarding a cab for the trip to the airport when another car pulled up beside it and two officers grabbed him and shoved him through the open back door, slamming it behind him. Sitting next to him was the detective who had interrogated him.

"At least you're not cuffing me this time," Golzari said as the car sped away from the hotel.

"Agent Golzari, we've been instructed to take you to the airport."

"You're wasting your time. I was just heading there. I appreciate your generosity though," he said sarcastically.

"We are to put you on a plane to the United States and watch you leave," the detective continued. "The government has instructed us to tell you that if you ever return to Singapore you will be arrested and incarcerated indefinitely."

"Lovely."

"Do not take this lightly, Agent Golzari. We were also told that if we did not arrest you and send you back to your country, your life would be at risk. Of course, it may already be wherever you go."

RHIB *Somers*

The rocket wasn't accurate, but it didn't have to be because it wasn't designed to hit another platform. In any case, the crew of the RHIB stopped firing at the catamaran, which was now listing to one side and taking on water through the many holes in its hull. All Stark and the others could do was wait. When the rocket reached an altitude of five hundred yards it exploded into an orange ball that expanded into lazy greenish-blue sparks. Stark could only pray that *LeFon* and *Syren* were far enough away to escape the EMP's effects.

The scene suddenly became deathly quiet as the RHIB's motor stopped. The boat lost momentum and stopped dead in the water. The two fishing boats also stopped. Far more discomfiting was the sight of the two littoral combat ships, which had been barreling toward them at thirty knots and were now completely devoid of electronics and engines. Their momentum continued to propel them over the fishing lines with the translucent buoys.

Stark tried to hail them, but to no avail. The RHIB's radio was dead, too. He could see through the binoculars that *LeFon* was under way, which meant she was outside the range of the EMP rocket's effect.

Life appeared unexpectedly on the bullet-ridden catamaran as the two men who had gone below emerged in the cockpit with weapons. Stark realized that they could have survived the gunfire only if they had up-armored the cabin. "Take them out, Gunny," Stark said coldly, and gunfire from the RHIB silenced them permanently. Stark's group still had to worry about the men in the fishing boats, but those were out of range for now.

In the distance Stark could see the fishing lines beginning to wrap around the hulls of the drifting LCSs. The lines were in no danger of fouling the propellers because the EMP had destroyed the ships' electronics and machinery and the props no longer worked. That didn't make sense. If the Sea Tigers knew the EMP would kill the ships' electronics, then why try to foul the props with fishing lines? Unless the propellers weren't the target.

The first buoy exploded just as Stark realized the implication. One by one and in succession the translucent buoys detonated along the waterline of each LCS. The Highland Maritime team watched helplessly as holes eight feet in diameter ripped through the thin hulls. Each ship, Stark knew, carried a minimal crew because the designers had insisted that automation would make large crews unnecessary for damage control. Stark wondered what the designers would say at this moment as he watched the hulls of two modern ships crumple and sink in a matter of minutes, taking their minimal crews with them.

Stark put a hand on Ranasinghe's shoulder to express his anger and sorrow. The Tigers had just killed two more Sri Lankan crews. Even if anyone had survived, the men in the RHIB could do nothing to help them. He ordered the security team to keep a sharp lookout. The last time the Sea Tigers had attacked the Sri Lankan navy they hadn't stopped until all the ships were sunk.

"Sir," Gunny Willis said pointing at the drifting fishing boats.

"What is it?" Stark said as he drew his own binoculars to the direction Willis was pointing. One of the larger fishing vessels, about 100 tons, was bobbing around like the others, but several men were gathered at the stern. Just as Stark tightened the focus the ship's double doors opened.

"This isn't good," he told Ranasinghe. "I've heard about these elsewhere. North Korea uses them—or at least used to. They're getting ready to launch a small boat."

Almost on cue, a thirty-foot speedboat with a low profile and three large outboard motors slid into the sea. It was the only operational platform in the immediate vicinity, it carried half a dozen Sea Tigers, and it was speeding toward the RHIB.

"More trouble, boss," Jay said as he pointed to a second speedboat easing down the ramp.

"Positions, everyone. Port side," Stark commanded, and the men took up prone positions from bow to stern, resting their FAL-308s on the port tube. Stark was in the middle with Ranasinghe and Warren to his right and Gunny Willis and the coxswain to his left. The other security officer held his position with the MAG-58. A couple adjusted their Kevlar helmets and armor-plated vests. Stark handed his Beretta to Jay.

"I'm not a shooter, boss."

"We're all shooters right now, Jay. I'd give you the bigger one, but I need the range that the pistol doesn't give me," Stark replied.

"Right. Hitting a target just like in the Olympics," Warren said.

"My targets in Seoul didn't move," Stark said as he focused on the Tiger boat.

"Captain, they're coming into our range," Willis said.

That's good, Stark thought. If the Tigers hadn't started firing yet, then his group would have a brief advantage based on the range of their own weapons. Most insurgent groups relied on AK-47s because of their availability. That gave them an effective range of a bit over 400 yards at best, while the FAL-308s had a range of at least 650 yards. Stark's own personally sighted weapon and expertise as a marksman added 200 yards to his effective range.

The first Tiger speedboat had veered to port to give the soldiers an opportunity to fire. Stark slowed his breathing in preparation. As the RHIB's port tube settled with the next swell, he trained his sights on the high-speed engines. He fired one round, hitting the Tiger boat's starboard engine and causing the boat to reduce speed, which in turn caused confusion among the five soldiers readying their weapons.

"Weapons free," he said, and the pedestal-mounted MAG-58 and FAL-308s opened up on the Sea Tigers' boat. With its other two engines still running, the speedboat pulled to starboard for a few seconds, then turned broadside again at 550 yards. Three Tigers immediately fell to the security team's gunfire while two other soldiers hid behind the boat's metal freeboard. The MAG-58 let loose, and every nonmetallic item on the speedboat splintered. After the initial MAG-58 volley, Gunny Willis and Stark both found their marks as the final two men were killed. Only the helmsman remained alive.

"Second—" the security officer managed to say before the impact of weapons fire from the second Tiger boat lifted his body and impelled him overboard. Stark shifted direction toward the stern and saw the speedboat less than 450 yards away and the coxswain's lifeless body draped over the transom.

Gunny Willis was about to shift when he was hit by debris from the MAG-58. He clutched his throat with one hand and tried to fire with the other as he put himself between the oncoming boat and Jay Warren.

Ranasinghe came around to Stark's left as Stark dropped to one knee. Stark flipped the FAL-308 to full auto mode just as two rounds hit his Kevlar chest protector, driving the air from his lungs and propelling him backward. He struggled to regain his balance and breathe, thankful for the body armor that had saved his life. Ranasinghe had just taken a prone position when he was hit in the head, his helmet flying back viciously.

Just as Stark raised his weapon again, fighting back the pain in his chest, a wall of water exploded between the RHIB and the second Tiger boat. He wondered briefly if the boat had a mortar, but no mortar round would have created such a high wall of water. A second later he heard the distinctive sound of the 5-inch/62 Mark 45 gun carried by Navy destroyers and realized what had happened. *LeFon* had taken a big chance with a friendly so close, but there wasn't much of a choice. Stark and Gunny Willis kept firing blindly through the wall of water. As it descended Stark saw *Syren* making her way toward the scene. Puffs of smoke showed that two of her .50-caliber machine guns were firing at the speedboat as well. The Tigers turned their boat around and made for *Syren*. Stark dropped his weapon, grabbed the pedestal, and pulled himself into position to fire the MAG-58. The stern of the second Tiger boat disintegrated, sending the occupants, already dead, into the water.

LeFon's 5-inch gun continued to fire—this time at the larger stern-trawler mother ship—and destroyed her with only a few rounds. *LeFon* next focused on the two fishing boats that had dragged the explosive lines earlier, and with a few more rounds the battle was over.

Jay was leaning over Gunny Willis, trying to stem the blood gushing from his throat. Ranasinghe was down as well and barely breathing. Stark picked up the ship-to-ship radio. "*LeFon*, request medical assistance. Two dead. Two severely injured." He removed his vest, lay back on the starboard tube, and lost consciousness, having forgotten that the EMP blast had rendered the radio ineffective.

PART II

DAY 8

Mullaitivu District

Outsiders knew the site as the Mullaitivu Breakers. The local Tamils who worked there called it hell. The Breakers was the reclamation site for more than a hundred freighters, tankers, passenger ships, and other boats whose engines were outdated, had been damaged, or otherwise were too costly to operate in a competitive global market. Some of the ships were less than thirty years old. They bore faded names like *Wei Express*, *Golden Pacific*, and *Katya P.* Two dozen of the ships lay like beached whales on the shore; the others, nearly a hundred of them, awaited their fate in the shallow waters offshore. Instead of maggots and scavengers slowly eating away at the great beasts, a legion of barefoot workers deprived the ships of their former glory, many using only their hands as tools.

Sparks flew inside and around the ships as men tore them apart piece by piece for the metal scrap that was now their only value. There was no Occupational Safety and Health Administration here. Falling steel plates could crush a worker who wasn't paying attention, and unstable decks could give way and plunge an unwary man to his death. Two or three men died every day at the Breakers, and most of the others who worked there bore "Mullaitivu tattoos"—the scars from close calls. And so it had been for forty years, with the only exception being the years of the civil war. Hundreds of men lost their lives or dignity to this trade for poverty wages while the government of Sri Lanka and the shipowners reaped the profits.

The Sri Lankan government had chosen the Tamils to do their cheap labor, men like Vanni, his brothers, and his father. Vanni was the only member of his family still alive and able to work. One of his brothers still lived, but a brain injury—there were no hard hats—had left him a helpless invalid in the care of relatives in one of the many tin-roofed shantytowns that lined the coast. Vanni had grown up in one of those shacks and had been lucky enough to attract the attention of an educated Tamil who had been condemned to the labor camp, for that was what the Breakers was.

During the day the boy worked at the Breakers. At night he learned his alphabet and then read eagerly. As a teenager he read the works of Hegel and Marx as well as the speeches of Ho Chi Minh and other great communist leaders. He read the words and thought about them every day at the Breakers as he saw his family, friends, and neighbors laboring for just enough money to keep themselves alive. And he saw that the workers must organize and rise up against their oppressors, just as Hegel and Marx and Ho said. When the uprising came and civil war tore Sri Lanka apart, the Tamil Tigers recruited Vanni and sent him to their maritime arm: the Sea Tigers.

While he had been dismantling ships at the Breakers Vanni had learned a great deal about how they were built, and he and the other Sea Tigers became innovative marine architects who constructed craft that could challenge the Sri Lankan navy. Together they built the fiberglass suicide boats and patrol boats that would eventually sink nearly thirty Sri Lankan navy boats. The Sea Tigers even maintained their own system of logistics ships far offshore.

The leader of the Sea Tigers, Colonel Soosai himself, had recognized Vanni's intelligence and had taken him as one of his closest advisers. Among his contributions was a communication system that relied on the old signal flags used during the Age of Sail rather than radios, to prevent the Sri Lankan navy from intercepting messages and locating the senders. Indeed, that was how his men had succeeded in their recent attacks at Trincomalee, Colombo, and Galle—by using signal flags from the launching catamaran and the Sea Tiger fishing vessels to coordinate their activities. He was well aware that his only chance to defeat superior forces was to use innovative means of disrupting them and destroying them.

On the deck of his command ship—a former Soviet *Ugra*-class submarine tender that had been at anchor for years off the Breakers—Vanni listened calmly to the report on the latest attack. Spies in Singapore had told him of the two littoral combat ships that the United States had transferred to the Sri Lankan navy, and he knew when they would arrive. Almost everything had gone as planned. The catamaran had nearly been taken but had launched the EMP in time. It was fortunate, he thought, that the American destroyer had not been damaged, because that would have brought down the wrath of the U.S. Navy.

Vanni closed his eyes and envisioned the attack as the messenger described it. The two Sea Tiger fishing boats had successfully towed the lines with the new C4-stuffed buoys that Gala's 3D printers had made. The buoys had wrapped around the ships just as expected and, set off by a trip wire in the fishing line, initiated a perfectly timed daisy chain of explosions.

Vanni swelled with pride. Two primitive fishing boats had sent two of the world's most modern warships to the bottom of the sea. And his vision and planning had brought it about. Of course, the lucky discovery of the mine that contained the exact substance needed to make the EMP weapons had made it possible. But Vanni was the one who had seen the possibilities and directed the project. Vanni's breathing was slow and steady, like his leadership.

"There was only one issue, Vanni," said the messenger who had been describing the attack.

"Go on," Vanni quietly replied, his eyes still closed.

"Another ship was reported in the area, one claiming to be a private security ship working for the Sri Lankan navy. And it nearly succeeded in stopping the attack."

Vanni's eyes flew open. "Continue."

"A small armed boat from the ship was near the catamaran and almost stopped the launch of the EMP rocket. The ship itself was too far from the battle to be affected. But we learned its name: *Syren.*"

Vanni hummed a simple "mmmm," acknowledging the statement but offering nothing else. He dismissed the messenger and looked out at the fleet of ghost ships, the two dozen already beached at the Breakers and another hundred at anchor awaiting their fate. That fate would have to wait. The workers had more important things to do. They would be fighting for their independence very soon.

He went below to Gala's labs. In the first, the 3D printers were manufacturing soda bottle–sized buoys for future operations. Gala and his assistants from China were working on the new EMP rockets in the larger lab.

Gala was making calculations on a computer and didn't look up when Vanni entered. His body was bathed in sweat, even though the old Soviet air-conditioning units were working hard to lower the temperature of the lab and cool the heat-generating computers and equipment. Vanni put his hand on Gala's shoulder. "Again, the Gala rocket succeeded, my friend. Two more warships sunk. How goes your work?"

Gala looked up and turned to Vanni. "We have much more to do."

"I have confidence in you," Vanni said with a smile. "We shall christen them the 'Gala IIs.'"

Seattle, Washington

When Golzari landed in Los Angeles he had more pieces of the puzzle. Most important, he now had the full name of the foreign scientist who had asked Dr. Sims to loan him a hydrostatic press: Viswanathan Gala, a Sri Lankan from the northern village of Alampil. Gala was twenty-seven and, according to his passport photo, extremely thin. Neither the State Department nor Interpol had any additional information on him, and several attempts to contact the Sri Lankan authorities had failed because of the continuing communications problems.

Golzari had also learned a great deal about the Tamil Tigers—far more than he knew when he was sent to Singapore to investigate Special Agent Blake's death. And what he learned was alarming. The Tigers—who called themselves the Liberation Tigers of Tamil Eelam, or LTTE, were among the best organized and most brutal terrorists the world had ever seen. The Tamil people were Hindus of Indian descent, which made them a minority among the largely Buddhist Sri Lankans, who marginalized and disenfranchised them. Since they organized in the late 1970s the Tamil Tigers had waged a war of terror against the rest of Sri Lanka. They bombed public buildings and assassinated the country's public officials—including President Ramasinghe Premadasa in 1993. They financed their operations with drug smuggling and robberies. The LTTE's first uprising, in 2006, had been aimed at carving out a homeland for the Tamil people in northeastern Sri Lanka. Their second major offensive had begun a few days ago, and Golzari found himself right in the middle of it.

If Gala was a Tamil, then the "borrowed" extruder was clearly going to play some role in the LTTE's new offensive against Sri Lanka. The fire at the Argonne National Laboratory office that killed Dr. Sims had apparently destroyed any hard copies of proposals he received, but Golzari expected to find summaries of research projects and loans in the lab's central database. Oddly, though, when he had contacted the lab, there was no record of the loan of the extruder; nor was there a record of how it was shipped.

Golzari remembered Dr. Paddock mentioning zirconium, so he searched online to find information on the element. He learned that zirconium is a malleable metal that resists corrosion and does not absorb neutrons. That latter characteristic makes it useful for coating nuclear reactor fuel. Now Golzari was really alarmed. *Does this mean the extruder has applications for a nuclear bomb?* He called Dr. Paddock again at Argonne.

"Not really, no," Paddock opined. "But Admiral Rickover and his research group did do some work on the idea."

"Hyman Rickover—the father of the nuclear Navy?"

"Yeah," Paddock responded. "He had this group called the Vulcans in the 1950s and 1960s—young scientists he hand-selected to test the characteristics of different metals."

"Are any of the Vulcans still around?"

"Yeah, there are a few. One of them used to stop by here a lot before he retired. Dr. Abraham."

Golzari managed to track down Dr. Dov Abraham, who was now living in Seattle. A short flight later and he was welcomed into the older man's modest home.

"Zirconium? Why the interest in that?" asked Abraham.

"I'm trying to find out if it has any special properties, where it comes from—that sort of information," Golzari said.

"It's not an uncommon element," Dr. Abraham said, his hands shaking badly from Parkinson's disease.

"Where is it found?" Golzari asked.

"Oh, many places. Mostly Australia, the eastern United States, China, Ukraine, and a few small pockets elsewhere—Uruguay, West Africa, northern India, and Sri Lanka."

Bingo. "And you used zirconium when you worked for Admiral Rickover?"

"Yes, we tested properties and applications for many metals," the veteran scientist confirmed. "I remember those days with great fondness. We were in Tennessee, you know, at the National Security Complex. Building 9211." Dr. Abraham smiled and his eyes took on a faraway look.

Golzari brought him back to the matter at hand. "Was there anything special about zirconium that would have interested Rickover? Something with nuclear applications?"

Abraham thought about it. "You know, my mind isn't as sharp as it once was," he finally said. "But I remember that we looked at different ways of separating zirconium from hafnium."

"Hafnium?" Golzari was puzzled. "What's that?"

"It's another element, almost always found in combination with zirconium. There were theories that hafnium might occur in its pure form, but no one to my knowledge has ever found a pure lode."

"What's special about hafnium?"

"Like zirconium, it's effective for neutron absorption in nuclear power plants. There *was* one other application . . ." Abraham trailed off as if reluctant to say anything more.

"What was that, sir?"

"High-yield explosives. Not on the order of a nuclear explosion, of course, but an order of magnitude greater than a standard chemical reaction—some fifty or a hundred thousand times greater, we estimated."

Golzari was stunned. "It's not something I've heard of before."

"There's no reason why you would, Agent Golzari. None of this was ever of much use. We spent years testing theories, but none of them panned out. We needed a pure hafnium isotope, and that was impossible to find. So Admiral Rickover had us move on to other projects."

"Did the government ever pursue this?"

Abraham shook his head. "Again, there was no reason to."

"Did anyone ever learn about these experiments?" Golzari pressed.

"Several of the Vulcan reports became public. I think the ones on hafnium and zirconium separation were declassified about ten years ago," the old scientist said.

"I find it odd that experiments with that sort of application were declassified."

"So did we, though there were only a handful of us remaining. We fought it, but someone at the Department of Energy overruled us."

Golzari thanked Abraham for his time and headed back to the airport on rain-slicked roads. On the way he made some calls to the Department of Energy and learned that the man who had declassified the material had been accused of removing files and selling them to the Chinese government a few years before. But there had been no trial. The matter was hushed up in the interest of national security.

As his rental car came around a bend, the rain now pouring down, a car began to pass him. *Stupid thing to do on a blind curve,* he thought. His instincts kicked in and told him to slow down. As he did, the window on the passenger side was lowered and a weapon emerged. The man in the passenger seat missed Golzari but managed to shoot the engine and front left tire, sending

Golzari's vehicle fishtailing as he eased it onto the shoulder. He immediately got out and pulled his Glock from its holster.

The other car braked and came to a stop fifty yards ahead in the middle of the road. Three men emerged, all armed and in classic shooter's stance facing Golzari, who lowered his profile behind the engine and stabilized his weapon on one of the men. A couple of their shots hit the car, but Golzari ignored them and calmly fired his weapon. He took out one of the men with a headshot, but at this distance he needed three rounds for the bullets to find their mark.

The other two men dashed off in opposite directions perpendicular to Golzari; they were trying to outflank him. A tractor trailer approached behind the gunmen's vehicle and slowed to a stop. Other traffic was visible in the distance. *This is a busy highway,* Golzari thought. *They're going to want to get this over with quickly.*

One of the men took up a position behind a tree thirty yards away, but the other had not yet reached cover. Golzari took careful aim at the second man and fired two quick shots. The first bullet struck the man in the leg; the next was a direct shot to his chest. It was now a duel between Golzari and the last man.

Golzari ducked as three more shots shattered the rental car's windshield. Then silence. *This one is better trained than the other two.* He waited patiently for his opportunity, aware that the shooter would be getting desperate as more cars approached and stopped. A couple of people emerged from their vehicles to see what was holding up traffic. As a federal agent Golzari had a responsibility to keep them out of danger. He fired two rounds then ran into the woods behind him, his leather soles sliding on the wet grass and moss. He had to draw the third man away from the civilians, so he quickly removed his shoes and ran toward the largest tree in sight.

Sure enough the man followed. He took shelter behind a smaller tree that almost hid him completely. But Golzari could see just enough, and with one stable shot the agent took off the left side of the man's face. Golzari breathed a sigh of relief. He stopped long enough on the way back to his car to take a close look at the shooter. Even with half his face gone it was clear the man was Hispanic, not Asian. The Singaporean detective had warned him that Zheng R&D had a long reach.

The good citizens who had come out of their vehicles to investigate the stopped traffic had disappeared at the sound of gunshots, but several had called 911, and Golzari could hear sirens in the distance. Good. He was going to need a ride to town.

M/V *Syren*

Dusk had given way to night, and Connor Stark closed the porthole to his stateroom and secured the curtain to ensure that no light escaped to betray *Syren's* location. His ears were still ringing from the firefight, and just raising his arms generated enough pain in his chest to make him wish he had accepted Doc's offer of treatment afterward. Gunny Willis and Ranasinghe had been in much greater need—so badly injured, in fact, that both had been transferred to *LeFon* with her superior medical facilities.

Syren and *LeFon* were sailing in company a few hundred yards apart some fifty miles off the coast of Sri Lanka at five knots. *LeFon's* helicopter was somewhere above them searching for approaching boats that might pose a threat.

Stark sat down at his desk and eyed the photograph that held a prominent place on it. He lightly traced the edge of the frame with his right forefinger. Maggie was standing in front of a rose bush on the Isle of Lewis. It had been raining that day, and her water-soaked red hair hung heavily on her shoulders and Shetland wool sweater. But she was smiling nevertheless. It was the first time she had taken more than a day off from the pub in a year. He had spirited her away in his boat without telling her where she was going. That had been just a month before he was recalled to duty in Yemen and everything changed. Before people died on *Kirkwall* and elsewhere. He understood why she wanted him out of this business. Did she understand why he couldn't leave it? He wasn't sure.

His left hand was shaking uncontrollably from the pain and in reaction to the day's events. When there was a knock at his door he grabbed a drawer handle with his left hand and loudly said, "Enter."

Olivia Harrison came in first, followed by Jay Warren. "Captain, we're ready to report," she said.

"Go ahead," he said, motioning with his right hand to have them take seats on the chair and bed.

Harrison took a deep breath before speaking. "Gaffney and Steiner have been transferred to *LeFon* for repatriation. We had the home office notify their next of kin."

"Should have waited for me to do that, XO," Stark said, feeling a pang of grief for the coxswain and gunner killed in the fight.

"I figured you had other things to handle, sir."

"Understood. I'd still like the contact information. As soon as we're out of this I'll get on the satellite phone with their families."

"Will do. The CO of *LeFon* and her navigator are coming on board momentarily."

"Have the steward prep some coffee for them."

"Already done, sir."

"Jay, what do you have to report?"

"The RHIB's back up and operational," the big scientist said.

"So fast?" Connor asked.

"The EMP fried the circuit cards in the engines and radio, that's all. We just had to replace them, and we've got plenty of spares," Warren replied.

"That's it? When they fire an EMP all we have to do is replace cards?"

"Not quite. If *Syren* had been hit, all our spare cards would have been fried too. I'm working with the guys on a Faraday cage to protect them."

"A what?"

"A Faraday cage." Jay said as if the term was commonly known. "Invented by Michael Faraday in the 1830s. We build a wire-mesh cage that looks like a chicken coop in the storage area that will block out electromagnetic pulses, superweld the corners, and then keep all the spare cards in there."

"A chicken coop? That's all it takes?"

"Pretty much, boss."

"Can we do the same with the ship?" Stark asked.

"Kind of a tall order," Warren laughed, but I'll see what I can come up with."

"Okay. Let's talk later about this. Send our guests in, XO," Stark said as he turned back to Harrison.

After Warren left the stateroom Stark could hear him in the passageway greeting their former colleague Jaime Johnson with his characteristic bear hug. "Jaime, girl! It's good to see you." The *hmmphh* of air being squeezed out of lungs was unmistakable.

The short, blonde Navy commander in blue coveralls entered with another officer behind her. She took a deep breath before greeting Stark. "That man is going to hug someone to death someday," she said, trying to elicit a smile from Stark. "How are you doing, sir?" He stood to shake her hand, keeping his still shaking left hand behind his back. "And I believe you remember my NAV," she said, turning to Ens. Bobby Fisk.

"Good to see you again, sir," Fisk said.

"Same, Bobby, although I wish it was under better circumstances. Jaime, how are Gunny Willis and our Sri Lankan liaison?" Stark asked.

"The commander is all patched up. It wasn't as bad as it looked. He was lucky. If the shot hadn't glanced off his helmet it would have been a lot worse," she said. "He'll be transferring back to *Syren* in the next boat."

"And Gunny?"

She shook her head. "I'm sorry, Connor. He didn't make it. Our corpsman tried everything, but even if we had had the facilities on an amphib or a hospital ship it wouldn't have mattered. He lost too much blood."

Stark sank into his chair and put his hands up to his face, trying to control the shaking as he remembered the first time he had met Willis in the gym at the U.S. embassy in Sana'a, Yemen. When Willis retired from the Marine Corps, Stark immediately took him on at Highland Maritime to train the security teams. He had become a close and trusted colleague. It was a bitter loss.

"You've got three of my people on your ship, Jaime."

"Don't worry. Remember, I worked for Highland Maritime too. I'll take good care of them. We're going to Chennai to transfer them."

"Chennai? Contact the Indian navy and see if Captain Dasgupta can meet you there. He'll be a big help to you. I'd appreciate it if you could fill him in on all the details."

"Okay," she said, then turned to Fisk. "Bobby? Can you give us a moment? I'll meet you down at the boat."

Fisk said goodbye to Stark and closed the stateroom door behind him. Jaime sat on the edge of the bed closest to Stark's desk. "You okay?"

"Yeah, why?"

"Because you've just lost three men and because I know you. I caught your hand shaking. I've seen it before."

"My responsibility. My fault we were out there."

"No, not your fault. Your job. You saw something. It was your job to investigate it. You weren't prepared for an EMP or the Tiger attack. And you were able to get off a warning. Connor, if you hadn't told me, *LeFon* would have been hit and possibly sunk with more than three hundred American sailors."

"What about the other two ships?"

"Blame the late Admiral Rossberg. He was just so damned arrogant. He wouldn't listen to me, and he sure as hell wasn't going to listen to you."

"Any survivors?"

"We didn't find any. We sent a small boat to the site to search. My chief engineer served in an LCS. He said those ships always have a lot of cracks in them. Once those Tamil weapons detonated, the ships went down fast."

"All those people lost because of Rossberg," Stark said grimly. "That insufferable ass."

"Agreed. As far as the Highland Maritime personnel on the RHIB? You all did the best you could under the circumstances." She removed her ball cap with the ship's crest and held it. "So, what are your plans?" she continued.

Stark had been thinking about that. He was still operating under a letter of marque, but the cost had already been high in lives. And he wasn't sure how to proceed. Clearly this was not a minor insurgent campaign. The Sea Tigers had used a completely new type of weapon, and so far, at least, the world's most advanced weapons had been helpless against it. What could one ship do against them? If he could get to the heart of their operations, though, he might be able to prevent more deaths like those that had happened on the LCSs and very nearly on *LeFon*.

What was it Gunny Willis had said a few weeks before, when he and Connor had been training, with Willis as always getting the better of him? Oh, yeah, "You have got to finish a fight a lot quicker. . . . I know you've been in a few scraps, but you've been lucky." At this moment Stark didn't feel particularly lucky.

DAY 9

Chennai

The FBI had no information at all on the three Hispanic men who had tried to kill Golzari outside Seattle. Their fingerprints were not on record. They carried no documentation—no driver's licenses, no passports. Their vehicle had been stolen near Green Valley, Arizona, south of Tucson. The only item of interest investigators found was an empty bag from a fast-food place that had been stuffed under the passenger seat. The greasy receipt inside pointed to a burger joint just north of Los Angeles. The FBI suspected that the three were drug cartel members who had crossed the border illegally and gotten weapons from colleagues in California. They thought Golzari was simply a target of opportunity.

Golzari thought otherwise but didn't share his suspicions with the FBI. If Zheng R&D had access to guns in Singapore, with its stringent regulations, then the Chinese firm would have no problem sending killers across America's porous border. Zheng was out to stop Golzari; he was sure of it—as sure as he was that Zheng's people had killed Blake and the Singaporean informant. The Iranian-born Diplomatic Security agent had never before been deterred from following a case to its conclusion. This was not going to be the first time.

He caught the first available flight to India. That was as close as he could get by commercial transportation because all of Sri Lanka's airports and seaports were closed to outside traffic. With the memory of his flight to Singapore still fresh in his mind, he had taken the government-issued coach class ticket and upgraded it to first class with his own money. He hadn't slept for two days, and if he was to have a chance at cracking the case, he needed sleep—a luxury not afforded those in the crowded, noisy coach cabin. The flight was uneventful, although he eyed every person on the plane with suspicion. Where would the next attack come from?

During the long flight from Los Angeles he had put together more pieces of the puzzle. His brief trip back to the United States had yielded a name—Gala—and his visit with Dr. Abraham had yielded a potential take on Gala's interests—the theoretical use of an element called hafnium to make explosives. Hafnium usually occurred with zirconium. Abraham had mentioned that zirconium was mined in Sri Lanka. Gala was from Sri Lanka. There had been reports of small explosions during Tiger attacks that had incapacitated electronics, but there was nothing that indicated the source. If the explosives were based on hafnium, Golzari thought, then a young Sri Lankan scientist had found a way to exploit the element in a way that Admiral Rickover's brilliant Vulcans had not been able to do.

Gala might have been conducting his research with funding from the Sri Lankan government, Golzari reasoned, but if he had, there would have been no reason to obtain the extruder through a shadow company. No, Gala was being funded by Zheng. And if Zheng had found a way to weaponize hafnium, then there could be broader implications well beyond a localized insurgency in Sri Lanka.

Satisfied with his conclusions, Golzari leaned back, closed his eyes, and let his thoughts drift. These were easier days for him in Diplomatic Security. No longer tied to protection duty for diplomats—domestic and foreign—he was free to conduct his own investigations. It certainly beat standing outside some diplomat's hotel room in four-hour shifts counting the dots in ceiling tiles or the threads in a hotel carpet. He could exercise the more analytical side of his brain now, the side that had been trained by his father's personal guard.

When his father, General Farhad Golzari, had fled Iran after the shah was overthrown, he brought ten loyal bodyguards from the Savak—the secret police—with him. Though Golzari and his father were close, it was the guards who were with him around the clock, especially in the early years when his father feared Iranian revolutionaries would track down the family in the United States. The most senior of the guards had been with Savak since its creation in 1955, when an American major general named Schwarzkopf—the father of the general who led the troops during the Gulf War—had been brought in to train them.

The hardened policemen had taught young Golzari a few of their more benign tricks—how to pick a lock, how to break in and conduct a search without being detected, how to tap phones, and how to tell if a man was lying, among others. And they trained him to shoot until he was better than any of them. That sure aim had enabled Golzari to take out the Zheng R&D assassination teams quickly and efficiently. The guards didn't teach him the harsh interrogation methods the Savak was better known for—at least not when he was a child. And they recognized and protected his sexual orientation without stigmatizing him.

Golzari, for his part, had simply absorbed everything they taught him. And during his career he regularly fell back on his Savak training, even during his brief stint as a police officer in Boston, never telling his superiors about the methods responsible for his unusual success rate. He was too skilled for his supervisors to realize that he had gone beyond the pale of the law. When he was the subject of regular polygraphs, he used tricks his father's bodyguards had taught him—which they had learned from the CIA—to protect himself; no one ever discovered his Savak training as a youth—or his sexual orientation.

He had once asked his Savak guards what it was like to kill a person. So they told him. They also told him that it got easier with each kill after the first because you lost part of your soul each time. Eventually, there was no soul left to feel sympathy or remorse. Golzari had lost most of his soul years before.

After the plane landed at Chennai, the gateway to southern India, he caught a cab to the Hyatt Regency Chennai, a stunning square building with glass sides and rounded corners that dominated the city's skyline. He was passing the lobby lounge on his way to the concierge desk when a few young Americans sipping beer at a table briefly caught his eye. A newsstand on his right displayed papers covering the new civil war in Sri Lanka, complete with photos of the devastation. He found a paper in English and was giving his charge card to the young woman at the register when he heard a voice behind him.

"Agent Golzari?"

Golzari turned quickly and smoothly, like a panther, and was surprised to recognize the blond young American standing behind him. "Ensign Fisk? From *Bennington*?"

"Yes, sir! Well, not *Bennington* now, of course. I've been in USS *LeFon* since Yemen. Damn, who'd have thought I'd run into you here?"

"Indeed," said Golzari. The odds of meeting a U.S. Navy ensign in an Indian city of nine million were quite high. "What brings you here?"

"*LeFon* pulled in a few hours ago. We got overnight liberty from the skipper. You wouldn't believe the week we've had. How about you join me for a drink and I'll fill you in."

"I think I'll do that." Golzari said. "Let me check in and drop off my bag, and I'll be right with you. Why don't you get us a table?" He continued on to the registration desk as Bobby went over to the bar and told his shipmates he'd catch up with them later.

"Hey, you'll never guess who I ran into yesterday," Bobby said after they were settled at a table for two. "Captain Stark."

"Connor Stark?" Golzari questioned.

"Yes, sir. My old skipper. I saw him on his new ship, *Syren*."

"Here? What's he—?"

"That's part of the story, Agent Golzari," Fisk said.

After hearing what Bobby had to say, Golzari couldn't help but think that serendipity had brought him here at this particular time. Serendipity had also quite possibly provided a ride to Sri Lanka.

Mount Iranamadu, Sri Lanka

The past several days had passed in a haze for Melanie. The last thing she clearly remembered was escaping the soldiers pursuing her only to find herself facing another group, all pointing guns at her. She froze and waited for the guns to fire, wondering if it would hurt when the bullets entered her body. Two journalists she knew had been beheaded by Islamists, and she had tried to imagine what their final thoughts were as the end was approaching, when the cold metal was about to slice across their necks. The terrorist would cut back and forth, wielding the knife like a saw, until the carotids and esophagus were cut, then the ligaments, and finally the neck vertebrae, freeing the head from the body for the hooded murderer to wave in front of a video camera for the world to see. Those journalists were the brave ones. At least she wouldn't have to face that. If Melanie was lucky, the soldiers would fire and kill her immediately and she would feel nothing.

The other group of soldiers—the ones she had been running from—came up behind her. She felt a strike against her right temple, and that was the last thing she clearly remembered. She phased in and out of consciousness. Once in a while a guard slapped her awake and poured water in her mouth or shoved in moldy bread or a piece of fish and forced her to chew. Her memories were vague, but a fire was always burning in the background, and there were never less than six insurgents in their tiger-striped camouflage uniforms eating and talking, and only occasionally looking at their prisoner. Whenever she had a spurt of energy she would gamely try to struggle out of the ropes that secured her arms to a tree trunk. The men would watch and laugh.

This time was different. She awoke to soldiers splashing water on her face and untying the rope that tethered her to the tree. They gave her a full meal, and after an hour had passed she had regained enough strength to remain awake. It was nighttime. The fire she remembered vaguely from the stress-induced fatigue was raging. By its light she could see a man enter the clearing. He waved the others away. When the others were gone the man walked over and sat cross-legged a few feet in front of her, silhouetted by the fire at his back. "Why are you here?" he asked.

She froze. Unable to think of a response she fell back on her instincts. Journalists *ask* questions, they don't answer them. "Why are *you* here," she answered defiantly. "And who are you?"

He brushed aside her question. "You are a stranger with no business here," he said.

Melanie struggled to concentrate. She squinted to make out his features. He wore a light white cotton shirt and khaki pants with a thin leather belt and sandals. He appeared to be in his forties, his skin darkened by years of work in the sun. His hair was thinning, and a goatee reminiscent of Ho Chi Minh's adorned his chin.

"I am not from here, that's true. But I want to know more about you," she said raising her chin. "That's why I'm here." She knew at that point that she was safe, at least for the moment. They were keeping her alive for some reason. Were they holding her for ransom? Did they think she was an intelligence agent? Probably not. She was clearly not Sri Lankan, and it was unlikely that a foreign intelligence agent would be here. She posed a threat to their operations, though, and why would they keep someone alive who threatened their operations?

"What is your name?" he asked softly.

"Melanie Arden," she said without hesitation.

He nodded. "Melanie Arden. And where are you from, Melanie Arden?"

"I'm originally from South Africa."

"Then you are a . . . tourist?"

"I am here to see your country," she hedged.

"Why?" he asked.

"Because I want to learn more about it," she said.

"What do you hope to learn in this jungle that you cannot learn from your computers and books?" he countered.

At first glance he seemed a gentle and very intelligent man. Quiet and reserved but exuding strength despite his diminutive stature. His eyes, though—his eyes revealed an intensity that frightened her.

"Do you not agree that firsthand experience is better than a book?" she asked. The longer she kept her identity a secret the longer she might remain alive. *Keep asking him questions*, she thought. *If he's answering my questions he won't be able to ask his own.* The game of questions could last forever, like the tales of the 1,001 Arabian Nights.

"I think you are someone seeking answers," he said intuitively. "You do not look like a tourist."

"Why? There must be many tourists in this beautiful country," she said.

He laughed softly. "Because this entire territory has been off limits to tourists for nearly a year. It is under private control, and we have patrols to keep outsiders such as you from entering."

"You can't control an entire region of Sri Lanka," she said.

"Perhaps. But you are not *in* Sri Lanka. You are in Tamil territory. And soon you will be in Eelam, our nation," he said defiantly.

She kept on the offensive. "What is your name?"

"You may call me what everyone else calls me—Vanni."

"Vanni," she said with a nod. "Are you the leader of the Tamils?"

He paused. "You ask too many questions," he said, his voice turning cold. "A tourist would not ask so many questions. A tourist would be too frightened. You are not an intelligence officer, I think." He smiled and nodded. "You are a reporter."

This man wasn't stupid. "And if I am?"

"Then you will tell our story—the story of the Tamil people's glorious struggle for freedom and the new nation they will create."

"What if it is not the story I came for?" she asked.

"Then you will tell no story."

Melanie felt perspiration dripping from the ends of her short black hair. She had been a week without a shower or much food. She was exhausted and sore. And now she had a choice. She would tell the story from the perspective of the insurgent Tamil Tigers or they would execute her because she would be worthless to their cause.

DAY 11

M/V *Syren*

The small-waterplane-area twin hull—SWATH to those who knew them—skimmed effortlessly through the waters east of Sri Lanka. Jay Warren and the team had been busy for the better part of two days preparing a container specifically to encase extra circuit cards to protect them from a Tamil Tiger EMP. The makeshift Faraday cage was ready. Stark remained skeptical. The problem was timing, he told them. The cards would be safe if the Tigers launched an EMP, but the ship would be vulnerable to attack during the time it took to retrieve them from the cage and install them.

He explained his strategy. Distance was their friend. *Syren* would remain just far enough from EMP-bearing ships to keep her circuitry from being fried if they fired a rocket but near enough to respond quickly. The power of the electromagnetic pulse was the issue. The detonations thus far had affected electronics within a one-and-a-half- to two-kilometer range. The pulse's effective range was like a bulls-eye, strongest at the center and dissipating out toward the edges. *LeFon* had experienced this already. She had been far enough from the detonation bulls-eye to avoid complete destruction of her electronics but was close enough for the EMP to fry the GPS antennas and NAVSSI—the navigation system.

Stark's major problem was reconnaissance. With the threat of an EMP, he couldn't launch the small boats lest their crews be rendered defenseless, as he and his team had been. Airborne reconnaissance was also restricted. There were no commercial airliners flying overhead into Sri Lanka for a reason. The Malaysian Airlines jet that that been hit by an insurgent missile over the Ukraine during a recent conflict with Russian separatists had proved that even civilian aircraft were not safe above insurgency zones. And Sri Lanka had sent no military jets or helicopters to the north out of fear they would crash.

Fortunately, *Syren* carried two commercial unmanned aerial vehicles in one of the containers. Just before dusk, Stark ordered the first UAV launched. The device carried enough charge for a twenty-hour dwell time overhead, and its embedded camera would transmit imagery directly to the CIC and to Stark's computer on the bridge. At its operating altitude the bird could see fifty miles in every direction and identify approaching ships. And unless the Sea Tigers had sophisticated radar equipment they would not know the UAV was there.

He watched the launch from the chair in the LSO shack directly above the bridge. He sipped his coffee as the bird gracefully slid off the starboard side of the deck, guided by Jay Warren, who pumped his fist in proud celebration at the takeoff. Another one of his toys was being put to good use.

Stark knew he could rely on his crew in the upcoming operation. Their professionalism kept them working even though they felt keenly the loss of their three colleagues. Many had served in the military before and understood that missions had to continue after the loss of personnel. There was no talk of Gunny Willis and the others in the mess deck at meals, but neither was there the boisterous laughter Stark normally heard among them. Each crewmember mourned the loss, but formal mourning would have to wait until after the mission was complete.

Connor toyed again with the idea of calling Maggie, but what would he say? That he had not immediately taken the ship to her original destination? That he had accepted an assignment in Sri Lanka? That he had already lost three of his shipmates because of his decision? That if he continued the mission more of his crew—and he himself—would be at risk? Or would he tell her that he might be the only asset in the area now that the Sri Lankan navy had lost not only its entire fleet but the two replacement ships as well? That he had seen a weapon that could eviscerate warships in minutes? If he told her any of those things he would lose her, and he could not bear to think of that.

As much as he wanted to hear her voice and savor its Scottish lilt, as much as he wanted to give up the mission and return to Ullapool to help with the most mundane tasks in the pub or her house, as much as he wanted to open a side of himself to her that no one else saw, he had chosen this path and he would follow it to its end. And then he pushed those thoughts aside. This was a personal issue. His priorities had to be the crew, the ship, and—for the time being—the mission. For now he had to concentrate on the immediate and potentially life-threatening situation. Crew, ship, mission; he could allow no personal thoughts to interfere.

Sea Tiger Command Ship *Amba*

A deck below the laboratories and manufacturing facility on the former submarine tender, two Tamil Tiger guards dragged their prisoner back into the makeshift cell. When he whimpered in protest, one of the guards kicked his legs out from under him, then kicked him in the ribs. He writhed on the deck and begged them to stop. The guards looked at Vanni, calmly sitting in a chair in the corner, for his orders. He nodded once, and they kicked the man in the groin and then removed his uniform to show Vanni the whip marks on his back. His Navy-issue blue-and-gray camouflage uniform had served its purpose well—no one had seen him in the water, not even the search-and rescue-teams. One of the guards handed the uniform blouse to Vanni.

He read the embroidery on one pocket: "U.S. Navy." The name on the other pocket read "Rossberg." The embroidered collar devices, one on each side, were silver five-point stars. "Admiral Rossberg," he said with his deceptively gentle smile. "Why is a United States Navy admiral helping the Sri Lankan government?"

Rossberg said nothing, trying only to pull free from the guards. One of the guards punched him in the stomach. "I was delivering ships," Rossberg finally muttered.

"Ah, yes. We sank those ships. Only you survived. And no one knows you are here. What are we to do with you?"

Rossberg's eyes bulged in terror. No one did know. *LeFon* hadn't found him. These terrorists could do anything they wanted.

Vanni's voice hardened. "What happens in this country is no business of the Americans, Admiral Rossberg. Do you understand?"

Rossberg nodded.

USS *LeFon*, Chennai

The destroyer was one of the youngest in the fleet, but she and her crew had already experienced and survived the first EMP weapon attack at sea. *LeFon* had survived only because Cdr. Jaime Johnson had the sense to recognize and act on Connor Stark's warning—and because she had disobeyed the orders of Rear Admiral Rossberg. The two littoral combat ships ostensibly under his command had failed to take appropriate action, failed to recognize the threat of the fishing boats towing the lines, and had gone down with all hands as a result.

The Flash message—disseminated immediately to the entire intelligence community—had taken only a minute to write and provided only the basics: the location, the ships involved, the nature of the attack, and the estimated loss of life. It did not matter that the two lost LCSs had already been transferred to Sri Lanka and that their crews were Sri Lankans. It did matter that an American admiral was on board one of them, and it mattered to the Navy that *LeFon* had been there and had also been attacked. Jaime's situation report to Seventh Fleet took six hours to write, including cutting and pasting relevant information from her department heads.

Navy logistics could not replace *LeFon*'s GPS and NAVSSI right away. The ship would have to continue on without surface radar, and positioning would rely on the crew's solid navigational skills. Jaime had contacted Captain Dasgupta when she arrived in Chennai, and he quickly facilitated the purchase of a commercial ship's radar, which *LeFon*'s crew jury-rigged into place. It could not interface with the ship's weapons systems, but at least Jaime and the ship's crew would have some basic situational awareness of their surroundings.

Jaime was in her cabin when she took the call from Adm. Maura O'Donnell, Seventh Fleet's commanding officer. She glanced momentarily at the rotating frame with photos of her children, who were staying with her parents until she returned from this deployment. She closed her eyes and focused on what O'Donnell was telling her. The admiral was clear on the country's and the Navy's position.

As had been the case during the previous civil war in Sri Lanka, the United States would not be directly involved. The loss of Rear Admiral Rossberg was tragic, but there would be no official response. Seventh Fleet had no platforms available to transfer away from those conducting the quarantine of North Korea, and airframes were out of the question until more was known about the threat of the Tamil Tigers' EMP weapons. *LeFon* was to operate independently in the region to protect any U.S. commercial ships that might come under inadvertent attack by Tamil Tigers.

"What are *LeFon*'s rules of engagement, Admiral?" Johnson asked.

"Fire only if fired upon or otherwise clearly and imminently threatened by the Sea Tigers. If you are protecting U.S. assets such as a U.S.-flagged commercial ship or lives, you will defend them appropriately."

"Ma'am, how much latitude do I have on that word 'appropriately'?"

"Commander, I understand that you were given command of *LeFon* by the former president under unusual circumstances. Perhaps your lack of formal training led to that question. If you don't think you're up for this tasking, I can send a more experienced captain to relieve you."

Johnson paused, recognizing her own limitations. It would be easy to accept relief and go home to her children. But she had personally trained this crew, worked side by side with them for months, and knew each of them by name—no mean feat with a crew of more than three hundred. And she would not leave them and take the easy way out. "No, ma'am. *LeFon* and I are ready for this assignment."

"Good. You're going into uncharted territory, Commander. There is one more thing that we're asking of you. We need more information on this EMP. We want you to provide us with updates as they come in."

"Aye ma'am."

"I also understand that if there's another attack, we may not hear from you. Just carry out your mission, Commander. Godspeed."

The ship was refueled and the crew recalled. Jaime stood at the quarterdeck and watched as taxis returned her sailors in groups of two to four as she had ordered. Each man and woman walked up the brow, paused, and turned to salute the flag on the sternpost. She looked into each face and saw determination: duty to the country, loyalty to the ship, desire to get the job done. All had enlisted or been commissioned for different reasons. But they were her crew on her ship. She would not let them down.

She checked the crew roster. Two dozen or so had yet to report back, but they were still trickling in. She was about to look in on the newly installed radar when another cab arrived. Bobby Fisk emerged, followed by a dark-haired man with a goatee. He was wearing a European-tailored suit and held a medium-sized carry-on bag. Another junior officer—Bobby's liberty partner—emerged behind them.

Fisk and the man came up the brow. Like the others, Bobby, in civilian attire, stood at attention toward the flag before he stepped on the ship and showed his identification card to the OOD. "Ensign Fisk returning from liberty. I have permission to come aboard." The OOD returned the salute and checked him off the list of still-absent crew.

"Captain," Fisk said as he turned to Johnson, "we need a moment of your time."

The suit fit the goateed civilian to perfection, except for the small bulge on the left side of his rib cage. Most people would not have noticed it. "I expect someone coming on board to report if they're carrying," Johnson said to him. "NCIS?" The guard nearby took notice and began to raise his gun.

"Captain, if I may, I have my credentials and would like to get them out of my coat."

She nodded, alert for any quick move.

"Diplomatic Security," he said offering his badge to her.

"I've worked with Agent Golzari before, Captain," Bobby put in. "In Socotra."

Johnson had not been present at the battle fought on the Yemeni island off the Horn of Africa. She still had been recovering from the injuries she had received a week earlier when *Kirkwall* was attacked and went down with two-thirds of her crew. But she had heard all about it in the months since Fisk had reported on board *LeFon*. USS *Bennington* under then-captain Rossberg had been working with Yemeni ships on a humanitarian mission to Socotra Island when terrorists working with Somali pirates had smuggled explosives onto the ship and detonated them in the wardroom. Most of the officers and chief petty officers had been killed, and Rossberg suffered head injuries that left him unconscious. Connor Stark assumed command as the senior officer present and ordered a counterattack. Agent Golzari had been on Socotra as well.

Jaime motioned them both out of earshot of the quarterdeck sailors. "We're about to get under way, Agent Golzari. We don't have much time. How can I help you?"

"Captain, I need to get to Sri Lanka. I'm investigating a murder, and the investigation has led to a possible involvement with the EMP weapons. I don't have any authority to request this, but I need your help."

"An EMP connection, huh? You're in luck, Agent Golzari. We can get you there. Or at least get you to someone who *can* get you there."

"Captain Stark?" Golzari took an educated guess. "Bobby told me he was in the area. I see trouble continues to follow him."

"Sometimes, Agent Golzari, he actually looks for it." She turned to Fisk. "Bobby, I believe you have an empty rack in your stateroom. And list Agent Golzari as a supernumerary in the logbook." She looked back at the agent. "Welcome aboard."

M/V *Syren*

Syren was thirty miles from the shoreline with no other boats in sight. Most of the commercial traffic had changed shipping routes to avoid the conflict in Sri Lanka. Stark ordered the helmsman to change course. Instead of running parallel to the coast in a northerly direction, they would make a heading of 270 degrees—directly for the coast—for the next thirty minutes at forty knots.

The sun had set over Sri Lanka and the moon was rising astern of the ship as she made her way in. The ship's crew had conducted four boardings that day. In each case the operating procedures were the same. Olivia Harrison remained in command of *Syren* while Stark, Warren, and Ranasinghe joined a security team on one of the small boats and boarded the target ship.

Three of the ships were fishing boats. The team thoroughly checked them for signs of weapons or components—one of the security team even put on a snorkel and fins to dive under the hull. Stark never overlooked that part of the inspection. Years before, as commanding officer of a PC—a small Navy ship— in the Gulf, then-lieutenant Stark had intercepted and boarded a ship the Office of Naval Intelligence was certain was carrying weapons. The inspection turned up nothing in any of the compartments, but Stark and a sailor looking around belowdecks noticed three large bolts in the hull that were out of place, and all were leaking water. Stark ordered his most experienced swimmer to check under the hull, and the man found a large canister bolted to the ship. When the boat was escorted into port, the canister was removed and opened, revealing weapons and ammunition bound from Iran to Gaza for Palestinian terrorists.

The fourth ship they searched was a five-thousand-ton Panamanian-flagged freighter named *Asity*. The captain and crew were largely Pakistani, although the steward was a Filipino. The inspection team found no canister mounted beneath the hull, but two of the searchers found a cache of weapons and ammunition in one of the holds. Stark, Warren, and Ranasinghe questioned the captain closely. The compliant captain presented a logbook that showed monthly transits between Myanmar and Pakistan and listed a variety of cargoes including corrugated steel, shovels, copper wire, lights, power sluices, picks, and sieves. When asked, the captain explained that he had a contract to provide construction supplies for the expansion of the port of Gwadar—a big project on which China and Pakistan were cooperating.

"And you always have a direct route from Rangoon to Gwadar? No stops?"

"Yes," the captain said nervously. "No stops."

"Why are you carrying weapons?" Stark asked.

"They are for the Pakistani military."

"Hmm, I see," Stark responded.

Stark motioned to Ranasinghe to join him on the bridge while the security team monitored the captain and crew. The two walked to the chart table, and Stark called Olivia on *Syren* asking for *Asity*'s exact coordinates and heading when she was first spotted. He picked up a ruler, then checked the fuel level and estimated usage. The estimate matched what might be expended if the ship originated in Rangoon. The problem was the heading. The ship had not been on a southwesterly course that would take her well south of Sri Lanka and India. She was on a heading that would take her to northeastern Sri Lanka.

Stark paced the bridge as he thought. He looked out onto the deck where the captain and crew stood in a group, all watched by the Highland Maritime security team. But someone was missing—the steward. Stark called on the walkie-talkie to his team and was told that the steward had been allowed to remain in the galley because he was busy preparing the evening meal.

"Follow me," Stark said to Ranasinghe as he went below.

The steward was indeed busy in the kitchen, chopping vegetables, boiling water, and moving plates about. He stopped abruptly when he saw the uniformed Sri Lankan commander and Stark standing in the doorway and took a step back when he saw the pistols at their sides.

Stark held up his hand. "You speak English?"

"Yes, some English," the steward replied.

"You have a logbook?"

The steward motioned to the small office across from the galley. "I show you?"

Stark and Ranasinghe broke apart to let him through as he went directly to the desk. Amid a stack of notebooks he found one with a green cover and handed it to Stark.

The steward's logbook was different from the ship's log. The latter noted ship positions, ports visited, and key events. The steward's log listed all the food purchased for the ship as well as receipts for all services, including garbage taken off the ship by port contractors. Stark scanned the past year. Rangoon was clearly listed, but Gwadar was nowhere to be seen. Instead, the other main port visited was Mullaitivu in northeastern Sri Lanka. Stark took the logbook with him and returned to the deck, where he and Ranasinghe presented the inconsistency to the captain. The captain looked from Stark to Ranasinghe but said nothing.

"Commander Ranasinghe," Stark said, "am I to understand that as a designated ship representing Sri Lanka under a letter of marque I am authorized to seize and impound this ship?"

"The Sri Lankan government so authorizes you, Captain. When the ship and its contents are sold, the money will be transferred to you, in accordance with the terms of your letter of marque."

"Very well." Stark turned to the captain. "Sir, you and your crew are now my prisoners." Stark turned to the security team leader. "Take them to the largest stateroom and keep them there." As the prisoners were leaving the deck Stark called *Syren* and ordered Charlie team to join them on *Asity*. When they arrived, Stark took the team leaders and Commander Ranasinghe to the bridge and leaned over the chart.

"Commander Ranasinghe, I'd like you to take the ship here," Stark said, pointing to coordinates seventy-five miles off the coast of Sri Lanka. "I request that you remain there until further notice."

"Understood, Captain Stark."

"You do understand that I have no authority over you, Commander, and that I can only request your help."

"Captain, you have my trust," Ranasinghe replied. "And I am pleased that I have yours. Let us resolve this issue together."

"Then do you see any problem with my having seized a Pakistani-crewed ship?"

"I do not. The ship was searched and seized in Sri Lankan territorial waters and found to have contraband. And we need not notify the Pakistani government until this crisis is resolved."

"Thank you, sir. I will be in contact as soon as possible."

They shook hands and parted.

Stark returned to *Syren* and advised Olivia that they were now down two of their four six-man security teams, then gave the order to make for the coast at forty knots. The moon rising astern laid out a path for them.

DAY 12

Mount Iranamadu

Melanie was now in full control of her senses, having slept, eaten well, and, more important, survived her interview with Vanni. She was busy formulating her next story, and it was not going to be the one the mysterious Tiger leader wanted her to tell. The only problem would be reporting it. She sensed that Vanni's group wasn't just a terrorist organization conducting a hit-or-miss insurgency. They were fighting a civil war far more aggressively and with far more focus than the Tamil Tigers had done in the past. Groundswells took time. Since arriving she had sensed their urgency. Prior to last week's events the Tigers had been invisible. No one anticipated that the Sea Tigers would reemerge unexpectedly and launch a major successful attack, or the attacks that followed. What she was seeing wasn't a groundswell, but it was effective silent groundwork.

Her ex-husband had attended English schools and was a rabid Sherlock Holmes fan. More than once in their very brief marriage he had referred to "the dog that didn't bark" from Conan Doyle's story "Silver Blaze." The dog didn't bark because the murderer was not a stranger. For some reason the Buddhist monk's story of the silence from the monastery at Mount Iranamadu kept reminding her of that.

The silent monastery, the abandoned village she had come across in the valley, and the mass grave she had found and photographed had not been reported in the media. And the Sri Lankan government had mounted no investigations. She thought she understood why. Vanni had told her the region was under private control. An entire government ignoring vanishing villages was unlikely, but she had been to enough war-torn areas to know that it took very little to bribe minor public officials in seemingly innocuous positions. Anything could be covered up for long enough to make a surreptitious purchase, cut communications, or close roads for something as mundane as "road work."

Her guards had been reduced to a team of four. Vanni had disappeared as well after telling her she was being moved to another camp where she would be provided paper and pens to write the Tigers' story for release. If he approved of it, she would continue to live. If he did not, then he no longer had a use for her. She enjoyed her relative freedom. For the first time in a week her wrists were unbound. One wrist was raw and bleeding from rope burns, but she had no way to treat it. She hoped it wouldn't get infected in this humid environment.

Dusk was approaching when they moved her. She noticed something different about these guards. Their discipline was notably slacker since Vanni's departure. But that happened everywhere when the boss left. Employees, soldiers, and reporters alike—they were all on good behavior in the presence of their superiors. And when the bosses left, the employees became more casual, less disciplined, and less cautious.

The well-beaten path wound its way another few hundred yards up Mount Iranamadu, and Melanie realized where she was going. Beyond the ferns and trees she could make out voices and the shimmer of firelight reflecting off stone. The group stopped at the edge of a flat terrace built of stone. To one side all was dark save the faint light of the newly risen moon, three-quarters full. The evening was clear enough for her to see moonlight reflecting off the sea perhaps ten or fifteen miles away. Hundreds of miles to the southeast was Thailand, her point of origin. She had found—or rather been brought to—the ancient monastery the monk had asked her to investigate.

In the distance ahead, some fifty yards away, she could see light coming from the side of the mountain and people pushing wheelbarrows out of a large opening. They dumped the contents on a pile where other people—children and a few older bald men in tattered robes and sandals—sifted through the soil with small rock hammers and their hands as a dozen soldiers stood close watch. This was clearly some sort of mining operation, and based on the size of the pile and the number of people it had been going on for a while. But what were they mining?

She had found the silent monks. She had also uncovered the mystery of the mass graves that contained only adults. The children were here, working with the monks as slave laborers. All of them were dirty and gaunt. *This* was the story she had come to report. If only she had her camera. More important than the story, she had to find a way to help them, to free them.

Three of her four guards left her and approached the men guarding the mine, who greeted them with backslapping and laughter. Melanie was appalled. These men—who were not only ignoring the plight of the bedraggled miners but were causing it—were laughing!

Melanie noticed that one of the monks kneeling by the stone pile had stopped working and was looking directly at her. He straightened slightly, and his dull face took on animation. Even at this distance she could see that his eyes had brightened. What was it that he saw when he looked at her? What was different from her as a new prisoner? It was hope, she realized; hope that the end of their work was near. He slowly nodded to her. She inclined her head just enough to acknowledge him. The complacent soldiers paid no attention.

The monk turned to another monk at his side and they too exchanged nods. The second monk summoned all his strength, jumped up, and ran into the jungle. The startled guards turned in his direction and away from the mine entrance. The first monk looked at Melanie again briefly, then rose and darted into the cave entrance followed by another monk. The guards meanwhile began shooting into the jungle. They fired haphazardly, but it seemed likely that one of the dozen men firing in the fleeing monk's direction managed to hit him.

Then someone realized that two other monks had gone inside the cave, and all of the guards except two began to chase after him. Melanie realized the event had been staged to give her a chance to escape. The monks were giving their lives so that she would have a chance to tell the world what was happening here.

She and her guard were still far from the entrance and the work area when she seized the opportunity. Her *muay thai* combat skills kicked in as she dropped and swung her left leg around behind her guard's knees, forcing him to fall backward. His AK-47 flew from his hands into some brush. As the man lay on his back, still stunned from the series of events, she jammed her elbow into his solar plexus. She rose to her feet and took a quick look at the children standing at the cave entrance. This was her chance, yes, but it was not for her freedom that she ran. She ran to find help for the children and the monks.

She sped back down the path. No one was chasing her yet, but she heard intermittent gunfire. Suddenly the ground beneath her began to shake. The rumbling increased in intensity. Struggling to keep her footing, Melanie turned and ran back toward the monastery, which seemed to be the locus of the sound, and the helpless children. She had almost reached the monastery when a blinding flash of light shot out of the entrance. The fireworks continued for nearly thirty seconds, then diminished into wisps of smoke. The shaking stopped and the ground settled.

She saw that the guards were holding the children down. There was nothing she could do for them other than get help. Melanie made her second break for freedom and succeeded. She had eluded the Tigers—for now.

M/V Syren

The ship settled back into the water as the helmsman reduced her speed a few miles from the coast. With the sun well down now, those on the ship could see little on the water except for reflected moonlight. Stark had ordered all ship's lights, including running lights, turned off. Running dark risked a collision with another ship, but the radar showed nothing except the ships anchored offshore at the Breakers waiting for demolition. Syren had another advantage—her camouflage paint scheme. In the daylight it made her more difficult for other ships to see; at night, even in the moonlight, she was nearly invisible.

Asity, under Ranasinghe's command, was forty miles away by now, along with twelve of Syren's twenty-four security personnel. They would eventually take up station and maintain radio silence until Stark and Syren returned for them.

Connor sat back in the captain's chair, the navigator seated diagonally to his left and the helmsman forward and to the right, as he sent an email to Commander Johnson on LeFon. Olivia Harrison stood behind him. The helmsman wore night-vision goggles—NVGs—as the ship turned slowly to starboard to regain a parallel track along the coast. Stark and Harrison both raised their NVGs in the direction of the horizon to confirm what the radar showed; there were no other boats here.

Stark's major concern was running into one of the long lines with explosive buoys that had sunk two U.S. Navy warships. Minefields were also a possibility, but Stark figured two factors minimized the threat. First, it was unlikely the Sea Tigers had set up minefields because they had sunk the entire Sri Lankan navy on the first day of the war. Second, the explosive buoys that had sunk the LCSs were on lines towed by Tiger boats, and Warren had told him the lines probably had detonator cord and needed a boat to detonate them.

It was also possible that the Sea Tigers had stealthy ships. Since taking this assignment Stark had learned what he could about their previous civil war. The Sea Tigers had designed and built their own boats, including stealthy suicide boats with a low enough freeboard to evade most radar. Were they here? Stark made sure the remaining security teams were using their own NVGs.

The radio cackled. "Boss, need you down here in CIC now," came Warren's staccato voice.

"You have the conn, Olivia," Stark said on his way down the ladder.

The door to the CIC module was open. Jay and one of the technicians were hovering near a monitor. "What have you got?" Stark asked as he stepped up behind them.

"Our UAV. I've had it mowing the lawn along the coast," Warren replied, referring to the flight pattern. "A few minutes ago the infrared camera caught this." Warren pointed to the monitor. The UAV image showed a wavering line that reminded Stark of the mirage above a hot road in summer.

"Heat," Stark said.

"Yup, but we're trying to—go back, go back. That's it," Warren said to the flight tech.

"What are you looking for?"

"The FLIR camera is showing something interesting. I also mounted something like our NVGs and an ultraviolet camera on the UAV to give us better night vision," he said. Warren typed on the keyboard as quickly as he spoke. The monitor changed. It cycled through various images until they merged into one grayscale as the bird circled the data point. "Boss, it's been thirty years since I worked in a mine in the Upper Peninsula, but that sure as shit looks like a mine fire to me."

"Have you got the coordinates of that location?" Stark asked. Without saying a word Warren turned to a second station and typed in a few commands. A second monitor displayed *Syren*'s location, a map of the coast, and the location of the site, which was about ten miles inland.

"Can you zoom in on the coastline?" Warren magnified the image, which showed mostly beach, and then zoomed out again and focused on the fire's location.

"What can you tell me about that spot, Jay?"

"Elevation is about 2,600 feet. It looks like it's on the side of a small mountain—Mount Iranamadu."

"How high up is the bird?"

"Five thousand feet."

"Can you fly her in closer?" he asked the tech.

As the UAV approached the site, the large fire separated into what looked like small campfires. The UAV's camera zoomed in on the site and showed bodies on the ground and a few people milling around nearby. Some appeared to be chasing another person running southward from the site. Small flashes appeared from some of the running bodies.

"Gunfire?" Stark asked Jay.

"Got to be."

"Jay, print out some maps for me from the coast to the site."

"You got it. You planning on going somewhere?"

Stark called for Olivia and the security team leader on watch. When they arrived in the CIC a few minutes later he explained what he had just seen and his conclusions. "Folks, it's been quiet here. This is the first sign of activity. If there's gunfire, I'm going to bet this isn't a simple mining operation. The Sri Lankan army isn't operating this far north, so I'm thinking all this must be connected to the Tigers. I want to see if that site will give us more information about their location."

"Who are you planning on sending, Captain?" Harrison asked.

"We're not storming a castle. This is simply a reconnaissance mission, so we're going in light. The security team will be with me until we hit the beach, then I'll go inland alone."

"Boss, what do you know about mines?" Warren asked, slowly for a change.

"Whatever you can tell me in the next couple of hours."

"Uh, uh. No way. Mines are freaking dangerous places. You need me to go with you."

"It's not that simple, Jay."

"Uh, yeah it is, boss. I know mines. You don't. Sounds pretty fucking simple to me."

"Sir, you should have some shooters with you," Olivia added.

"I appreciate that, Olivia, but I *am* a shooter. I want a light footprint. Just to find out what's going on. I want the teams to stay on *Syren* to defend the ship. Get one of the small boats ready. They'll insert us on the coast at 0100 hours and then return to the ship. I want you to hightail it back over the horizon and return in forty-eight hours to extract us. That should give Jay and me time to get to the mountain and find out what we can."

"Aye, Captain," Harrison acknowledged. "We'll have the gear ready for you. Standard issue?"

"Yeah, XO. The ship is yours."

"I'll take good care of her, sir."

Sea Tiger Command Ship *Amba*

Vanni reentered his headquarters—his home—and made a quick tour. Much of the ship's interior had been gutted to make room for the labs and production areas. The ship would never sail again, so structural integrity in heavy seas was not a necessity. On one deck were quarters able to house more than two hundred soldiers and sailors. The two-man composite suicide boats were also constructed on this level. Their design had been improved in the decade since the last civil war. With an even lower freeboard and more powerful engines, they had already proven their worth during what the Tamils now called Muragan Day, named after the Tamil deity of war and victory. Vanni had thought to discourage the idea because religion had no place in the Marxist world he was trying to build, but he realized that it promoted unity and would eventually serve his purpose.

The next deck below held Gala's beloved laboratories. Vanni came through as little as possible to avoid disturbing Gala, but often enough to show his support. Vanni stopped briefly at the door and looked through the small port-hole into Gala's primary lab, where he was shaping the processed hafnium and cesium charges with the new equipment they had stolen from the Americans. Several young Chinese engineers and scientists on loan from Zheng Research & Development were assisting him. The labs contained a variety of equipment, including casting units, a tantalum crucible welder, and a variety of furnaces—chill casting, high-temperature vacuum, and electron beam. Vanni looked but did not enter.

In the next area a team was assembling the rockets modeled on the Qassams the Palestinians used constantly to harass the Israelis. Two Palestinians were teaching a handful of Tamils how to blend the sugar and potassium nitrate propellant and then include that with the rocket and payload. The Tigers' fight was local, but Vanni was smart enough to consult experts from elsewhere who had experience fighting their own wars. Along the bulkhead were row upon row of tubes ready to be assembled into EMP rockets.

The last area on this deck was the production facility for the sea mines, the buoys constructed using the industrial 3D printer that the Sea Tigers had also stolen through their ghost company in Singapore. The translucent bubble surrounding each explosive was one-eighth of an inch thick. Each buoy contained several pounds of C4 explosives and a blasting cap. Unlike the old stationary naval mines with a series of protruding Hertz horns that detonated the mine when contacted, the Sea Tigers' explosive buoys were strung on detonating cord and towed through the water. The racks lining the bulkheads here held buoys ready to be deployed for potential seaborne attacks. The Sri Lankan navy was no longer a threat and the two transferred American warships had been destroyed, but Vanni expected trouble.

Further below, on the ore-processing deck, Vanni smelled old diesel fuel—the sub tender's former cargo—and the more than one hundred slaves processing the raw ore. Many had been taken from villages that opposed Vanni's forces. They lived in filth down here and worked until they died. The ore was initially sent through crushers, where water was added to turn it into slurry. One machine after another played a role in the process: leaching tanks with cyanide, electrowinning cells, and smelting furnaces. A guard had given him earplugs when he entered; the workers were given nothing. They deserved nothing. Their villages had not joined the movement, and now they suffered the consequences.

Vanni and his men struck quickly and in a well-ordered fashion against villages that opposed them. First they detonated a small EMP to cut communications and cause disorder. Then his Tigers rounded up the villagers. Those who resisted were immediately executed. The others were forced at gunpoint to dig mass graves and bury the bodies. Then the survivors were led back and put to work either in the mine or on the ships.

At the end of this deck, guarded by an armed team, was the final product of the mining operation—small plates of pure hafnium. No one else in the world had this material. Few outsiders even knew the lode had been discovered. That had been a serendipitous accident—Gala had been the one who found it on Mount Iranamadu. He had visited the monastery as a boy. A silvery piece of metal sticking out of a rough-hewn column caught his attention, and when no one was looking he had chipped it out and saved it as a good-luck charm. It was unlike any metal he had ever seen. Only years later, after the civil war ended, did he satisfy his curiosity and discover the metal's value. Then he told his friend and savior Vanni about it. And Vanni, one of the survivors of the original Tamil Tigers, had known how to use it.

Vanni removed the earplugs and went down another deck to the cell where they were holding the American. The stench was even worse on this deck. Two guards stood aside as Vanni walked past them into the cell. He crouched to look at the battered, nearly naked American whimpering in the corner, his face turned away from the doorway.

"Turn around," Vanni said quietly. The American didn't respond.

"I said turn around," he repeated, loudly this time. Again the American did nothing. Most of his clothes were in a bundle in another corner. Some of the pieces had bloodstains on them. Bruises covered the back of the small man's body.

Vanni said something to the guards in Sinhalese. They rushed over to the American, took him by the arms, and slammed his back up against the bulkhead so that he faced their leader. Before Vanni could say anything further another guard burst into the cell. Vanni turned to chastise him, but the guard insisted on speaking to him. Vanni's face hardened as the man spoke.

"That is all we know, Vanni," the messenger insisted when Vanni demanded more information. "There was an explosion in the mine. One of the operators radioed the base camp on the shore, but no one there knows what happened. Also," he almost whispered, "the reporter may have escaped."

"Prepare boats and men. We are going to find out." He jerked his head toward the cell. "And bring him."

USS *LeFon*

The destroyer had just completed a high-speed run past a second fleet of fishing boats, giving them a wide berth. The jury-rigged commercial navigational radar was still having glitches despite the furious efforts of the electronics technicians. Jaime Johnson stayed away from their work area. She knew better than to mother-hen them. They knew their jobs, and she trusted them to tweak the radar until it was working perfectly. She was busy enough as it was, shifting between the bridge and the CIC.

Shorter than most of her sailors, she still stood tall on the bridge. They respected this captain who worked beside them rather than standing back and barking orders. She was more likely to be in the engine spaces than in her stateroom in her time off the bridge. She was everywhere on the ship, maintaining situational awareness and knowing what her people were doing, but not interfering. That was a lesson young Lieutenant (jg) Johnson had learned from Connor Stark when she served on his boat in Bahrain. *LeFon* was exponentially larger than that old PC boat, but the application was the same. The crew needed to know the captain was around. On her next deployment she had served under a captain who rarely left the upper decks and interacted with the sailors under his command only to give orders. Most of them wouldn't have recognized him if he showed up in their workspaces.

Johnson had just secured the hatch to the CIC behind her and had started toward the ladder to the bridge level when someone called to her.

"Captain, a moment?"

She turned to see the Diplomatic Security agent who had arrived with Fisk. "Agent Golzari, let's walk and talk."

"I appreciate your conveying me," he said politely, "but I still need to make it ashore."

Two sailors hit the bulkhead at attention as she passed by and recognized them. "Doing my best, Mr. Golzari, but my orders are specific about maintaining neutrality—not to mention the safety of my ship and crew," she informed him.

"I understand, ma'am, but the—"

She stopped and pivoted toward him. "Mr. Golzari, the safety of my ship comes first, period. Not to mention that we lack diplomatic clearance to put anyone ashore here, in port or anywhere else. Understand that you are a supernumerary, not a special warfare asset assigned to us. That being said, I received an email a few hours ago from an intermediary. I think I've found a way to—"

"Captain to the bridge!" the voice crackled on the 1MC.

Jaime raced up the ladder with Golzari following close behind.

"Captain on the bridge," announced the helm as she looked for her XO in the dim ambient light. She found him at the navigational display.

"Two boats on CBDR, Captain," said the XO. "We were going around another patch of fishing boats when they broke away and came at us. I think they spotted us in the moonlight."

Jamie had a momentary flashback to the Gulf of Aden when lethal speedboats had sunk *Kirkwall*. "Flank speed. Left full rudder," Johnson ordered the helm. The Sri Lankan coast was to starboard and she wanted to keep *LeFon* in open water.

The small boats continued to close on the ship. *Damn, they're fast.* She wished she had the luxury of a helicopter in the air, but an EMP rocket would bring it down. She couldn't take the risk. She called down to the tactical action officer, "TAO, this is the captain. Are the two boats within range?"

"Yes, ma'am."

"Weapons free."

A moment later the forward 5-inch gun began to lob one shell after another at the oncoming boats. Just forward and below the bridge, the staccato of the Phalanx Close-in Weapon System whined above the 5-inch gun's methodical bass. Jaime, Golzari, and Bobby Fisk stood on the starboard bridge wing, covering their ears as the gunfire lit the area around them. One of the 5-inch rounds found its target. Soon after that the Phalanx ripped apart the second boat.

"TAO, Captain. Any more targets?"

"Negative."

"Very well. Cease fire."

The guns fell silent, and once again only the moon lit up the night. Jaime called her operations officer. "OPS, have the communications officer get a Flash message out. Message to read: 'USS *LeFon* approached by two suspected Sea Tiger boats. *LeFon* opened fire destroying both boats.' Include our latitude and longitude."

The OPS officer acknowledged the order, following standard operating procedure. Any incident of an imminent or actual attack had to be reported within ten minutes.

"I think we can expect more of those attacks as long as they have ships and rockets," Jaime said to Fisk and Golzari. She motioned to them to follow her into the pilothouse. "Let's get you off this ship, Agent Golzari." She pointed at an X penciled on the chart marking a spot seventy-five miles off the coast. "That, Mr. Golzari, is where you're going."

"There's nothing there," he replied.

"On the contrary. That's the location of a merchant ship seized by Captain Stark. Ensign, Mr. Golzari is still in a suit. How about you help him find something more appropriate? We should be at the rendezvous point in an hour."

At the appointed time and place, *LeFon* pulled near a ship half her size. Jaime Johnson, carrying a Navy-issue nine-millimeter, stood by the small boat davits as Golzari and Fisk prepared to board. Instead of a business suit Golzari wore the black tactical uniform of the ship's VBSS teams. At his side was his own Glock 19 nine-millimeter handgun. He looked far more dangerous now than he had in the exquisitely tailored suit.

"Thank you again for your assistance, Captain."

"There's been a change in plans, actually. *Asity* doesn't have a small boat for you, so we're loaning you one of ours."

"We're what, ma'am?" Fisk asked.

"Ensign, *Syren* is sending their team ashore now. We're an hour behind and to the north of them," the CO said.

"Aye, ma'am, we'll get our team to—"

"Hold on, Bobby," Jaime broke in. "No one from *LeFon* is going ashore. Mr. Golzari, how are your nautical skills?"

"Minimal, Captain, but I believe if you point me toward land I can get there on my own," Golzari replied.

"Good. Just make sure to kick the RHIB into high speed. You need to get there before dawn." She called to a chief, who arrived with an ammunition box that he handed to Golzari. "Spare circuit cards for the engines in case you're around one of those EMP rockets. The chief here says he's modified this box to shield them. We're not sure it will work, but it's worth a shot if you get into trouble. You'll also find flares on the boat."

"Ma'am, if we're not allowed to send our crew ashore, how will we justify sending one of our RHIBs?" Fisk asked.

"Mr. Golzari needs to get ashore and find the man who's building those EMP weapons," she said, and then turned back to Golzari. "You have enough fuel to get there and return back here. We'll be here the same time every day until we recover you—unless my chain of command reassigns us away from this area."

Golzari raised his eyebrows at her caveat but said merely, "Thank you, Captain."

Golzari and Fisk got into the boat and were lowered into the water. Fisk brought up the RHIB's engines and handed the helm to Golzari, then made his way back up the ladder to the deck. Deep in thought, he watched the agent steer the RHIB clear of *LeFon* and toward the shore of Sri Lanka. Then he shook his head and went about his duties.

DAY 13

Mullaitivu District

Stark held tight to the starboard-side lifeline as the RHIB bounced across the water. Warren did the same on the port side. Stark's hand was shaking again. He tried to convince himself that it was because of the engine's vibrations. He had almost e-mailed Maggie before he left the ship but decided against it. Then he pushed all thoughts of her to the back of his mind. He was forward deployed at what they used to refer to as the "pointy end of the spear." His mission and his responsibility to protect his crew were paramount. The more he allowed himself to think about Maggie, the more distracted he became. He hoped that if anything happened to him she would somehow know. But he was determined that nothing would stop him from returning to her.

He looked over at Jay, who was hanging his head over the side. The whine of the motor masked the sound of Jay vomiting, but Stark could see the droplets flying. Fortunately, the boat was going fast enough to outrun the stench. He had known Jay long enough to know it was nerves, not seasickness. And he couldn't blame him for that. They were going into unfamiliar territory and might find themselves face to face with an unknown number of violent insurgents. Warren had never been in a fight before—excluding the battle of the boats earlier—but he had put aside his fear and volunteered to help Stark negotiate the mine. Stark reached across the boat with his left hand and gave Jay's shoulder a squeeze. Jay lifted his head for a moment and nodded in grateful acknowledgment.

It wasn't yet the blue hour—the time before dawn when the sky gently fades from onyx to turquoise. They still had enough time before daylight to make it ashore and get the coxswain and security team back to *Syren*. When the boat slowed a few hundred yards from shore, Stark grabbed his backpack; Jay did the same.

"You sure about this?" Stark said.

"I got it out of my system," he said calmly. "We're doing this."

The boat slowed again as it slid up the beach. Stark looked at his watch and donned his NVGs. "See you in forty-eight hours," he said to the crew. Then he and Jay made their way across the sand and over a palm tree–lined berm.

"Which way, Jay?"

Warren looked at his GPS and shook it. "It's acting funky, boss."

"What do you mean?"

"Numbers aren't aligning, and I can't get a read on enough satellites."

"Then we go old school," Stark said and pulled out a map and compass. After a moment he pointed in the direction of the mountain. "This way. That should give us a good enough landmark for now."

Ten minutes later they came to a two-lane paved road. The map showed it to be the B297 highway, which paralleled the coastline. A series of lights appeared in the distance in the southbound lane. Stark pulled Warren into a thicket of trees and both men went down to the ground.

The first truck in what turned out to be a large convoy passed by at high speed. Most of the vehicles were white Toyota pickups, the transportation of choice for insurgents worldwide. Stark and Warren might have been in Iraq or Afghanistan. Armed soldiers packed the bed of each truck. The soldiers' heads hung low, a sign they were asleep. They had probably been on the road for at least an hour or two, cheap guns at their sides. Insurgents almost always used cheap guns. In Connor's experience people's lives in these affairs were cheap too.

It took twenty minutes for the convoy to pass.

"Lotta soldiers," Warren observed.

"I counted about 240 trucks. Only a few looked like they were carrying supplies, so they're going light. The pickups had about ten men each, including two in the cab. Figure about two thousand. That's a regiment—a lot for a small terrorist group. If that's what they have in one convoy, they must have a lot more people to the north." Stark immediately regretted saying that out loud. Jay was already aware of the odds.

"How many do you think are at the mine?" Warren asked.

"More than two," Stark said sarcastically. "Come on, we need to make time. The sun will be up soon."

They were four more miles inland when dawn broke over the sea. Twice they spotted foot patrols in the distance, both times squads of five men, weapons drawn. Each time, Warren and Stark crouched low until the squad was out of sight. Each time, Stark instinctively reached into his boot and stroked the jeweled pommel of the *sgian dubh*. He pushed its sheath deeper into his boot. He didn't want to lose his lucky charm.

The pair hiked up a hill and down again into a valley with a single road that took them into a small village. It took Stark only a moment in the brightening light to see that the village was abandoned. Nevertheless, he guided Warren along the tree line and kept his FAL-308 at the ready, though hoping not to get into a firefight.

Stark slipped quietly into the thick forest on the other side of the village. The big redheaded scientist crashed along beside him, oblivious to the racket he was making, so Stark was the first to hear intermittent gunfire ahead of them. Motioning Warren to stop, Stark listened intently. Based on his experience, the distinctive rattle of AK-47s on full auto sounded more than a mile away.

"What now, boss?" Warren asked quietly.

"Sounds like two or three guns, no more. Let's keep moving forward, but slowly."

When they came to a small clearing about twenty feet in diameter Stark motioned Warren to stop. The gunfire had ceased. He kept his rifle at the ready as he extended the mouthpiece of his CamelBak and took a long drink. Jay did the same. The rising sun lit the clearing and gave them their first good look at the vegetation. Stark immediately thought of snakes.

"Ready to move again, Jay?"

"I'm good. I'm the one who does hot yoga, remember?"

"Trying to forget that, thanks."

The going was slower on the other side of the clearing until they found a small footpath that led them in the direction of the mountain. A troop of macaques eyed the two men cautiously as they passed beneath. The monkeys suddenly began darting about and jumping from tree to tree, then raced away. Warren's gaze instinctively followed them through the treetops, but Stark kept his eyes trained on the direction from which the monkeys ran. Something had disturbed them. Over the sound of their shrieks he heard someone running toward them at full speed, crashing through the shrubs and oversized ferns. Stark was raising his weapon when he realized that he was facing not a Tamil soldier but a broad-shouldered woman nearly his own height. She was looking back over her shoulder.

Stark called out, "Hey!" just as she turned around and broke through to the path a few feet away from him. Quicker than Gunny Willis in a training match, she hit him in the solar plexus, kicked him in the groin, and clubbed him with a branch as he went down. As he was hitting the ground he watched her do the same to Warren, a man half a foot taller and a hundred pounds heavier. Then she took his gun.

"You're not Tamils," the woman said. She towered over the men lying helpless on the ground, holding tightly to the rifle and aiming it at Stark.

"What was your first clue?" he replied, trying to ignore the pain in his groin.

"Shut up. Who are you? You're not Sri Lankan and I've never seen uniforms like that before." Both men wore the light gray shipboard coveralls of Highland Maritime. Stark also wore a khaki explorer's vest with numerous pockets.

"Why don't you tell us who *you* are? You're the one running away from something," Stark returned. A closer look showed that she was covered in dirt and looked much the worse for wear.

"Because I'm the one holding the gun."

"Fair enough. I'm Connor. This is Jay."

"You're Americans," she said. "But you're too old to be with their special forces."

"Thanks a lot," Jay said sarcastically.

"So why are you here?" she asked.

He and Jay had just been taken captive. And now came the interrogation. But was she a threat? From her accent, Stark figured her for a South African. She was running from the general direction of the mountain and the gunfire. Given the dirt and the cuts and bruises on her face, he guessed she had been a captive of the Tigers. She wore a vest similar to Stark's. Many journalists covering international conflicts wore that kind of vest. He took a chance. If he lost, he still had his Beretta strapped to his waist, although her reaction time told him it would be a poor choice.

"We're with a private maritime security company hired by the Sri Lankan government to find the Sea Tigers. The guns have stopped," he added. "They probably gave up chasing you."

She lowered her gun. "How did you get here?" she asked.

"We have a ship off the coast. A small boat dropped us off to investigate the mine fire."

The woman looked back in the direction of the mountain. "I was there," she said shortly.

"Are you working for anyone, or are you a freelance journalist?" Stark asked.

"Freelance. How did you know?" she said.

"Educated guess. We can help you," Stark said.

"Really? Then why am I the one holding the gun?"

Stark rose slowly and Warren followed his lead, both avoiding quick moves to reassure the woman holding Jay's weapon.

"I'm Melanie Arden."

"Well, Ms. Arden," Stark said, "how about you tell us what's on that mountain and in the mine."

"People enslaved. Monks. Children. And a lot of soldiers. But there was an explosion and a fire." She quickly recounted everything she knew about the site but told them nothing about her personal experiences.

"I need to go. I have to find my equipment," she said.

"Out there? Even if you can find what you're looking for, there are more insurgents roaming around. We saw a big convoy of them heading south," Stark said.

"I . . . I don't care. I have to find my equipment."

Stark knew the signs of exhaustion. She was running on adrenaline. At some point, and soon, she would crash.

"What kind of equipment? And where is it?" Warren asked.

"Basics. Food, video camera, digital recorder. I even have a mobile phone," she said. "And I don't know the exact location. It's under some ferns on the way to the mountain. It was a few hours' walk north of an abandoned village."

"Maybe we can figure that out," Jay said. "You were probably going through the jungle at around a mile per hour, at best." Jay showed her a map of the region and pointed to a valley. She pointed to several villages she had seen but said nothing about the mass grave at the last one.

Jay got the faraway look that indicated he was dreaming up an idea. Stark had learned long ago to be quiet and wait for the moment when all would be revealed. In the meantime, he kept a lookout for any signs of insurgents.

"Is he okay?" Melanie asked Stark, catching Jay's expression.

"Not really, but just wait a minute."

"Hey, boss," Warren said, "I got an idea if our satellite phones are still working." He reached into his backpack for the satellite phone and made a call to *Syren's* aviation technician. He gave the tech some coordinates and mentioned a "URE module." After he ended the conversation he took out his own mobile phone and fiddled with one of the apps. "Yeah, yeah, we can do this," Warren said.

"Time to fill me in," Stark said.

"We can find her stuff."

"What are you talking about? How?" Melanie asked as Stark pulled food and water out of his pack for her.

"Boss, the bird still has a few hours of juice. She's on her way to our coordinates now, but I just turned on the URE module."

"You just lost me, Jay."

"Remember last year when the media reported the Department of Justice was flying UAVs inside U.S. airspace with surrogate cellular base stations, essentially picking up cell phone traffic like a cell tower? Well, I started playing around with my own version in *Syren's* lab. I've got a module that can do that and detect powered electronics like digital recorders. The other UAV is tricked out with some other sensors I've been playing around with."

"How?" Melanie asked again.

"Simple. All equipment gives off electromagnetic radiation. They leak UREs—unintentional radiated emissions. I have a sensor that picks up on that because I was working on a deterrent for the Sea Tigers' EMP weapons." Three beeps on his mobile phone interrupted Jay's explanation. The bird was already in range.

"But that assumes the batteries are still working," Stark said. "Melanie, were they fully charged?"

"They were, yes, but I don't know if they'd still be on at this point. That was ten days ago. I suppose it's worth a shot." She sat down in the shade of a tree and ate a protein bar and drank the water Stark had given her.

"Jay, our bird's been up for a while. What about its batteries?"

"I'm showing three hours left, and this will soak up some power. We can use it safely for an hour, but then we need to send it back to the ship," Warren replied.

Stark continued to monitor the jungle while Melanie rested and Jay manipulated the app. The bird's track started at the last abandoned village Melanie had pointed out on the map, then took a direct route for the mountain. "The URE module has an effective range of five miles," Jay said, "so as long as

Melanie didn't veer more than two and a half miles off the track, we should be able to find her equipment."

"What company did you say you're with?" she asked Stark suddenly.

"Highland Maritime."

"Highland Maritime. I've heard that name. Don't you do work off Yemen and Somalia?" she said, surprising him.

"Yes, we do. How do you know that?"

"I was based in East Africa for a while. I heard all about the private security companies working there when piracy was big."

There were more beeps from Jay's phone. "Got it, boss," he said with a grin.

Stark smiled. Warren never failed him. "How far?"

"Three hours' walk; maybe four."

"Melanie, how bad do you want your equipment?" Stark asked the rejuvenated and excited journalist.

"What's the trade you're offering, Connor?"

"The three of us go and get your equipment, then you take us to the mine. Jay and I just planned to get more information on the Tigers, but if they're using slave labor up there, I want to see if we can get those people out. That convoy we saw wasn't a patrol. The insurgents are either getting ready or have already started an offensive to the south. That means their rear might not be well protected. Those people you saw might have a chance at freedom. Are you with us?" Stark asked.

"Yes, absolutely," she replied.

Stark offered his hand and pulled her up from the ground. "Let's go. I'll walk point. You stay next to Jay for now."

North of Mullaitivu

Golzari had stashed *LeFon*'s RHIB and left the beach hours ago. He had accomplished one goal, at least. He was in Sri Lanka. All that remained now was to find a young scientist named Gala and bring him to justice—in the chaos of a full-blown civil war. He suddenly wished he had thought it through more fully. But he had confidence in his ability to get the job done. Even as a beat cop in Boston, before being accepted to the Diplomatic Security Service, Golzari had thought himself uniquely qualified to do this sort of work.

His Boston patrol area had been in District B-2, the area that included Roxbury. The police called it "Glocksbury" for the prevalence of firearms there. Roxbury was on par with other high-crime areas such as Mattapan—"Murderpan"—and Dorchester—"Deathchester."

That job had also been the first and last time Golzari worked with a partner, with the exception of multiperson security details as a DS agent. Tom Sullivan was a twelve-year veteran of the Boston Police Department. Golzari had already been accepted to the Diplomatic Security Service and had three days left with BPD before leaving for training at FLETC in Glynco, Georgia. It was the middle of their shift in the early morning hours, well before the T—Boston's subway—was operating. Golzari remembered every detail of that shift, right down to the moment they stopped a holdup at a twenty-four-hour convenience store. They ordered the two men to get down on the floor. They didn't see the third man, the driver.

Tom had been closer to the door and bore most of the brunt of the shotgun blast. Golzari had pivoted quickly enough to take the assailant down with three rapid shots. When the other two men started to get up off the floor, Golzari turned and paused just long enough to allow them to retrieve their weapons. Then he shot them both. Three men dead in a matter of seconds—and a lot less paperwork than arresting them would have entailed. Justice was swift in Golzari's world. "Officer down," Golzari had said into his radio. Sullivan lived, but the damage to his spine left him paralyzed.

Golzari had been outnumbered many times since. There had been the attacks in the Gulf of Aden, when he reluctantly gained a temporary partner in Navy officer Connor Stark. And, of course, the Chinese assassination team in the Long Bar at Raffles and the killers outside Seattle. And with each dead man he lost another piece of his humanity. Would Gala be terrified, Golzari wondered, if he knew what kind of man was on his track?

LeFon's chief had set him up well for the mission. In addition to the black tactical VBSS uniform he was wearing his pack contained a tactical vest and bulletproof chest protector and an M4A1 carbine with two hundred rounds of ammunition. He carried his Glock 19 as well, along with five extra magazines.

Golzari had never been to Sri Lanka, but his reading on the long flight to India and his antiterrorism training had made him familiar with the nation's history. The northern region in which he now found himself had been the site of a major battle between Sri Lankan forces and the Liberation Tigers of Tamil Eelam, a leftist terrorist group founded in 1976 that had tried to carve out a separatist state for its people, the Tamils. The insurgents waged a thirty-year war against the Sri Lankan government. The Battle of Kilinochchi in late 2008, just to the north of where Golzari was now, had marked the beginning of the end for the Tigers. After the government consolidated its position the Sri Lankan air force dropped leaflets over the city of Mullaitivu urging civilians to leave for safe zones. This was the last major territory controlled by the Tamils and their maritime branch, the Sea Tigers. The city's population dropped dramatically, in part due to migration and in part due—allegedly—to ethnic cleansing by both sides. Whatever the reason, the Tamil population in the Mullaitivu District dropped from more than 250,000 to less than one-fourth of that by war's end.

Golzari had given careful consideration to his plans as he made his way inland. It would require every skill he had to find one man in such a large territory. But he knew that Gala would require certain things. He needed at the very least a safe place to work, power to operate his equipment, and a logistics network to get raw materials. There were many safe places for a laboratory, and Gala would surely have his own generator. The chokepoint was logistics. He had to be able to bring in supplies. And Golzari knew one other thing, from his discussion with Dr. Abraham: Gala was interested in hafnium, which was usually found with zirconium.

Golzari had used *LeFon's* computers and Internet connections to locate several mines in central and northern Sri Lanka. Golzari dismissed the sites to the south, which were ostensibly under the Sri Lankan government's control. There were a few zirconium mines in the north in the hills near Mount Iranamadu, home of an ancient Buddhist monastery under the protection of the Sri Lankan government, which allowed no visitors from outside. The government no longer controlled this region, though, and Golzari wasn't sure if the monastery was even still there. In any event, it seemed a good place to start.

He made his way north through dense flora, skirting agricultural communities because he had no idea how the local population viewed the latest insurgency. People were an unnecessary complication. He checked his gun frequently, a habit of extensive field operations, and kept it at the ready.

Golzari finally took a chance and walked along a road with farmland to the west and tall vegetation to the east. His eye caught something in the sky moving in a straight path. It was flying low, and it was far larger than a bird but much smaller than a plane. As it passed overhead he realized it was a drone flying at an altitude of about a thousand feet. Thinking that perhaps the Tamils had adopted another piece of advanced technology, he jumped into the vegetation, but the drone simply went on its way.

The move proved fortunate because he heard vehicles coming up the road from the south. Two small white pickup trucks passed him at high speed. Each carried half a dozen soldiers in tiger-striped camouflage and weapons. They continued north toward the hills that were his destination. Clearly something was going on there. More certain that he had made the right decision, he increased his pace toward the hills.

Iranamadu Range

Syren's drone had long since returned to the ship, but before that it had led the threesome to the exact spot where Melanie had hidden her equipment. The batteries were low, but they still had enough juice remaining to serve as an unintended beacon. The three- or four-hour walk had stretched out into five hours because taking a straight line to the site was impossible. A vast plain of rice paddies lay in their path, and Stark thought it best to walk around them rather than potentially expose themselves to Tiger patrols.

Warren's mobile phone app had allowed him to use the UAV's sensors to scan the area before it left. The UAV spotted several five-man patrols in paddy fields and local roads. Who knew how many more were beneath the cover of the thick vegetation? While they rested for food and water Melanie took a solar battery charger from her pack and connected it to the camera.

"How long did it take to get to the mine from here, Melanie?" Stark asked, taking a bite from a protein bar and sipping from his CamelBak.

"About half a mile from here is a field," she replied. "There are a few scattered trees. Just beyond that there's a footpath a couple of miles long that leads to the mountain and the mine—I should say the monastery. I doubt the mine's been there long. The monks would have never permitted it. They lived in total seclusion. Locals and tourists weren't allowed inside the monastery or even to approach it. Just before the path reaches the monastery there's another clearing with some small, flat stones on the ground and a larger one about the size of an altar. I think the clearing is where the monks would accept novitiates or food."

Stark crouched as he finished the last of the protein bar. The sun in the cloudless sky was past its apogee, but there was plenty of daylight remaining to get to the mine given the distance and potential obstacles. Melanie had seen a few monks and twenty or so children outside the mine entrance and only about a dozen guards. If that held true, then maybe they had a chance to free the enslaved workers.

As Melanie waited for the camera to fully charge, she inspected the nine-millimeter Warren had given her. Stark watched how she handled it. She was no novice.

"I haven't known many reporters familiar with weapons," he said as she checked the sight.

"My ex-husband taught me. He was an expert in firearms," she said casually, chambering a round.

"Military?"

"No. No, he was studying at George Washington University when I met him," she said.

"South African?" Stark asked.

"No, American—sort of. He was originally from the Middle East. Can we dispense with the questions, Mr. Stark?"

"No problem." Stark's mind returned to *Asity*. "Jay, here's a question for you. Would the shovels, picks, sieves, power sluices, and copper wire we found on that freighter be used for mining?"

"Absolutely. It's primitive, but mining usually is, especially where it isn't regulated very well," the scientist replied.

"I doubt this one's regulated at all. Let's get moving. Jay, you've got the rear again."

The three slung on their backpacks and began their trek. An hour later they were on the footpath to the monastery.

They had just gone around an uphill a curve when Jay heard the sound of running feet behind them. He hissed at Melanie and Stark and motioned urgently toward the vegetation beside the path. They barely had time to take cover behind some thick shrubs when ten soldiers raced past them, not bothering to look to either side of the path. Ten Tigers, all armed, were on their way to the mine.

When the soldiers were safely ahead, Stark came out and listened for the sounds of others coming up behind them. Assured there were none, he called softly to Jay and Melanie.

Jay looked doubtful. "Might be a good time to turn back, boss."

"We're not just here for answers anymore, Jay. There are people who need help," Stark replied.

"You still coming?" he asked Melanie. She nodded and began walking.

They had covered another half mile when they heard a shot in the distance and then its echo. All three immediately stopped. After another shot and then a third, the way ahead erupted in the staccato sounds of several AK-47s firing at once.

"That first shot wasn't an AK," Stark said.

"Then what was it?" Melanie asked.

"It sounded like an M-16, but I can't be certain."

The gunshots continued intermittently. A crack from the mystery rifle would echo, and AK-47 shots would follow.

"I'm going up ahead," Stark announced. "There's a battle, and that means someone's fighting back against the Tigers. Can you both keep up?" They nodded. Stark took off in a sprint. As he got close to the gunfire he slowed and looked over his shoulder. Melanie was right behind him, but Warren had fallen back out of sight.

Stark crept up the path until he could see a clearing. He heard shouts from somewhere nearby. The stones and the altar were just as Melanie had described them. A few Tiger soldiers lay motionless on the ground. Several more had taken cover behind the altar and a couple of trees and were firing, apparently randomly, into the jungle. Stark heard the lone gunman fire another round and watched another Tiger reel back. The shooter was methodical, almost surgically precise.

The Tigers were all facing away from Stark's position. He had come here to investigate the mine fire and keep a low profile. But that plan had gone by the wayside. He knew that the men in front of him were terrorists who had already killed hundreds of people both at sea and ashore and were part of the operation enslaving monks and children, yet he hesitated to shoot them in the back.

Lying prone Stark tried to steady his weapon, but his hand was shaking again. He inhaled deeply and then again until his hand relaxed. One of the Tigers was shouting commands at the others. Stark lined the leader up in his sights and fired twice, silencing him. The others turned around in shock as Stark shot another man. The other gunman took out yet another. Two Tigers remained and were about to fire in Stark's direction when more gunfire erupted behind Stark. It took half a dozen rapid shots from the nine-millimeter, but Melanie dropped her man. The lone Tiger still alive dropped his weapon and was raising his arms when a final shot rang out from the other side of the clearing. The last Tiger was dead.

"What should we do now?" Warren whispered as he knelt beside the still prone Stark.

"Wait," Stark said as he slowly pivoted the barrel of the FAL-308 back and forth in search of a target. The circumstances didn't make sense. One man had just taken out two Tiger squads, albeit with a little help from Stark and Melanie. Given the precision of the gunfire, Stark was fairly certain the gunman would have succeeded even if the three of them hadn't come along.

The question remained: who was the gunman? Was he or she Sri Lankan military? It seemed unlikely that the military would send only one sniper after showing such a propensity for using overwhelming force in the previous civil war. Plus, the Sri Lankans didn't use American military-grade rifles.

"Melanie," Stark whispered to his right where she was standing behind a tree. She inclined her head in acknowledgment. "Can you call out loud enough to be heard?" He was risking their lives, but if the gunman was part of an American unit, then a woman's voice in English might let the shooter know they weren't the enemy.

She took a deep breath and in a loud voice simply said, "Hello?" She repeated it.

A few seconds later a baritone voice with a hint of British accent replied: "American?"

"No," she said immediately.

Stark watched her closely. She had narrowed her eyes and tilted her head as if she recognized the disembodied voice. Then again, so did Stark. He stood up next to Warren and motioned the larger man to stay back as he made his way into the clearing. "Don't shoot. I'm coming out," Stark chanced.

There was a rustle in the brush fifteen yards away as the other shooter emerged. Both continued to hold their rifles high.

The gunman was clad in the plain black coveralls, boonie hat, and black vest Navy boarding officers wear. The boonie hat was tilted, but Stark could make out the man's goatee resting on the butt of the rifle. Stark was the first to lower his gun. The gunman did the same as they approached each other.

"Unexpected surprise, Golzari," he said as he offered his hand.

"Lovely. Well, we can't start a war without Connor Stark, can we? I appreciate the assist, old man. I was running short of ammunition."

Warren and Melanie entered the clearing, the latter picking up speed as she came.

"Dear God!" Golzari managed to say before she cocked her arm and hit him squarely in the nose. He dropped to his knees, blood dripping from his face onto the ground.

Stark grabbed her to prevent further violence, or worse yet murder, but then realized that she could already have shot Golzari had she wanted to.

"Hello, Melanie," Golzari said still holding his nose.

Stark released her when he realized that Golzari not only knew her but wasn't going to retaliate.

Melanie immediately spun around, walked over to her pack, and dug out a camera.

Golzari wiped his bloody nose on his sleeve and rose.

"Does everyone do that when they first meet you?" Stark asked him.

"Not everyone, no," Golzari replied. "Just you and my ex-wife."

Stark nodded and began to check the bodies while he let that sink in. All the men had been killed by clean shots. Then he checked their weapons and pockets.

"Care to fill me in?" Stark asked. Melanie continued to photograph the scene, ignoring the living men in the clearing.

"What else is there to say? Melanie and I were married," Golzari said matter-of-factly.

"Briefly," she snapped. "But I wasn't his type."

"I see," Stark said. "Well how about we keep this reunion short? Jay, keep an eye on the trail back there. Our little shootout at the OK Corral has surely warned the guards at the monastery."

"You don't have to worry about them. I just came from there," Golzari said.

"Just you?" Stark asked.

"There weren't that many, and they weren't that professional. Not unlike the band you and I encountered at Old Mar'ib," Golzari said.

"Then you were lucky. What about the monks and children?"

Melanie stopped taking photos of the soldiers to hear Golzari's response. Golzari knew his ex-wife well enough to understand that this was the reason she had come.

"I would normally tell you it's not worth going up there, but I suspect Melanie needs to see it for her report."

Melanie picked up her pack. "Then let's go," she said stoically.

The group repacked and started up the trail, Stark and Golzari in the lead.

"How's your nose," Stark asked.

"No worse than when you assaulted me at the embassy in Sana'a."

"Assault is a strong word. Given what *she* just did, I'd call that a greeting. So what the hell brings *you* here, Damien? This isn't exactly an embassy."

Golzari shared the basics as they walked up the trail—a DS agent had been murdered in Singapore for investigating the theft of scientific equipment; the trail had led him to a young Tamil scientist and zirconium mines; and a fortunate encounter with USS *LeFon* in Chennai had led to his presence here. In exchange, Stark told him of *Syren*'s letter of marque, the seizing of *Asity*, and the mine fire seen from their drone.

Melanie bolted ahead of them when they reached the outskirts of the monastery. Stark tried to hold her back in case reinforcements had arrived since the battle in the clearing.

"No," Golzari said to him. "Leave her alone. You can't stop her. And she needs to see this."

Melanie walked past the bodies of the guards Golzari had killed. There were at least a dozen. Some were slumped behind the ancient columns, having vainly tried to hide from Golzari's expert shooting. Others were lying face down, shot in the back. Golzari clearly hadn't distinguished between the men who were fighting and those who had elected to run from him. Her ex-husband, she knew, could be as vicious a killer as the Iranian Savak guards who had trained him.

She approached the bodies of the victims, the monks she had seen when she was brought in as a prisoner. They had been lined up, and each had been shot twice in the head. The monks of the ancient monastery at Mount Irana-madu were no more.

But where were the children? She looked around for shallow graves like those she had seen at the abandoned village but saw nothing to indicate that they had been killed. She turned to Golzari as Warren took up a position at the head of the trail and Stark checked the bodies of the dead Tigers, as he had done in the clearing.

"Where are they?" she asked Golzari.

"Who?"

"The children. There were children here. They were working as slaves."

"I saw none, Melanie," Golzari said. "They were executing the final few monks as I arrived, before I was close enough to respond."

USS *LeFon*

The ten-thousand-ton warship slid smoothly through the water at eight knots. Normally a destroyer traveling so slowly bobbed like a cork with every wave she struck. But *LeFon* was no ordinary destroyer. She was the newest—the seventy-fourth—of the *Arleigh Burke* class, one of the best-designed warships of the past century. Jaime Johnson stood on the bridge and admired her command. She knew good luck had brought her here—despite her unorthodox return to active duty and her lack of formal training in the command pipeline.

Johnson had served as chief engineer in USS *Stout*, another *Arleigh Burke* destroyer, before leaving the Navy to raise her kids after the divorce. She had remained in the Navy Reserve but had jumped at the chance to go back to sea when Connor Stark hired her for Highland Maritime. He needed an experienced young officer to command his small fleet's flagship, and she fit the bill. *Kirkwall* provided security to the offshore supply vessels coming out of Yemen and bound for the oil rigs under construction south of Socotra Island during the height of the Somali piracy crisis.

She had nearly died when *Kirkwall* went down and had thought her days at sea were over for good. And then, as Johnson was recovering from her injuries, Stark somehow managed to get her command of one of the Navy's latest warships. The order had come down from the president himself. She still wasn't sure how Stark had managed it. Regardless, she was grateful to be back at sea and serving her country once again, even though it meant leaving her children with her parents while she was on deployment.

She walked into the CIC, the ship's eyes and ears. *LeFon* was steaming independently for now, the only U.S. warship in the region. The Sri Lankan theater was just another backwater for the United States, which had its hands full dealing with far more serious threats off North Korea and elsewhere. Jaime's orders from Seventh Fleet were clear: fire only if fired upon or otherwise clearly and imminently threatened by the Sea Tigers, and protect and defend U.S.-flagged commercial shipping. Ensign Fisk had been right to question her loan of the RHIB to Golzari, but the potential loss of a RHIB was the least of the Navy's worries right now.

Jaime sat in the captain's chair in the CIC gleaning everything she could from the wide tactical screens before her. Ensign Fisk was standing behind the TAO, working on his qualifications even during the current high alert. Bobby had the potential to be a good captain someday. She knew that he had reacted with good sense and courage in the battle at Socotra, and she intended to do what she could to help him on his path. Adequate officers were common in the Navy. Excellent officers were far harder to find.

Only the occasional necessary chatter between the stations and the bridge broke the quiet of the CIC. Every hour Jaime shifted her position between the CIC and the bridge, stopping only to get fresh coffee. As the day progressed, more ships emerged over the horizon. She kept *LeFon* a healthy distance from them and made sure that each was monitored for any sudden moves that might suggest Sea Tigers were operating it. She wished again that she could put up a helicopter because surface radar simply could not provide the same

situational awareness than an airborne monitor offered. But all flight operations in the area remained suspended. The ship had carried two Scan Eagle
UAVs, but those had been removed in India and shipped to Navy assets operating off Korea. The Navy had even taken her two RQ-21A Blackjack UAVs.

She sat back in the starboard bridge chair and read her e-mail. Operational security under the current conditions limited e-mail access to the captain, the XO, and the operations officer. The daily unencrypted traffic included
a message from her eleven-year-old daughter with her Christmas wish list.
Jaime smiled as she read it. Dolls, a dollhouse, a kite, a skateboard, and a jump-
rope were far more traditional requests than the robot, new iPad, goPro camera, and self-sustaining aquarium her nine-year-old daughter had asked for.
Though Jaime had more in common with her technologically savvy younger
daughter, she appreciated the simplicity of her older daughter's tastes. How
much simpler could one get than the paper, wood, and string of a kite? She
imagined flying the kite with her daughter when she returned from deployment, guiding it in the wind and making it dance in the air, all with a just piece
of string held in her hands. A kite didn't need anything but the wind—and it
wasn't affected by technology either. But that didn't mean it couldn't work *with*
technology, now did it?

Jaime picked up the phone and called the command master chief. "Master
Chief, I need a couple of your sailors to help with a little project."

"No problem, Captain. What do you need?" he asked.

"I need a camera. And I need someone to build a kite."

Mount Iranamadu

The grounds of the monastery rose in tiers formed by retaining walls built of
flat granite stones. The level ground in between the walls held the remnants
of untended gardens interspersed among the pillars and rudimentary statues of
Buddha. At least four dozen small caves had been carved into the mountain-
side behind the large main plaza. These were where the monks lived. One cave
opening was far larger than the others—clearly the mine entrance. A few overturned wheelbarrows were strewn about near it, as were some simple tables. The
plaza itself bore Golzari's methodical work. Each Tiger had been shot—once.

"Is this the only trail up here?" Stark asked Golzari.

"There's a smaller path on the other side of the plaza that's only wide
enough for one person," he replied as his eyes followed Melanie. "That's how
I came up."

"She's really your ex-wife?" Stark asked as he checked another Tiger's gun and pockets.

"Yes," Golzari said curtly.

"She slugged you pretty good," Stark said, failing to add that he too had been a victim of her fighting skill. "What happened?"

"We wanted . . . different things," Golzari said, scanning the perimeter.

"Yeah, well that happens," Stark said noncommittally. He supposed it did, but when it came to relationships, Stark had no clue. He had never married. His work had been everything to him. He couldn't figure out Maggie. And all during the Yemen incident he had had no idea that Ambassador Sumner and the president of the United States were lovers.

"You've been ransacking the bodies rather thoroughly, Stark. Found anything?"

"Nothing much. Extra ammunition. No food or water. They must have supplies back in their trucks. We saw plenty of those earlier. It's the AK-47s that bother me."

"What about them?" Golzari asked.

"No serial numbers on any of them; nothing to identify their point of origin. That means mass production of untraceable weapons."

"Third party?"

"Has to be. Do you think the Tigers could manufacture these in large numbers?" Stark asked.

"Doubtful." Golzari took an AK and examined it more closely.

"Best guess?"

"I can narrow it down to the three likeliest."

"Russia, China, and North Korea."

"You're smarter than you look, Stark."

Stark laughed. "Smarter? No. Just getting wiser with each new gray hair and adventure. Player A, B, or C gives them unmarked guns. Why? What do they get from the Sea Tigers? They always get something in return. Maybe it's as simple as money. But then the Tigers would have had to come up with the money. This isn't exactly a wealthy region," Stark observed.

"Someone trying to destabilize the country? We've seen that before."

"Yeah, but what would any of those three have to gain? Whoever it was knew about the attacks in advance—knew the Tigers were going to need a lot of weapons for a full-scale civil war. You don't just make and deliver that many weapons overnight." Stark turned to Warren. "Hey, Jay, let's go get what we came for." Warren took one last look down the main trail and started walking toward the large cave.

"What did you come for, old man?" Golzari asked Stark.

"A good look around. We're trying to find the Sea Tigers' base."

"You think it's here?"

"We had a UAV up last night that saw a mine fire. I figured it was enough out of the ordinary to check out," Stark said.

"Your hunch proved right."

"It would have helped if you hadn't killed them all, Golzari. We might have been able to get some information."

"I'll try to be a poorer shot next time."

Stark and Golzari joined Warren, and the three walked toward the mine entrance. Melanie remained where she was, deep in thought and quietly recording the activities in the plaza. Stark looked back at the trailhead from time to time.

"Huh," Warren said aloud as he inspected the work area and the mine entrance. The overturned wheelbarrows, hammers, and piles of broken rock confirmed that the ore had been mined inside the cave, brought through this entrance in wheelbarrows, and then broken up with hammers. The monks had probably been forced to do the heavy work with picks while the children had separated the metal from the rock with hammers.

"What do you think?" Stark asked Warren.

"I think it's good that you brought me, boss," he said with his hands on his hips. "This is new."

"What's new?" Golzari asked.

"The mine. The whole operation. Look at the entrance and the wood they used for supports. You use better-quality structures if you've been working on a mine for years. I'd say this one is maybe a year or so old," he said as he felt the hewn rock around the opening. "But why go to all this trouble for zirconium? And then why throw it away? Look at this," he said, showing them some fragments from the pile of discarded rocks. "It's full of zirconium."

"What if it wasn't zirconium they were looking for?" Golzari asked.

"But what else would they . . . aw, shit," Warren said. He quickly pulled off his pack and dug through it to get at a piece of equipment. Like a child finding a toy, he flourished a gray box with a display panel and a probe connected to it by a wire. He carried it to the work area, and the display came alive when he passed the probe over the ore. It did when he scanned the mine entrance as well. "Gamma fucking rays. This is why I couldn't get the right readings in Trincomalee with the EMP," the scientist said.

"Hafnium?" Golzari said.

Warren froze. "Yeah, how did you know?"

"An educated guess based on a conversation I had a few days ago with a retired scientist, one of Admiral Rickover's Vulcans. I asked him about zirconium, and he mentioned that it sometimes occurs in combination with hafnium."

"Yeah, Admiral Rickover's guys spent a while trying to find a way to use this," Warren said.

"Jay, how about condensing this for the rest of us?" Stark interjected as Melanie drew closer to the group.

"Sure, sure. Hafnium is a rare earth element usually found with zirconium. About fifty years ago Admiral Rickover's outfit started playing with it because of its potential for high-explosive weapons."

"Like atomic bombs?" Stark asked.

"No, not quite on that scale. But pretty darn close."

"So why didn't it happen?"

"According to the scientist I spoke with," Golzari interjected, "they needed pure hafnium, but no lode was known to exist."

"Yeah, that's right," Jay said. "So they scrapped the program. There's only one problem."

"What's that, Jay?" Stark asked.

"I think there *is* a pure lode of hafnium. And it's in this mine."

"How much is here?"

"I'd need more time and a better look to tell you that. Most likely specks of dust with a few nuggets interspersed. They'd have to sift through a lot of earth to get enough to be useful."

Stark grimaced. "Not a problem if you have slave labor."

Hong Kong

The Mercedes-Benz pulled off Wharf Road on the north side of Hong Kong Island, and the driver stopped in front of one of the city's newest high-rises. The bodyguard exited the S-class sedan first and greeted one of the two security officers stationed at the entrance. The bodyguard adjusted his suit coat then stood by the door.

Tao Hu picked up his briefcase and leaned over to kiss his wife. She reminded him not to be late to their younger son's concert that evening. He gently pointed out that he had never missed any of their children's performances.

She smiled and touched his hand. "I didn't say you would miss the concert, my dear, only not to be late," she said.

He smiled broadly. After all these years she knew how precise he was in his use of words. That precision had helped him throughout his career negotiating deals. It worked less well with his wife. He tapped twice on the window, and the bodyguard immediately opened his door. After Hu exited, the bodyguard closed the door and the car pulled away.

When the car was out of sight, Hu took out a pack of Benson & Hedges cigarettes, tapped the pack against his forearm until one slipped out, then turned to the bodyguard, who already had a cigarette lighter ready. "I promised her she would never *see* me smoke again," he said. The bodyguard chuckled. Hu allowed himself to enjoy half the cigarette because they were early for the meeting. Then he and his bodyguard entered the building, crossed the ten-story atrium with its nine-story waterfall, and walked to the elevator. The bodyguard made sure the elevator was empty and then, after Hu entered, pushed back a couple of businessmen hoping to get on as well. The elevator took them smoothly to the thirtieth floor at five hundred feet per minute.

The doors opened to reveal a spacious marble lobby with mirrored walls that made it appear to be quadruple its actual size. The receptionist and other employees in the lobby stood when they saw Hu and remained standing until he passed. He recognized them with a quick nod as he made his way to the conference room. The floor-to-ceiling windows that formed one side of the room offered a breathtaking view of Hong Kong harbor and Kowloon, where glass buildings reflected the rays of the risen sun.

The nine board members and chief financial officer of Zheng Research & Development were already seated at the oblong onyx table. Hu shook their hands one by one as he made his way to the end of the long table. Most of them had coffee or tea, and a few had elected to try the croissants made by the firm's French chef. Hu believed that food relaxed people. As for himself, he attended so many meetings that he had found this luxury to be a necessity. His executive assistant was making last-minute adjustments to the papers before them as Hu took his seat.

Sitting in chairs against one wall were three of Hu's top staff—his chief scientist, his chief of security, and his corporate information officer, an innocuous title for intelligence chief. The latter two were Westerners. The burly chief of security had served with the Russian navy for twenty years. The slender, blonde intelligence chief was an American—or at least had been an American. She had done more to advance his company—and China—in the past eight years than many of his scientists. But success always came with a price.

Hu began the meeting when the chairman of the board looked imperiously at him from across the table. The CFO spent the first half hour discussing the firm's revenue and expenses along with projections. When a board member asked a question about the large spike in the out-years, the chairman replied that Hu would give a full report on that after the financial report. Ten minutes later the CFO closed his folder and deferred to the firm's president.

Tao Hu slid back his chair and called up a map of Sri Lanka. He motioned to his executive assistant to pass a black box around the table. The velvet-lined box contained a dull silver nugget of metal about the size of a raisin. "Gentlemen," he said as the box was making its way around the table, "the contents of that box will pave the way for that spike in revenue along with placing China ahead of every other nation in the world in terms of first-strike weapons. This small piece of hafnium—pure hafnium—in your hands is more than anyone outside our operation has ever seen. In fact, few people even know that pure hafnium exists."

He asked his chief scientist to explain hafnium's properties and how it might be weaponized. When he concluded, Hu continued his briefing.

"As you know, we have many projects around the world, and many eyes and ears. One of those came to fruition eighteen months ago with a young Sri Lankan scientist. He was educated in Beijing, and we supported his research with money, transportation, and assistants. That research has produced stunning results. Almost as important, this young man is a close friend of a man who was a mid-level leader of the Tamil Tigers during their civil war."

"And this is the insurgent who is leading the new civil war, Tao?" the chairman asked.

"Yes. We provided him with a shipment of weapons a few months ago. The cost of the weapons is a pittance compared to what we expect to receive in return," Hu said as he tapped his finger on the onyx table and smiled. "With the weapons we gave them the Tamils gained control of the lode of hafnium in northern Sri Lanka."

"How are you ensuring that this mineral will come to us?" another board member asked.

"Yes, and what happens if the Americans learn that pure hafnium exists?" asked another.

"Is that how the insurgents took out the Sri Lankan navy?" came another voice.

The chairman's voice overrode all of the others. "Tao, this firm must not fail as it did with the oil platforms off Yemen."

Hu's smile faded at this reminder of his only failed project. "Gentlemen, I assure you that while the extraction process is largely in the hands of the Tamil Tigers, it is we who control the hafnium. Due to operational security, I'm not at liberty to discuss the details." This was technically true, but he simply didn't want to tell them. The board meeting broke up, and Hu's executive assistant closed the lid of the box and returned it to his office.

Hu held back his chief of security and intelligence chief until all the board members had left. "What of the American agent asking questions," Tao Hu said to the Russian.

"He was too fast for the team in Singapore. For the American operation, it was easier to subcontract the hit to one of the Mexican cartels," the burly man responded in a rich baritone voice.

"Easier, perhaps, but did it work?"

"Apparently not," the Russian said dryly. "He was last seen boarding a flight to Chennai."

"We picked him up there," the intelligence chief said. "An American destroyer was in port by coincidence," she added. "We believe he boarded that ship."

Hu thought about this for a moment. "Forget him for now. Even if he got to Sri Lanka, he wouldn't have the means to find Gala. No, let's focus on the operation in Mullaitivu. Once they've extracted and processed the ore for us, we can deal with the American agent." He dismissed them and stood by the window to admire the view, secure in the knowledge that the material for this new EMP weapon would provide him with a needed boost up the next step of his career ladder.

Mount Iranamadu

Melanie wrote in her moleskin notebook while Golzari walked the perimeter and Jay wandered among the caves that had been the monks' quarters. Stark looked out at the water in the distance and tried to unwind. Dusk was approaching, and a few fishing boats meandered offshore. He wondered if one of them might be a wolf in sheep's clothing—or in this case a Tiger in sheep's clothing. It was time to get moving. The four of them were deep in enemy territory, and it was just a matter of time before more Tigers came to the site. This was the source of their power, literally and figuratively.

Stark knew that his hunch to come to the mine had paid off. If they were going to find the Sea Tigers' base, this was the only immediately available clue. The mine was clearly crucial for their weapon making, but there was no facility here to process the ore or to build the rockets. The material was being taken to another spot where the weapons were manufactured. He had seen no evidence that they used the trail he and the others had followed to reach the monastery. And as far as he knew, the Tigers lacked the ability to transport the ore by air.

The other trailhead was the key. Beyond the wheelbarrows were large backpacks. One of the murdered monks had been wearing one. Stark opened the backpack and sifted his hand through the chunks of ore it contained. This was a primitive operation. Everything was carried from the mine to the processing facility. How far was it? How far could aging monks carry tons of earth?

"Think I got something," Jay said as he approached Stark. "There's a pretty large cave. Normally a mine entrance will have a shack for equipment, the supervisor, and paperwork. They were using the cave for that. Probably less noticeable from the air." Warren handed him a stack of papers.

"Great. I can't read Sinhalese or Tamil," he pointed out.

"I have an app for translations. I read through a few of them. They're essentially accounting records. That ship we took? *Asity*? It's listed here. You were right that it was carrying mining equipment here. They used some other ships as well."

"Then they're not just using small boats, they've got an entire logistics network. But they have to keep it hidden from the Sri Lankan government," Stark said. He used Jay's translator to find the names of shipping companies and ports of entry and departure. The departure ports were scattered throughout Asia, but he saw no ports of entry in Sri Lanka. Most of the times recorded in the papers were in the evening. After allowing Melanie to photograph the papers Stark told Warren to put them in his pack. Then he thought about what he had learned. *How would the Tigers get large freighters close enough inshore to offload their supplies without being noticed? They probably do it at night. A ship could easily make it into Sri Lankan territorial waters at night, transfer the supplies, and then be back over the horizon by daylight.* Stark decided he had to see where the other trail led.

As he turned to suggest that the team move out, a hair-raising howl issued from the mine tunnels behind him.

"Mother of God," Warren gasped. "What was that?"

"Probably just the wind," Stark said uncertainly. But there was no wind. They hadn't felt so much as a breeze since they'd landed on the coast. He turned and drew his weapon. The haunting, ghostlike wail intensified. "Any chance there's a second entrance to this mine?" he whispered to Warren, who shook his head.

"Not in a cheap operation like this."

Golzari joined Stark, his own rifle raised. The howling was approaching the entrance now, becoming clearer and louder. Stark realized he was hearing more than one voice. *What kind of animal makes a noise like that? Are there wolves in Sri Lanka?*

A small, shrieking shape burst through the mine entrance. Stark was about to fire when he realized what he was seeing. The first child raced out into Jay's giant bear hug. Two more followed. All looked like they had just escaped from hell. Melanie grabbed the second child, and Stark dropped his weapon and scooped up the third. The children stopped screaming and started talking when they realized they had not run into the arms of Tamil soldiers, but Stark and the others couldn't understand them. Warren tapped his smart phone, said a few words, then hit another key, and his words, translated into Tamil, spoke from the phone to the startled children.

"Jay, ask them if there are any other children in the cave," Stark said.

Through the translator, the first child was able to convey that there were seven more in the mine, where they had taken shelter when the soldiers massacred the monks. Stark grabbed a headlamp from his pack.

"How far back are they, Jay?"

"He said as far back as they could go, but they were worried about being lost."

"Nothing more specific?" Stark asked.

"No. And I don't think the kids are likely to go back with you to show you."

"Stark," Golzari said. "This could take a while. How much longer do you think we have before more Tigers arrive?"

"I'm sorry, Damien, but we can't leave them down there—especially if the Tigers are going to return. You stay here. If they do come back, hold them off if there's a few of them. If there are more, just get out of here. Jay, you keep those three kids close to you."

As he walked into the entrance, Melanie pulled a flashlight from her pack and walked behind him. "I'm coming, too," she said.

Within minutes Stark began to feel claustrophobic. His breathing became labored, and he broke out in a cold sweat. He hadn't prepared for this. He could see the frayed wire tying the primitive lights together, but the wires had been severed, probably during the explosion he had seen on the UAV image. There was no noise except his own beating heart and Melanie's footsteps. Every few minutes they called out. There was no response.

The tunnels were wide enough for a couple of people to walk abreast, but the wooden planks holding up the ceiling and sides were falling apart. The deeper they went, the more dangerous it became. They arrived at the first transfer station between two of the tunnels. He realized that without his headlamp and her flashlight they would be blind and helpless. His hand began to shake again and he considered turning back. But seven children would die if he did.

Melanie took the lead and called out. Perhaps it was her voice—a woman's—that made them brave, but she and Stark heard a whimper down one of the tunnel branches. They arrived to find six children huddled together. Nearby lay the body of the seventh; already frail when he entered the mine, the trauma of the past two days had been simply too much for him to survive.

They spoke calmly to the children, who shielded their eyes from the painful light shining from Stark's forehead. He took one child's hand and then another's. Melanie gathered the rest in front of her and they brought the little ones out of hell.

Stark hadn't wanted to start the trek down the mountain at night, but there was no choice. More Tigers would certainly arrive soon, and neither Stark nor Golzari had enough ammunition for another firefight. In addition, they now had nine children to worry about who were still in shock from their ordeal. Even after they had food and water several of the children could barely stand.

Melanie and Warren had been able to communicate with them in a very simple fashion. The children were all from the same village, but they were only the most recent bunch brought to work in the mine. Many children from other villages had come before them. Some had still been there when this group arrived. A few of the strongest had been taken elsewhere to work. The others either died or were killed when they could no longer work. The Tigers had no trouble finding replacements. To her horror, Melanie learned that their village was apparently the one with the mass grave that she had visited before being captured. The children were free to go home now, but they no longer had homes and families.

Golzari led the column down the back trail from the monastery, followed by Warren, then the children with Melanie, and last Stark. The moon had not yet risen, and only the four adults had flashlights or headlamps. When a child fell, Stark or Melanie would pick him or her up, administer a hug, and give a gentle push in the right direction.

The group had gone a little over two miles before Stark finally whistled to Golzari to halt and went to the front of the column to consult with him. They agreed they had to stop for the good of the children, who barely had the strength to keep up. The vegetation was sparse enough at this point to move off the trail, so Warren and Golzari quickly cleared out an area thirty yards off the path large enough for the nine children to be gathered together.

Stark and Warren took out the rest of their food, which had not been much to start with for a simple two-day mission, and distributed it to the children, then showed them how to sip from the CamelBaks. With food and water taken care of there was another issue—even here in the tropics the nights were cool. The best they could do after the children ate was to huddle them together to keep warm. Most fell asleep immediately.

"Golzari, our boat isn't scheduled to pick us up for another thirty-four hours," Stark said quietly. "Can we get to *LeFon*'s RHIB?"

"Assuming it's still there, we can get there by midmorning if we pick up the pace. With these children slowing us down it will be noon at the earliest." His emphasis on the word "children" indicated his distaste for the situation.

"They're not just children, Damien. They're orphans," Melanie said.

"You don't know that," he said.

"Yes, I do," she said softly. "I was in their village before I was taken. I saw the bodies of their parents in shallow graves. They have no one. We are not going to leave them here to fend for themselves."

"Fine, Melanie," he said to his ex-wife. "I was merely pointing out that we will be in broad daylight for a good bit of the time. If we encounter more Tiger patrols, how do you propose we defend ourselves and them?"

"We just do," Stark said simply. "How many rounds do you have left?"

"Seventy. I was careful."

"We may not have the luxury of being judicious with our shots this time."

Stark tried to call *Syren* on the satellite phone, hoping to bring in his security teams to help extract them, but had no luck. Despite Jay's best efforts, communication problems continued to plague them. They really needed help if they were to succeed. Even if they got to *LeFon's* RHIB by midday, they would be exposed once they were on the water.

"Jay, Melanie. The two of you get some sleep. Keep close to the kids to keep them warm." While the journalist and the scientist settled in with the children, Stark pulled out the NVGs. He handed one pair of the goggles to Golzari as they moved closer to the trail. They agreed to divide, one on each side of the path and about ten yards off the trail itself. Golzari would focus on the path coming down from the monastery while Stark watched for anyone coming up from below.

Stark was weary, but his early career training as a surface warfare officer had accustomed him to long watch hours in the night. He allowed his body to relax while his mind stayed on high alert. Just past midnight Stark saw a flicker of light in the distance, then another, and another. "Down!" he whispered loudly to Golzari. He hoped that Warren and Melanie and the children were sleeping soundly and would make no sound that might attract the attention of the approaching insurgents.

As the lights approached, Stark counted at least thirty Tigers walking up the path with torches. He knelt next to a tree and removed the NVGs so the torchlight wouldn't blind him. He steadied his rifle and kept it trained on the approaching Tigers. He knew that Golzari was doing the same. The insurgents were making far better time on the trail than the foursome with the children had.

Although his rifle barrel was steadied against a tree, it wavered as Stark's hand continued to shake. He took a deep, quiet breath and cleared his mind, focusing on the targets. Based on their pace, and because they had not unslung their weapons, he thought Golzari could take out half of them before any managed to get off a shot. That left fifteen against two. The odds were too great. And if he and Golzari went down, the Tigers would certainly find the children. Melanie and Jay would try to protect them, he knew, but it was a risk he couldn't take. And, of course, Stark couldn't know if another company of soldiers was right behind this one. The only option was to let them pass.

One by one, the Tigers walked in between Stark and Golzari, unaware that they were one wrong move away from death. Stark held his breath as they went by. As the light of the last torch, the thirty-fourth, faded in the distance up the trail, Stark slipped across to Golzari's hiding place. "How long do you think it'll take them to get there?" he asked.

"Less than an hour, I should think."

"They'll see the bodies and radio it in right away. Then all of them will know that someone is killing their guys," Stark surmised.

"We can't go deeper into the land and hide out. We don't have enough food or water or shelter for those children," Golzari responded.

Golzari was right. Besides, if they went into hiding they wouldn't be able to give the warning about the hafnium mine. They had to move out now and start the race to the ocean and the boat.

M/V Syren

Syren's speed saved her. She could accelerate to more than fifty knots in less than thirty seconds, but it was only because of Olivia Harrison's quick thinking that the order to do that had been given, and not before the ship paid a price.

Syren was operating, as Stark had ordered, just over the horizon, waiting out the forty-eight hours before sending a RHIB to extract Stark and Warren. Harrison had been in similar situations when she was a lieutenant serving in a Royal Navy frigate in the Persian Gulf. The worst part of it was the waiting—the edginess that interfered with people's sleep, rest, and work.

The ship was humming along at a slow, easy seven knots in a box pattern. The Sri Lankan coastline was barely visible from the bridge level, with the lights of Mullaitivu off to the northwest and the aura of Trincomalee's lights reflecting in the night sky well to the southwest. Occasionally they saw the lights of fishing boats to the east. Perhaps a few of those were Sri Lankan, but more likely they were the Chinese long-line trawlers that Syren's crew had seen en route to their current assignment. The larger trawlers were easily identifiable from their lighting scheme.

Syren had just completed a box when radar reported that one of the trawlers to the east was approaching the Highland Maritime ship at seven knots—the standard speed for fishing vessels dredging the sea to serve the markets in Shanghai, Hong Kong, Beijing, and elsewhere. The ship fit the pattern, but Harrison remained skeptical, particularly when she was informed that another trawler to the north had changed direction and was now operating in a large circular pattern. She made a decision. "CIC, bridge. I'd like to get some eyes in the sky again. Is the bird ready to fly?"

"Fuel cells are recharged, XO," came the reply. "She'll be on the flight deck in five minutes."

Harrison summoned the on-call security team to the deck just in case. The men positioned themselves at their six stations at the foredeck, mid-deck, and aft as the UAV was awakened and lifted from the small elevator on the starboard side of the pilothouse. When Olivia was new to the ship Stark explained that the admiral who had helped design *Syren* fifteen years before had anticipated the wide use of UAVs and had offset the pilothouse to the port side of the ship to allow room for them. The flight deck was designed to hold two standard helicopters, but an area on the starboard side of the pilothouse was set aside for UAVs.

The UAV lifted off as the aviation controller below in the CIC ordered the device to an altitude of two thousand feet. "Which direction, XO?" he asked.

"North first. I want infrared on that trawler. Then we'll check out the one to the east."

The trawler to the east had closed to seven miles now while the trawler to the north was six miles away. The UAV sighted on the closer trawler, and the aviation technician began patching in the feed to one of the monitors on the bridge so Olivia could see what the UAV was recording in real time. The feed showed the darkened outlines of a few figures walking aft along the port side of the trawler to join more figures. Olivia blinked as the size of the ship seemed to change. She stood up to take a closer look at the monitor.

She had seen this happen just a few days ago. This was another trawler with stern doors. A small boat squirted from the trawler's stern like from a calving whale. Another part of the ship lit up as the contrail of a rocket blinded the UAV. Olivia and the bridge crew could see well enough from their vantage point to know that they were looking at a Sea Tiger attack.

"All ahead flank, right full rudder, come about to one-two-zero degrees!" she ordered as a small fireball lit the sky.

"Bridge, CIC. We've lost contact with the UAV," came a voice.

Olivia knew what that meant. The Tigers had fired a tactical EMP, and the UAV was now dead and falling to the ocean, where it would sink to its final resting place.

"Speed?" she asked the helm.

"Forty knots. Forty-two. Forty-four."

She had to hope they could outrace the small speedboat, which likely had its own EMP rocket launcher. Harrison checked the radar again. *Syren* would soon be in the vicinity of the second trawler. What if that too was a mother ship? "Security, this is the bridge, aft fire teams focus on the small speedboat approaching us from astern. Weapons free," she ordered on the shipwide intercom. The two fire teams took a few seconds to locate the small boats—the trawler had released a second one—with their NVGs. Both speedboats were heading straight toward *Syren* at top speed; then they started zigzagging.

Harrison kept a close eye on the radar and watched the boats' patterns. Her teams couldn't train their weapons on the small boats, which quickly closed to three miles. At this range *Syren* couldn't outrun a rocket. Harrison was about to order the forward fire team to train their weapons on the second trawler, now on *Syren's* forward port quarter, when light exploded from its deck—once, twice, and again. Olivia heaved a sigh of relief. Those weren't rockets. She was seeing the steady fire of a warship's main guns. The only warship in the area she knew of was *LeFon*, which must have changed her lighting pattern to imitate a trawler's. Otherwise she would have been running completely dark to minimize detection.

"Helm?"

"Fifty-one knots, ma'am!"

One of *LeFon's* shells hit close enough to a speedboat to capsize it. The other boat closed to two miles. The weapons teams managed to hit the speedboat, but two seconds too late. It had fired its rocket. The EMP detonated a mile from both *Syren* and *LeFon*. Sparks burst from the equipment on the bridge as the three crewmembers reflexively shielded themselves with their arms. The warship's gun went silent and the ship turned to starboard, out to deeper water. Harrison picked up the mike for the ship-to-ship radio, but it was dead. The shipwide intercom still worked, but *Syren's* radar had gone blind.

"Helm, follow *LeFon* but keep us at the current distance," Harrison called before ordering the operations officer to gather damage control reports. Grabbing a large flashlight, she went onto the bridge wing and began flashing in code: "No radar. No comms. Request accompany *LeFon*." She repeated the message several more times before she received a reply from the warship: "Take station three hundred yards to our port. We have no radar or comms either. Stand by."

Two ships operating in such close quarters without modern communications or radar created a dangerous situation, but Harrison was far more worried about her captain and chief scientist. Their satellite phone could no longer communicate with *Syren*. They were stranded ashore, and she had no way to find them.

DAY 14

Mullaitivu District

Stark felt oddly like Gandalf in *The Fellowship of the Ring* as he shepherded his little group toward the coast. Except the children under his protection were not hobbits but very real boys and girls. Using his translation app Warren had managed to inform them that the four adults were taking them to the ocean and their boat to save them from the Tigers. The children accepted that but said little in return.

They stuck close to the vegetation to avoid being spotted as the sun began to rise. The children tugged at Stark's clothing, begging him to stop. Stark finally gave in and let them rest. He had no more food to give them, but the CamelBaks still contained some water. It would have to be enough.

"How far, Golzari?"

Both Golzari and Warren pulled out maps. Golzari pointed to a spot, and Stark was dismayed to see that they would have to pass by a couple of villages and cross some roads, including the coastal highway where Stark and Warren had seen the convoy going south.

"Five miles as the crow flies. Maybe an hour and a half to two hours depending on our protectees," Golzari said.

Stark just shook his head. There were too many unknowns. Would they encounter more patrols? What would happen if they reached the boat and it had been discovered? Were the children more at risk with them than they would be if left on their own here? *People in a nearby village would look after them.* Stark immediately dismissed that idea. These children had witnessed the horrors at the mine. The Tigers would never allow them to live.

He checked the map. The boat was in a heavily vegetated area, but the vegetation didn't extend all the way to their current location. They would benefit from some cover for another three miles but would have to traverse one mile of open area until they reached the final mile with cover all the way to the water. He checked his watch, realizing they had already stopped for ten minutes. Time was not on their side.

"That's it, folks. No other options. We keep going until we get to the boat," Stark said. "We carry the younger ones if we have to."

Twice more they spotted patrols in the distance, but each time, fortunately, before they were seen. Their luck continued for the time being. After an hour they reached the open area. The thick vegetation stopped abruptly about twenty feet above the fields and a road. Half a mile away, between them and the next patch of vegetation, sat three trucks carrying twenty Tigers with drawn weapons. Stark and Golzari had faced this situation before, but they had had cover, there were no children with them, and they didn't face potentially hundreds of other soldiers converging on them.

The normally optimistic Warren, carrying one child on his back and another under his left arm, hung his head in resignation. Stark heard Melanie mutter something like "not again" as she took out a long-range lens in what she assumed would be her final photos of this mission.

Golzari just took a calm breath and assessed the situation. "End of the line, old man," he said with a smile. "This isn't Old Mar'ib."

Stark smiled back as he recalled that firefight—if one could smile about such a thing. It had been one hell of a battle. Stark and Golzari had literally been at each other's throats before the ambush. But the battle had forced them to work together and forged them into an effective team for the remainder of their respective missions in Yemen.

"What was it you said then, Damien? I thought it was the Alamo and you preferred the Siege of Malta?"

"Indeed. But this is no Siege of Malta. I can't think of any battle in history that would apply to the current situation," the British-educated agent said.

Stark assessed the situation. If soldiers were posted here, it was likely that other trucks and soldiers were posted on the road north and south, to the west, and elsewhere. Stark closed his eyes for a few moments, enjoying the warmth of the midmorning sun and listening to the hard breathing of the children and the adults and the occasional click of Melanie's camera. He had a sudden memory of the first time he worked with Warren; it had been on the *Sea Fighter* project. Warren had tested positive during a random drug test. He had a thing for marijuana back then, and it had destroyed his government career. Stark's eyes flew open. *Yes!* And he realized his hand had stopped shaking.

"Not history, Damien. *Movies.*"

"Movies aren't real, Connor."

Stark handed his rifle to a surprised Melanie and removed his vest and blouse, giving those to her as well. He gave his backpack to Golzari.

"What are you doing?" Warren asked him.

"Damien, I believe your education is deficient in one area—American pop culture. Have you ever seen *The Breakfast Club*?" Stark asked.

"No," Golzari said distastefully. "Why?"

"Oh, boss," Warren interrupted. "You're not thinking of going Bender here. No, sir, we're in this together."

"Who is Bender?" Golzari and Melanie asked simultaneously.

"Classic decoy move," Stark answered. "Five kids are in detention. They escape the detention room and wander the halls; then they realize the assistant principal is about to intercept them. Bender starts yelling and singing, leading the assistant principal off in a different direction while the others get away."

"You can't, boss," Warren said. "I've heard you sing. They'll run in the other direction for sure."

"Very funny, Jay. Golzari, get these people to your boat and then to either *LeFon* or *Syren*. As soon as I take off, follow the jungle north a few hundred yards. If the soldiers follow me, wait and then make the dash to the other side. Tell my XO to get the ship out of here and warn the Sri Lankan government about the hafnium mine and weapons. Got it?"

"Understood," Golzari said. He knew Stark was following the only option available to them, whether or not it was viable.

Stark shook Jay's hand, but the big scientist pulled him closer and hugged him. "We'll come back for you," he promised.

Then Stark looked at Melanie. "Save these kids," he said. "And cut your ex-husband some slack. Try not to shoot him in the back. I hit him when I first met him too." She couldn't suppress a wry chuckle. Then she raised her camera and took a photo of him in his black T-shirt and gray coveralls. He reached down to push something further down inside his right boot, then unholstered his Beretta and headed back the way they had come.

A few minutes later they heard three shots and then, in the distance, saw Stark running at full speed across the open field. Golzari carefully watched the reaction of the Tigers. Their attention was focused completely on Stark, who was a mile away from them at that point. One of the men waved to the others, then all three trucks sped off in Stark's direction. Stark diverted into a rice paddy where the trucks would not be able to chase him. That meant the Tigers would have to pursue him on foot.

As soon as the trucks were well to the southwest, Golzari led the band on a direct path to the other side of the road. There were no other soldiers in the vicinity. They continued to hear gunfire. When they reached the cover that would shelter them on the final mile of their journey, Warren turned back one final time as he realized the gunfire had stopped.

LeFon's RHIB

Golzari had come ashore in search of Gala and instead found himself playing nursemaid to a different scientist, nine children, and his ex-wife. Stark had left him with this mess, and he intended to have the American mercenary make amends—if he ever saw him again alive. He recalled the route he had taken after landing on shore, and thirty minutes later the group reached the water.

The RHIB was exactly where Golzari had left it. He cleared away the brush and then began inspecting the boat from stem to stern, from top to bottom.

"What the hell are you doing, Damien?" Melanie asked. "We can't waste time."

"Patience, my love," he said with a hint of sarcasm.

"I know what you're doing," Warren said, sticking his hand into his bag of magic tricks. "Let me help." He inserted a wand into his smart phone and began the same process he had used to find Melanie's equipment. Within five seconds he found what he was looking for inside the engine. He removed it, remarking on the simplicity of the homing device.

"So they've been here." Golzari checked the fuel. "Still half a tank left. If you hadn't found that thing they would have tracked us right back to *LeFon* or *Syren*."

"Want me to break it?" Warren asked, still admiring the craftsmanship, elegant in its simplicity.

"No, no. Hang onto it and don't lose it. I have an idea." Golzari walked toward the muddy shoreline and saw a trio of deserted fishing boats anchored just offshore a few hundred yards to the south. He double-checked with his binoculars, but there was no sign of people on the boats, nor did there appear to be anyone on the shore.

Warren continued trying to reach *Syren* on the satellite phone but finally gave up in frustration. "Hey, man, I can't reach the ship. My satellite phone is working just fine. Either the ship is gone, or they got hit with an EMP," he said to no one in particular. Without Stark, Warren wasn't sure whom to report to.

"If we don't know where the ship is, then how do we find it?" Melanie asked as she distributed the last of the water to the children. "We can't take these children out in that boat without food or water. Have you ever seen the effects of dehydration?"

"Actually, Melanie, I have, and I'm quite aware of our predicament," Golzari snapped. "Mr. Warren, would you kindly assist me in getting this boat in the water?" He added somewhat sheepishly, "I would be willing to entertain ideas on how to find the ships."

"What if we don't look for *Syren* or *LeFon*?" suggested Warren.

"What do you mean?"

"I have the coordinates for *Asity*'s position. Captain Stark told Commander Ranasinghe to hold that position."

"How far?" Golzari asked.

"About forty nautical miles. Half a tank will give us fuel enough for that. If they're still at those coordinates, we should be fine."

"Do we have any other option, Damien?" Melanie asked.

"None that I can think of," he admitted. Stark had just sacrificed himself to give them this opportunity, and he was determined to take advantage of it. "Just point me in the right direction, Mr. Warren. Or do I call you Dr. Warren?"

"How about Jay?"

"Fine. Let's get going." The boat had been too heavy for Golzari to bring all the way ashore, so he had fashioned a crude pulley system on one of the trees to get it part of the way out of the water before securing it and hiding it. Golzari released the line from the pulley, and the boat slipped down until it was floating freely. Warren held the boat still as Melanie lifted up the smaller children and gave the larger ones a hand into the boat. Once all nine were safely in, Melanie joined them and got them to lie down. Warren hoisted himself over the side, and Golzari followed quickly.

"See if the motor will start, Jay." To the relief of everyone on board, it did. The Tamils apparently hadn't tampered with it, probably hoping for bigger game in the form of the large ships. Golzari eased the throttle forward, trying to ignore the people jammed into the bottom of the boat like logs. The sea was calm, and as the boat slowly accelerated to ten knots the group barely felt the motion.

"Hey, why are we going toward those fishing boats?" Warren asked Golzari, keeping his rifle trained on the coast.

"Because you're going to start the engine on one of them."

"What?"

As the RHIB closed on the fishing boats, Golzari pulled back the throttle and pulled alongside one of them. From this angle he could see shacks on the shore that likely belonged to the boats' owners. The shacks looked deserted too. Golzari was betting that these three boats had been abandoned when their owners were either killed or drafted by the Tigers.

Warren got onto the boat and effortlessly started the engine, though he noticed it only had a third of a tank of fuel.

"That doesn't matter. Does it have an autopilot?"

Warren went back into the pilothouse and gave a thumbs-up to Golzari. Melanie stood watch for any sign of Sea Tigers or the soldiers whom they had escaped.

"Put the homing device on board and set the autopilot for due south."

The scientist smiled and quickly complied. Golzari kept the RHIB alongside until Warren accomplished his task and returned. When they separated from the fishing vessel, Golzari pushed the throttle forward and the RHIB pulled away. Warren gave him the heading, and Golzari steered course zero-eight-seven, looking back at the fishing boat now and then to ensure it was on course away from them. When he was certain that it was, he accelerated the RHIB to thirty knots.

They saw a few fishing boats on the horizon but managed to avoid encountering more Tigers for the seventy-five minutes it took to reach a worn-looking old freighter that was barely under way.

"Are you sure that's *Asity*? It would be a shame to board a Sea Tiger ship after coming all this way, Mr. Warren."

Jay peered through the binoculars and confirmed that the ship was indeed *Asity*. Far better, though, was what he saw beyond her: two more ships, a smaller boxy one and the distinguished profile of an *Arleigh Burke*–class destroyer. "Whoo-wee," he yelled. "Salvation!"

"Thank God," Melanie said, relaxing against the gunwale.

Privately, Golzari doubted God had anything to do with it. They had been saved by Warren's equipment and by Connor Stark, who had given his life for twelve others.

Mullaitivu District

Stark made it another fifty yards through the paddy before his boot slipped and he went down. The old knee injury from the terrorist attack in Italy tripped him up, and he fell face-first into the dirt. The gunfire continued to erupt behind him as twenty men raced across the paddy toward him. They were three hundred yards away now, there was nowhere to hide, and he had long since exhausted his ammunition, save for one bullet he had been saving just in case. At least he thought he had one left. It was hard to keep track while running and firing.

I will lie me down and bleed awhile, then I'll rise to fight again. He forced himself to kneel and face the line of insurgents coming toward him. Although they vastly outnumbered him, their approach suggested caution. These weren't professional soldiers. The Tigers' organization may have been planning this war for some time, but they hadn't had the opportunity to recruit and train soldiers en masse. Of course, with the EMP weapons the Tigers didn't need highly trained ground or maritime forces.

These would be the last insurgents he faced—the last of many during his life. There had been the terrorist attack in Italy when he was a junior officer who happened to be at the wrong place at the wrong time. He'd played cat and mouse with Iranian Revolutionary Guards when he commanded a PC boat in the Persian Gulf. There was his final act as a naval officer, challenging a terrorist group in Canada, where his career and the lives of allies and enemies had ended on a tarmac. The list scrolled through his mind as he waited. His time with Highland Maritime dealing with Somali pirates, and the Yemeni coup attempt, when he had condoned the vicious torture of a young terrorist who had been part of his extended family and the near-execution of a senior administration official. All along the way there had been dead bodies. His would be the last.

If helping his friends escape was the last thing he ever did, it was a good end. How would Maggie hear? Would Golzari tell her? Or Warren? Would she forgive him? Would she put his picture up on the wall of heroes alongside those of her other family members and friends who had been killed in military operations?

As the insurgents drew nearer he recalled the first time he met her. He had left Yemen and was traveling through his mother's native Scotland, wandering the Highlands before coming to the small coastal town of Ullapool to catch the ferry to the outer islands. The rain had stopped and he had time for just one drink when he sat at an empty table at the side of the room. Tourists wandered in and out while the regulars enjoyed their drinks and watched a football match on the television above the bar. She came out of the kitchen, her arms full of plates for a table of tourists on the far side of the bar. Her long red ponytail swayed as she twisted and turned, effortlessly distributing the plates. As she finished she turned and caught him staring. She lifted her chin and smiled at the burly, bearded American who had found his way into her pub. That was when he knew he would miss the ferry. He stayed for one more drink, and then another, and after the other tourists left and the football match was over, they talked long into the night.

The gunfire slowed, and he could hear footsteps nearby. It was time. He looked to the azure sky, took two quick deep breaths, and said aloud "Maggie," then pointed the gun at his right temple. Before he pulled the trigger he saw her face before him. *If I do this I'll never see her again.* He lowered the pistol. There was little chance they would let him live—but if there was any chance at all, he'd take it. He threw the pistol away and waited for whatever fate had in store for him.

USS *LeFon*

One of the watch standers on *Asity* was the first to spot the small boat. She raised a red flag and waved it at the watch standers on *LeFon* and *Syren*, who acknowledged it. Signaling was a primitive form of ship-to-ship communication, but since the last EMP strikes had effectively wiped out their bridge-to-bridge radios and other systems, they had no other. Commander Johnson, Olivia Harrison, and Commander Ranasinghe had worked out some basic but effective signals because neither *Asity* nor *Syren* had Navy signal flags like *LeFon*'s.

Fortunately, *LeFon*'s general announcing and alarm circuits had already been EMP-protected before the attack. Johnson called for all hands to battle stations. As *LeFon* pulled from the lee of *Asity*, Johnson went to the port bridge wing and peered through the lenses of the hull-mounted binoculars. Bobbing in the water was a U.S. Navy RHIB. "I'll be damned," she said. "Prepare for recovery of the boat, officer of the deck."

Ten minutes later the RHIB pulled alongside the warship and boatswains guided its recovery on the crane. Johnson awaited the passengers on the deck. When the boat was flush with the deck, Johnson watched in astonishment as Jay Warren handed nine children across to the waiting sailors. Then he, a woman, and Agent Golzari made their way on deck.

Golzari offered a brief explanation of the boat's passengers and suggested that the children would be better off with Ranasinghe on board *Asity*—as, he pointed out, would Melanie.

"No way," she objected. "The kids are safe now. I'm following this story to the end."

"Whoa," said Jaime. "Slow down, everyone. We need a command conference to sort all this out. Let's get these children cleaned up and fed while I get Commander Ranasinghe and Commander Harrison over here. We'll reassemble in the wardroom in two hours."

Vadduvakal, Mullaitivu District

Stark remained on his knees and put his hands behind his head as the armed soldiers neared. It was up to them now: execution or capture. The Tigers kept their guns trained on him as their leader approached. He shouted an unintelligible command at Stark, who found himself wishing he had access to Warren's translation app. The leader motioned for Stark to get up, then drove the butt of his rifle into Stark's stomach. Stark doubled over in pain.

Other soldiers surrounded Stark, grabbed his arms, and marched him back to one of the trucks. They threw him in the truck bed and piled in on top of him, kicking him and laughing as he lay helpless at their feet. The younger ones—conscripts, clearly—seemed energized by their first military action. Stark looked past their faces at the sky and tried to ignore them. The truck made four turns in its twenty-minute journey, passing through a small town just before the end. When the engine stopped, the men threw him out of the truck. He landed in soft, white sand. He was only thirty yards from the water, although a four-foot-high dune obstructed his view.

To his left in the distance—toward the north—he could see dozens of rusty, dilapidated freighters and containerships anchored offshore. He surmised that this was the famed Mullaitivu Breakers, where old ships went to die. They rode passively at permanent anchor, waiting to be picked apart like a Thanksgiving turkey. More were beached in various stages of disassembly. Behind him was a causeway that connected the small town with this isolated spot. To the south he saw anchored fishing boats as well as some commercial speedboats probably used for patrolling the waters. There were two bunches of soldiers on the beach, each of about a dozen men. He had found the Sea Tigers' headquarters.

His captors pushed Stark toward a square wooden building with a tin roof and shoved him inside. The building had no windows, but dusty sunlight peeked in through cracks between the wooden planks and the corrugated tin roof. A few large boxes, one of which was open and empty, were scattered about the floor. Above were wooden beams with pulleys. The building had probably been used to store supplies for the local fishermen until the Tigers had reignited the war.

The soldiers pulled Stark's coveralls down to his waist and ripped off his black T-shirt. They bound his hands tightly together. He didn't try to fight them. There were too many here and outside, and he had to conserve his energy. They secured the rope that bound his hands to one of the pulleys and raised him so that his feet were off the ground. It took four of them to hoist him to that height. He heard another vehicle stop outside. He took long, deep breaths and waited.

A small, thin Tamil in khaki trousers and a white shirt entered with two soldiers ahead of him and two behind. These men weren't like the conscripts who had captured him. These men were older, and they had the severe and determined look of men who had seen battle. These were veterans of the first Sri Lankan civil war.

"I grow weary of foreign visitors," the man said curtly as he nodded to one of the other soldiers behind Stark. Stark heard the unmistakable *whoosh* of a whip just before it snapped on his back. He cried out with the first stroke, then regained his composure and clenched his jaw during the subsequent four strikes. He was able to bury the pain deep within himself but lost the ability to control his breath.

"Shall we talk now?" the man said, pacing in front of him. "You are in Tamil territory and you were armed. You killed many of my men. I may kill you now." He nodded, and the soldier whipped Stark twice more. Stark grunted and snapped his head back toward the pain at each blow.

"Why are you here?" Another nod. Another slash. "Have you come to rescue someone?" Another nod. Another blow. Stark tried to ignore the sonic booms caused by the crack of the instrument of pain.

Rescue someone? Stark thought. *Who needs to be rescued? Melanie? The children? Surely they're safely away by now. Someone else?* By now Stark was having difficulty getting enough air.

"Talk."

"Go to hell," Stark whispered. The man punched Stark in the groin. Stark's eyes watered with the pain, but even with blurred vision he was able to see soldiers drag a man into the room and drop him on the ground near the leader's feet. The man's face was obscured, but he was obviously in pain, and his bound hands revealed that he hadn't come with the Tamils willingly.

"What is his name?" the Tiger leader asked the man on the ground.

"His name is Stark," the man answered dully. "He has a ship." Even through his agony Stark was shocked to recognize the whiny voice of Rear Adm. Daniel Rossberg.

"Thank you, Admiral. Tell me about your ship, Captain Stark."

"Are you Vanni?" Stark shot back, regaining his composure. Rather than answering, the man grabbed a tire iron from atop a box and struck Stark's left ankle. Stark still had his boots on, but they did little to dull the sharp pain. He wondered if something had just been broken.

"Better answer him, Stark," Rossberg said. "He'll just keep hurting you until you do."

"Yes. The admiral has been very cooperative," Vanni said, guessing the thoughts running through Stark's mind.

When Stark was silent for a moment longer, Rossberg ventured, "His ship is—"

"Shut your fucking pie-hole, Rossberg," Stark yelled just before Vanni took the tire iron to his thigh. He stiffened in agony, unable to stifle a scream.

"Tell me more about him, Admiral."

"His name is Connor Stark. He was a Navy commander once, but now he is a mercenary. He stole my ship, my command," Rossberg said as he cowered on the dirt floor.

"Very good, Admiral. Are you a mercenary or a Navy commander now, Mr. Stark?" Vanni asked.

"I'm a man on a pulley," Stark said defiantly.

"Were you here to rescue Admiral Rossberg?" he asked.

Stark closed his eyes and focused on the pain and his breathing.

"Very well. Now I have two hostages. You will both serve a glorious purpose in a few days. And how fortunate that you know one another. You can spend the time getting reacquainted."

The Squadron

Melanie had just enjoyed her first shower in more than a week, courtesy of the destroyer *LeFon*, and had donned the camouflage "blueberries" worn by most sailors on deployment in the fleet. A female crewmember with an extra rack in her stateroom had offered it to Melanie so she could have some peace and quiet. She took a short but very refreshing nap, and then a sailor escorted her to *LeFon*'s wardroom, where Jaime Johnson, Ranasinghe, Olivia Harrison, and Golzari were already seated. Golzari had bigger bags under his eyes than normal, but she hadn't known him to sleep much anyway during the brief time they were together. Jay Warren entered just after she did. He carefully avoided looking at Olivia Harrison.

Harrison rose, walked straight up to Warren, and grabbed his meaty arm. "Where's the captain, Jay?"

After a moment of silence, he choked out, "He's still there. The captain's the reason the rest of us made it out."

"Please have a seat, Ms. Arden," Johnson said. She stood and went to the galley window, where a mess crank handed her a plate of greens, rice, beans, and bread. Johnson walked it over to Melanie's place. "Agent Golzari told me you're a vegetarian. We can make something else for you if you prefer."

"No, thanks. This is perfect. Thank you very much for your kindness, Captain," Melanie said.

Jaime Johnson took her seat and looked around the table. "Ladies and gentlemen, we find ourselves in unusual circumstances. The last EMP attack left our ships without radar and navigation systems. While it's not the optimal situation, we can get by without those. Humankind sailed the oceans for thousands of years without modern technology. My junior officers have all been brushing up on their MoBoards," Johnson said, adding, "maneuvering boards, Ms. Arden," after she noticed Melanie's quizzical look.

"More troubling is that we find ourselves without the ability to communicate with anyone on the outside. The last rocket was close enough to wipe out our communication systems. We are left with only a few choices on how to proceed," Johnson said. "And I want to be clear at the outset why I have allowed Ms. Arden to remain here. First, she has been with the Tigers and I'm hoping she can enlighten us. Second, she's a journalist. Normally our public affairs officer at Seventh Fleet would have to be consulted about this, but that isn't possible. Because of the circumstances, I want to be as transparent as possible without violating security constraints. Ms. Arden, you are our guest. You are free to take notes and eventually to report on what we do, because there should be a record and accountability. We have been drawn into a war zone. The Tamil Tigers have demonstrated that they are a threat not only to the Sri Lankan government but to neutral shipping as well.

"Our three ships represent the United States, Sri Lanka, and a private security company operating in the interests of the Sri Lankan government. We need to learn what we can from one another before our three respective ships make decisions on their next course of action."

With that, Jaime went around the table asking each stakeholder to share information. Golzari explained his search for Gala and the tie to hafnium. Melanie briefly recounted most of what she had seen and done from the time the Buddhist monk in Thailand asked her to go to Sri Lanka. She described the soldiers and her interview with Vanni.

Jay, who was standing against the bulkhead sipping coffee, offered what he knew about the weaponized hafnium, which, to Jaime Johnson, represented the greatest immediate threat to them and the Sri Lankan government. "Dr. Warren," she said, "is there any indication how much of this pure hafnium they have?"

"Lots."

"Let me rephrase the question," she said calmly, brushing her hair back with one hand. "Do you think they have the capability to make multiple high-explosive weapons?"

"I scanned the area outside the mine," he replied. "The dust contained high levels of pure hafnium. As I understand it, weapons such as the rockets and buoys we've seen require only very small amounts of hafnium. I did some calculations based on the previous attacks, and I'd say each rocket contains about three milligrams of hafnium." He raised his hand and touched his thumb to the tip of his little finger. "About that much. The size of a raisin. If the Tigers have the right equipment and enough people, yes, they can mass-produce the weapons."

"Can you estimate how much hafnium they have?" Johnson asked again.

"That mine was about a year old. Apparently they've been bringing in large numbers of slave workers, so they've probably extracted several tons of raw earth. Based on the percentage of dust and the piles at the monastery, I'd guess they probably have fifty kilograms by now."

"Fifty kilograms!" exclaimed Ranasinghe. "That's enough to make thousands of rockets. Or they could even build a massive bomb. They could destroy my country!"

"Whoa, whoa, Commander, it's not that straightforward. They may have the raw material, but they need a lot more—components for rockets, detonators, the ability to process it quickly—lots of stuff. Unless they have access to all those things they just can't make that many."

"But what about a much larger warhead?" the Sri Lankan commander asked again anxiously.

"Well, I guess it's possible if they have the right setup," Jay said rubbing his chin. "I'd have to see their lab to know for sure. And they'd need something a heck of a lot bigger than the Qassams they've been using against us. I'd have a tough time believing that the United States, China, or Russia couldn't see something like that from space."

"Are you saying it can't be done or is unlikely to be done?" Jaime asked.

"Ma'am, until I went to that monastery I would have told you that a hafnium-based EMP couldn't be done," he said.

"Very well." Johnson took a deep breath and reached for her bottled water. "Folks, we need to get word to someone what the Sri Lankan government is facing. I'm going to give my crew six hours to see what we come up with on the radios. In the meantime, we'll make a high-speed run to Chennai. I recommend *Asity* and *Syren* remain on station to gather more information."

Ranasinghe and Harrison concurred. Golzari remained silent. Only Warren spoke up.

"What about the captain?" he asked quietly.

"From what you've told us he's gone, Jay," Jaime said. "We have to continue the mission."

"His body is back there somewhere," Jay countered.

"He's right, Commander," Golzari said in Jay's defense. "It is unlikely that any of us would be here had it not been for Stark's sacrifice. We owe it to him to retrieve his body if we can."

"Look, I knew Connor Stark before any of you did," Jaime said in an unusually sharp voice. "I served under him as a junior officer and he hired me at Highland Maritime. If it hadn't been for him, I wouldn't be in command of this ship." Jaime stopped when she realized what she'd said and pointed to Melanie. "You never heard that, understood?" It was less a question than a command and warning. Melanie nodded and raised her hands to indicate acquiescence.

"We all owe him," Jaime continued. "Jay," she said, walking toward him and reaching up to lay her hand on his shoulder, "if you can figure out where his body is and a way to get him home, we will."

Vadduvakal

The sun beating down on the corrugated tin roof heated the interior of the windowless structure like an oven. The dirt floor beneath Stark's body was muddy from the mixture of his perspiration and blood. The angle of the sunbeams poking through the wooden planks was Stark's only indication of the time when he awoke. At best guess it was just after noon.

He heard the muted banter of several men on the east, ocean side of the structure and two more outside the door on the north side. A truck started up beyond the door and rumbled down the causeway. Admiral Rossberg sat with his back against the east wall, arms wrapped around his legs, staring blankly at Stark.

Stark shifted his hands in an attempt to unhook the rope that bound them from the pulley, then he started swinging forward and backward to loosen it. Neither worked, and he was quickly out of breath from the pain of his raw wounds.

"Cut me down," he said to Rossberg. The admiral simply stared and said nothing. "Cut me down," Stark said again.

"They put you up there. They'll take you down if they want to. If they find you loose they'll do something bad to you," Rossberg whined.

"Like what? Hang me, whip me, and hit me repeatedly with a tire iron?" Stark said.

"There's nothing here to cut with," Rossberg said.

"Check those boxes. Maybe there's something in them. Break them apart. Get a sharp piece of wood, a nail, a screw, anything."

Rossberg shook his head. "No. If they come in here and see me doing that, they'll hang me up there too."

"So, leaving me hanging again, are you? Just like the last time." Stark asked.

"What does that mean?" Rossberg snapped before realizing he'd raised his voice too much. The guards outside the door quieted their chatter.

"It means I was on *Kirkwall* when she was attacked by Somali pirates. Two-thirds of the crew were lost. The rest of us were in the water praying for rescue. The ship's captain, Jaime Johnson, was badly injured. And you did nothing to save us."

"Johnson?" Rossberg asked. "That female commander who disobeyed my orders on *LeFon*?"

"Shut up, Rossberg. She almost died in the water that night while you delayed *Bennington*. If it hadn't been for your exec and operations officers, the ship and its helicopters would never have arrived in time to save her and the rest of us."

"You have no proof of that," Rossberg responded cautiously.

"Oh, yes I do. I saw the logbooks for that night," Stark said coldly. "And the charts. What did your officers get for doing what was right? You killed them with your incompetence. Nearly every officer and chief petty officer on that ship died because of you."

"That's not true! I was the captain. I got a medal for *Bennington*'s actions against the pirates. You were the real pirate. You took my ship."

"That's a lie, Rossberg. You're completely delusional. You were unconscious in sick bay. There were only three officers left. I took command."

"No, that isn't true."

"Washington covered it up—the entire engagement—because it wasn't approved by the chain of command and the White House. But people know about it. Some of them are on *LeFon*, which was almost destroyed too when you led the two LCSs to the bottom of the ocean."

"You'll hang for those words, Stark."

"A little late for that," Stark said sarcastically. He knew he was essentially alone here. Rossberg was less than useless. Stark's left knee and ankle were swelling from the tire iron strikes. He wasn't sure he could walk if he did manage to free himself. If only Vanni had struck the other boot, Stark reflected, the *sgian dubh* might have protected him. *The* sgian dubh! *I'm an idiot!*

Stark rested a moment, focused, and summoned all his strength to lift his legs straight up—and dropped them immediately at the unexpected pain in his back and abdomen. He paused for a minute, took another deep breath, then raised his legs again, this time getting them above his head next to the pulley. He hooked his right boot around the chain to stabilize his leg, then brought it closer to his hands. His wrists were bound together, but his hands and fingers were fairly unrestricted. He reached into his boot, careful not to let the knife slip out and fall onto the dirt floor, where, he was sure, Rossberg would only sit and look at it impassively.

His fingernails found the jeweled pommel. Inch by inch he tugged it out until the pommel was free of the boot. Once it was secure in his grip, he let his legs fall back to their dangling position, panting from his exertions. He concentrated on each tiny movement of his fingers. His hands were sweating, and he didn't want to relax now and accidentally drop the knife. Had the sheath been made of plastic instead of antique leather, it might have simply slid away.

He slipped the knife free and placed the serrated edge against the hemp, methodically sawing back and forth, each movement bringing more pain from the open wounds on his back.

"Stop that, Stark. If they catch you with a weapon they'll kill us," Rossberg whispered up to him.

"They're going to kill us anyway, Sherlock. Vanni's not keeping us around for intelligence. He's going to use us for something. My guess is we'll be human shields." The knife was now a quarter of the way through his bindings.

"Oh, my God. He promised to release me. What are we going to do?"

"I'm trying to do something, Admiral. Tell me how you ended up here. I thought you died when the LCS you were on was destroyed."

"Well, there was an explosion, and I guess the ship sank. I don't remember what happened. I was in the water for a long time; then I blacked out. When I woke up I was on a ship. Down below in a little cell. Everything looked old and rusty. They beat me," he whined. "But I didn't tell them anything."

Stark suspected Rossberg had given up every bit of information he knew about Navy ships but figured the admiral would never admit that to him. Rossberg was a broken man.

"Then they put a smelly blindfold on me and made me climb up to the deck and then down another ladder into a small boat. Vanni was on it. I could hear him talking. And then we came here."

"How fast was the boat going?" Stark asked.

"Slow. Maybe eight to ten knots," Rossberg said.

"Any idea how long you were on the boat?" The *sgian dubh* had sawed through three-quarters of the binding and Stark prepared himself to land on his good right leg.

"I'm not sure. I was blindfolded. Maybe forty-five minutes to an hour."

Stark stored that information away. Their predicament was starting to make sense. Just then the last thread of the bindings split, dropping Stark two feet to the ground, right boot first. He lay prone for a few minutes, breathing hard and trying to control his pain.

He slid the *sgian dubh*—Maggie's lucky charm—back inside his boot, then got to his feet and approached Rossberg.

As the much larger Connor Stark loomed over him, Rossberg had only two options: cry out to the guards for help or beg for mercy.

Unwilling to take the chance, Stark wrapped his hands around Rossberg's throat and began to squeeze.

M/V *Syren*

As soon as he was back on board *Syren* Warren wasted no time in preparing the ship's last UAV. Golzari, with nothing else to do, watched over his shoulder. Jay worked furiously to establish the appropriate connections between the UAV's systems and his control panel. Golzari admired Warren's determined effort to retrieve Stark's body. Golzari had no doubt that Stark was dead. His life ended when the gunfire stopped. A man who had sacrificed himself for his friends in that fashion deserved the loyalty of individuals like Dr. Jay Warren.

"When do you launch it?" Golzari asked.

"I just have to confirm one more connection—there, have it. Okay, we can launch in five minutes." Warren called two crewmembers over to help get the device to the flight deck.

Melanie, who had been standing in the background watching them prepare the UAV, pulled Golzari aside and told him to follow her to the wardroom.

"May I get you something to drink?" he asked politely before sitting down. "Tea? Coffee?"

"Water," she said stiffly. "I know you didn't tell them everything in that meeting. You withheld information, and I want the backstory," she demanded.

Rather than answering her he said, "You didn't have to hit me. It was uncivilized."

Uncivilized. That was the first word he had said when they met ten years ago. She was a young college student from South Africa at American University in Washington, D.C., and a popular rugby player. She and her team had invaded an upscale bar in Georgetown after a victorious game, still in their dirty, sweaty gear, to the visible dismay of the elegant clientele. The young women had a few beers in them already when they stormed in and ordered drinks. After that round, Melanie's roommate turned and vomited on the Italian shoes of a patron sitting at the bar.

"Uncivilized!" the patron said loudly in a British accent. He took a napkin and wiped off his shoe in disgust. Although he was dressed in a suit befitting an older man, Melanie realized that he was probably no more than five years her senior. He was rising to leave the bar when Melanie stopped him and apologized for her roommate. Then she paid his bar tab.

"Did you at least win your rugby match?" he said grudgingly. "It's been a while since I've seen a decent one."

She was immediately taken with the worldly and suave Iranian American who was studying foreign affairs at George Washington University. After a short courtship they eloped. It took her a few months to realize her mistake. Damien spent his days and weeknights studying. On Saturdays he took her to a firing range and taught her how to shoot various guns. Sunday afternoons were spent at one of the museums in Washington. During their brief, cold marriage, however, he flew to England no less than five times for long weekends. When she finally learned more about his background and came to understand that neither she nor any other woman was Damien Golzari's type, she divorced him. This was the first time she had seen him since.

"I'm sorry," she said. "I should have said hello first."

He smiled wryly. "Very well, Melanie. I'll give you a little information."

He was interrupted forty minutes and ten stories later when Commander Harrison walked into the wardroom and advised them that Dr. Warren needed to see them immediately in the CIC. When they arrived, Warren was providing guidance to the aviation technician piloting the UAV. Both wide-screens displayed imagery from the bird.

"What are we seeing, Dr. Warren?" Golzari asked.

"Bird number two is flying over that rice paddy we watched the boss run into," Warren said as he gently pushed aside the aviation technician. "I know the lay of the land, Jerry. Might be faster if I fly her." Warren pressed a button and zoomed in on the last spot he remembered seeing Stark running, and then had the UAV follow in that direction, zigzagging to pick up a trail.

Melanie was astounded at the resolution of this commercially available camera. She could see individual rice plants quite clearly.

The bird flew slowly over the paddy until Warren found footprints tracking in the same direction they had seen Stark run. The scientist maneuvered the camera and followed the prints until they stopped in a larger imprint in the mud. A nine-millimeter handgun lay just off to the side. This had to be the spot where Stark had been gunned down, but there was no body. Around the larger impression were a series of other footprints that must have been made by the soldiers who were chasing him.

"They took his body," Golzari said. "Unless he was still alive and they took him prisoner." A flutter of hope entered the CIC.

"Dr. Warren, may I film this?" Melanie asked.

"Commander Harrison has to make that call," Warren said.

Melanie glanced at Harrison, who nodded her approval. "You can record the video, but not the faces in this room," she said.

"I understand."

The bird followed a path made by more footprints until it reached the dirt road nearby. The tracks stopped as the path turned onto the main paved road.

"Dr. Warren, can you zoom out and see if there's any general activity in the area?" Golzari asked as he inched closer to one of the screens. As the view panned out he saw a small town connected by a narrow causeway to a beach. Several vehicles and some small-boat activity were visible near a square building.

"There," he pointed. "Focus on that."

Three groups of uniformed soldiers were milling about an old building near the beach just east of what the map told him was Vadduvakal, a small village north of Mullaitivu. Two soldiers guarded the building's door. A few other men nearby were dressed in the tiger-stripe pattern of older Tamil Tiger military uniforms. It was a style Melanie had seen before, quite recently. These men were about to enter a truck.

"Zoom in on those men," she said urgently. As the camera focused in, one of the men turned his head. "It's Vanni."

"Are you sure, Mel?" Golzari asked.

"Positive. That's him."

"That building is too small to be a base for the entire operation," Harrison offered. "Jay, can you see anything inside the building?"

"I have infrared on this bird, but there's a metal roof." Warren dropped the UAV to five hundred feet, but well away from the area and to the south. From this vantage point the infrared detected the rough shapes of two figures inside. One was sitting against a wall. The other was hanging by his hands a couple of feet off the ground. Warren froze that image.

With another dance of his hands he switched the screen from infrared to radar. Data began streaming in on the screen. "Two people. One larger than the other," Warren said, then made a few changes to the controls and pointed to another image and data. The radar image showed the faint outline of a knife hugging the hanging man's leg. "Yeah, yeah, look at those numbers . . ."

Harrison nudged him.

"That data, XO, tell me the basic composition of that knife—steel blade, iron plate on the sheath, and a quartz pommel. Bet you a paycheck that quartz is cairngorm found primarily in Scotland. Wait, there's the other data now. It's definitely quartz. The infrared spectrometry stuff is pretty easy. We beam IR out of the UAV and get a signal ID in return. It's small but it's definitely quartz. That's the skipper's *sgian dubh*. That has to be him. Wait, I forgot about the audio recorder."

This UAV carried a more sophisticated pod of equipment and sensors than the first one had, one of which could pick up conversation coming from hand-held radios. He flicked another switch, and the speakers on each side of the screens began to share voices from the ground. There weren't many conversations, but Jay was able to apply the translation app to the data they were receiving. Most of it was typical banter from bored soldiers. They spoke of home, their next meal, and the heat. After fifteen minutes the sensors caught a different feed; that voice spoke of preparing the Americans for transfer at night.

Americans. There were two people in that building. If one was Stark, and that was a safe assumption at this point, then who was the other? A tourist? Another journalist? Either way, the crew of *Syren* now knew where to focus their operation.

"Bridge, get a signal to *LeFon* and *Asity*. Request the presence of their COs on *Syren* immediately."

When the council met again, Warren summarized the information from the UAV for Commanders Ranasinghe and Johnson. There were two people inside a wooden building at the Mullaitivu Breakers, and one of the Tigers outside had mentioned two Americans. One of the people inside appeared to be hanging from the ceiling, and the other was sitting against the wall, apparently able to move about. They weren't certain that the hanging person was Stark, although the *sgian dubh* seemed to confirm that.

"Is he alive?" Jaime Johnson asked.

Warren shook his head. "I don't know for sure. What I do know is that the temperature inside the building is 87° Fahrenheit, and at the time the UAV acquired the data both bodies were radiating a normal human temperature of 98° Fahrenheit."

Golzari interpreted for the group. "A body loses one and a half degrees of heat per hour after death until it matches the ambient temperature. That means that the hanging person in the image, whom we believe to be Stark, was either alive twenty minutes ago or had been dead less than half an hour."

The team agreed that in either case they would risk a rescue regardless of who the two Americans were. Commander Johnson decided this mission fell within the rules of engagement Admiral O'Donnell had outlined: "Fire only if fired upon or otherwise clearly and imminently threatened by the Sea Tigers. If you are protecting U.S. assets such as a U.S.-flagged commercial ship or lives, you will defend them appropriately." Two American lives had to be protected. The only way to defend them "appropriately" was to rescue them.

The next question was when to do it, but the biggest question was how. The UAV transmission said the Americans would be moved after dark. Sunset was only three hours away. In effect, they had two hours at most to launch a rescue. *LeFon* would take nearly ninety minutes to arrive close enough to conduct operations even at her top speed; her RHIBs would take about another hour after that. *Syren* was the fastest ship there—capable of more than fifty knots, she could be there in less than an hour. If it moved in close during daylight, however, either ship would be visible to those on shore long before the rescuers arrived, allowing the Tigers ample time to move or execute the prisoners.

Johnson, Harrison, Ranasinghe, Golzari, and Warren sat around the wardroom table with a map of the area in the center and penciled in resources, ideas, and options. *LeFon*'s executive officer, operations officer, and navigation officer stood behind Johnson. Jaime placed utensils and salt and pepper shakers on one side of the map to visualize the platforms available to them. For the next thirty minutes they debated options for a military operation that should have taken hours or days to plan.

Finally, Commander Johnson pushed back her chair and stood. "We're out of time, and we may not have another opportunity to rescue these people. We have to move now with the resources we have regardless of the risk. Here's what we're going to do," she said. "Listen up, OPS." For the next five minutes Johnson ran down the tasks for each platform, the times, and the distances involved. She concluded simply, "That's it, ladies and gentlemen. Let's make this happen."

Johnson, followed by her three-member staff, cut through the cargo bay on her way back to her small boat. Before she could reach it Melanie waylaid her and begged for some idea of what was about to happen. Johnson held up her people and pulled the reporter aside, out of earshot. "Ms. Arden," she whispered, "I can't tell you what's going to happen. But I will tell you that when this is over and you're able to file your stories, if anything goes wrong on this mission, it has been my responsibility and mine alone for any risks, mistakes, or deaths. Do you understand?"

"I do," Melanie responded. "Good luck, Commander."

USS *LeFon*

By the time Johnson returned to *LeFon,* now positioned forty nautical miles off the coast of Sri Lanka, preparations were already under way both on the destroyer and on *Syren.* It was now 1545, and they had a little more than two hours of daylight remaining. Chief Petty Officer Omar Garcia and the other boatswain's mates assembled working parties to prepare the small boats and hastily paint their exteriors two shades of blue in the old wartime camouflage pattern. The air boss was in the hangar checking out the second helicopter as the first began warming up on the landing pad.

Thirty minutes later Johnson took her place on the bridge and signaled to the other ships to commence. *LeFon* broke away as she steered into the window that allowed the first helicopter to take off and head due south for its wide arc. Johnson prayed for the safety of the three souls on the SH-60R, designated Starfire One-Seven. Of all the components of this mission, she was concerned most for them because the helicopter was vulnerable to an EMP rocket.

As soon as Starfire One-Seven launched, Starfire One-Eight was rolled out of the hangar and the eleven-meter and eight-meter small boats were launched, immediately speeding toward *Syren* half a mile away. Both had full complements of twenty-four and eight sailors and officers respectively—*LeFon's* entire VBSS teams.

LeFon closed on *Syren* as the small boats were brought up the stern ramp of the SWATH ship. As the second boat came up, the pulley system failed again and *Syren's* boat handlers were forced to secure it to the kingpost with rope. Once all four small boats were on board *Syren,* Harrison signaled to *LeFon* that she was ready. Johnson gave the word, and within a minute *Syren* was racing away at fifty-two knots, her underwater plane keeping her steady and level in the calm seas. No one on the ship realized how fast they were going until they saw the Navy destroyer behind them doing her best speed of thirty knots and still falling behind rapidly. And so the run to the hostages began.

Chennai

The burly Russian passed an envelope of cash to the ship captain on the bridge of the offshore support vessel *Alexander.* Sergei Stepanovich Makarov despised the Ukrainian seated across from him, but the man and his ship served a purpose in the underworld of illicit maritime commerce. It wasn't the illicit trafficking that bothered Makarov; he just hated Ukrainians. He was certain the former Soviet satellite would soon be firmly back in Russia's control now that his country finally had a tough and competent leader—the first he had known since he joined the Soviet navy two years before the fall of the Soviet Union. He had been based in Crimea with the Black Sea Fleet then, on board the cruiser *Slava* before he was given command of a patrol boat as a junior officer with the Caspian Flotilla.

"Will we have time to get supplies and extra fuel?" the captain asked.

"No. We go now. We will get food, weapons, and fuel at one of our floating armories," Makarov said.

"Who will be on board? How many staterooms do you need?"

"Three people, two staterooms."

The Ukrainian captain recognized that all three had arrived; an Asian man was standing near the door with a beautiful blond woman. He was about to make a comment about the arrangements when Makarov reached out and grabbed him by the lapels.

"Captain, I have paid you well," he hissed, "but I will kill you if you say the wrong thing right now. Of course," he mused, "she would do even worse to you."

"My apologies," the Ukrainian said hastily. "I was only going to say that it is my pleasure to do business with you once again."

"Very well. Get under way. We wish to rendezvous with *Nanjing Mazu* by tomorrow evening. Here are the coordinates," Makarov said as he released the captain and handed him a slip of paper with the longitude and latitude required.

Off Vadduvakal

The rescuers had been fortunate thus far. They had seen neither commercial ships nor fishing vessels on the run in to the coast—though they knew from experience that the latter were probably back in their harbors by now. *Syren* arrived on station twelve nautical miles off the coast, just over the horizon from the view of any Tigers who might be watching from the beach at sea level. According to the plan, two boats—both from *Syren* and carrying six-person security teams—would begin the high-speed run from here, followed by *Syren* herself at a slower speed. Golzari was in *Somers* while Warren was in *MacDonough*. The security teams lay low, hoping the hastily painted camouflage would hide the boats from casual view for another four miles.

LeFon followed behind at a pace ten knots slower. Her .25-caliber machine guns had a maximum range of about 7,500 yards but an effective range of only 3,200 yards. That was still too far for Johnson's plan to work because the structure in which the hostages were being held was directly behind two groups of soldiers.

Syren's UAV circled two thousand feet directly above the building beaming images of the shore. The two groups of soldiers on the beach were seated around fire pits eating their dinner. Nearly all were behind the dune, focusing on their meals and guarding the shack; only two guards were looking out at the slightly choppy ocean, scanning from north to south but clearly seeing nothing out of the ordinary. The camouflage paint scheme had bought the teams the additional four miles they needed.

Two guards stood outside the building's only door, and three pickup trucks were parked thirty yards northwest of the structure just before the causeway. Jay radioed the UAV for an update. It would be the last transmission for Warren's beloved bird. The controller on *Syren* set a timer, and the bird began to descend directly at the truck farthest from the building. Warren watched the death flight on his monitor as the UAV dropped hundreds of feet, its transmitted image of the soldiers getting larger and less stable. One Tiger appeared to hear something behind and above him and turned to look, then called out to the others. The last image Jay saw before the crash showed the two Tigers monitoring the ocean turn as well. Jay pumped his fist in victory. The distraction had worked for now. The teams had twelve minutes.

Nearly all the soldiers ran to the crash site. They pointed at the UAV's wings and what remained of the fuselage, mystified as to its origin. Once again the teams from *Syren* and *LeFon* were fortunate—the soldiers in the dunes, the first they would have to face, were inexperienced conscripts. Stark was not as fortunate. The men guarding the door of the wooden building were seasoned Tiger soldiers.

When the small boats closed to four nautical miles Golzari popped his head up just enough to be able to watch the next segment of Johnson's coordinated attack. He had difficulty distinguishing it because he was looking directly into the setting sun, but he expected it at any moment according to his watch.

Right on time, Starfire One-Seven flew out of the sun. After corkscrewing down from five thousand feet to five hundred before leveling out west of the mountain range, the SH-60R bore down on the truck the UAV had destroyed. The helicopter slowed and pivoted directly above the structure and faced south so that the crewman manning the GAU .50-caliber machine gun faced the soldiers massed around the remains of the truck. The gunner let loose, mowing down several Tigers in the first few seconds while others tried to run for cover. A few attempted to fire before the SH-60's pilot flew off to make another pass. The crew never saw the two Tiger guards enter the structure.

Vadduvakal

When Connor Stark was ten years old he had ventured through the woods of what remained of the Stark estate in Dunbarton, New Hampshire—named after Dunbartonshire in Scotland, home of his ancestor Archibald Stark, the first Stark to emigrate to America. The town had once been known as Starks town, and when Connor lived there it was a sparsely populated town of two thousand residents and horse farms, including the Starks' own.

He was more than a mile from the house and stables with his dog when they crested a hill and the dog suddenly barked. Connor looked up to see a Siberian husky slowly approaching them. Saliva dripped from its mouth and its head was weaving from side to side. When the husky saw Connor and the other dog it began to bark viciously. Connor recognized the signs of a rabid animal. Holding desperately to his dog's collar he tried to calm his pet and send him back home, but to no avail.

The husky first trotted and then ran toward Connor's dog. Connor thrust his pet behind him as the husky lunged. The young boy stuck out one arm to stop the husky's forward momentum and with the other grabbed the thick fur at its nape and yanked it back and to the ground. Boy and dog struggled on the ground as Stark tried to gain the advantage on top while avoiding the husky's snapping teeth. He took hold of the animal's neck with both small hands and forced the husky's head down before squeezing, ignoring the barks of his own pet. He didn't know how long it took, but eventually the husky breathed its last in Stark's hands. He swore never to kill another animal after that.

Now, decades later, Stark continued to squeeze Admiral Rossberg's neck with all his strength as Rossberg struggled vainly to let out a scream or beg for his life. His kicked out with his short legs and Stark tightened his grip. "You worthless son of a bitch. How can you wear that uniform after what you did?"

The admiral's face was turning blue when Stark heard a metallic crash and then the unmistakable sound of a Sikorsky SH-60 overhead in the distance. He turned and released his grip. Rossberg rolled over and curled up into a fetal position, his hands covering the back of his neck. Stark was relieved. They had somehow found him and were attempting a rescue. But he knew a helicopter alone could not get the job done. There were too many soldiers nearby as well as the possibility of an EMP rocket. Then he heard the .50-caliber pepper the area beyond the building. Stark immediately ran toward the door, leaving Rossberg curled up like an armadillo on the ground.

The helicopter stopped firing, and the sound of its engines faded away. Rossberg struggled to speak: "Where are they going? They have to come back for us."

Stark held up his hand for silence. If he knew Jaime Johnson, she wasn't attacking with only a helicopter. She'd throw everything she had at them. That meant troops, and the only way they'd get here was by boat. He heard men yelling in pain and others shouting orders. And then he heard the sound of his guards opening the door. Stark and Rossberg had no value as hostages if they were rescued, and they posed a huge threat to the Tigers' operations if they were allowed to tell what they knew. The Tigers had to eliminate them.

After the first Tiger entered, his weapon drawn, Stark threw all his weight against the door, slamming it against the second guard. The first guard, still focused on the only target he saw in the room, did not see Stark's muscular arm until it was wrapped around his neck. Stark lifted him up and then threw him to the ground, but not before the guard fired three shots at Rossberg. Stark quickly grabbed the guard's gun, whirled toward the door, and fired four rounds as the second guard tried again to enter. The man was dead before he hit the ground. Stark turned back toward the prone Tiger, who defiantly rolled away from him. Stark fired once and missed before the gun jammed.

The Tiger was half a foot shorter than Stark, but he smiled when he realized the injured American had no gun. It was one man against the other. The Tiger ignored the American crumpled against the wall as he looked about for a weapon. Stark threw the gun aside and crouched as if exhausted and in pain, exposing his left side to the Tiger. It wasn't far from the truth—he knew he'd be useless in a fight right now with a barely functioning leg. His right hand slid down inside his boot.

Stark tried to remember every move Gunny Willis had taught him in hand-to-hand combat on the training island off Ullapool. The Tiger closed on Stark and attempted a kick. Stark had foreseen this move; Willis had once done something similar. He quickly grabbed the man's left leg and flipped him to the ground. As he did that he slipped out his *sgian dubh* and thrust it into the unsuspecting man's throat. Stark stuck the knife in deep and twisted it. The man's blood spurted onto Stark as he struggled for oxygen to fuel his dying brain. Stark pulled out the short dagger and stood aside to allow the man his final moments.

More gunfire sounded from the east side—the ocean side—of the building.

"You . . . you killed him," Rossberg gasped behind him. "And you tried to kill me." He held a bloody hand over his arm where the guard's bullet had found its mark.

Still holding the *sgian dubh* Stark limped toward Rossberg, his bare chest splattered with the guard's blood. "And I may yet." He raised his arm, pointing the weapon toward the admiral, then knelt beside him and struck him with his fist, knocking him unconscious.

The gunfire from the ocean was becoming more intense. The helicopter was back, its .50-caliber firing again. Stark put the blood-covered dagger back into his boot, then collapsed from exhaustion. He had no real weapon to defend himself if more Tigers came for him. He had to trust the assault the others had planned. He heard fewer and fewer Tamils until the gunfire stopped and men approached the building.

"Americans," someone called as the door burst open.

"I used to be, too," he said weakly.

Two Highland Maritime security officers entered and swept the room. *Syren*'s medic and Special Agent Damien Golzari followed close behind them.

"Are you ready to get out of here?" Golzari asked as the medic checked Stark quickly for life-threatening wounds.

"I think I'd like to stay," Stark said right before he passed out.

PART III

DAY 15

Mullaitivu

Vanni had bided his time since the defeat of the Tamil Tigers in 2009. He still believed that the Tamil people deserved a better life and would have one if they followed him. He hoped for revenge against those who had defeated his comrades. So he organized the remaining loyal Tigers into a new cadre. He sought resources. When he found them, like the hafnium, he exploited them. When people opposed him or seemed ambivalent in their support, he had his most loyal Tigers execute them—all the great Marxist leaders had done this, he knew. It was efficient, clean, and necessary. He just had to be patient and wait for the right opportunity. And so he waited. And his time had finally come.

He believed the earlier Liberation Tigers of Tamil Eelam—the LTTE, as the world knew them—had lost because they had spread their resources too thin by fighting both on land and at sea. Colonel Soosai himself had summoned Vanni to fight with his forces at sea after the Sea Tigers' leader had heard of Vanni's successes on land. And while he was at sea Vanni had seen the future of his rebellion. Although ships and boats cost more initially than trucks and arms, they required fewer personnel than an army and their versatility allowed the LTTE to grow as a whole.

Fighting at sea offered major benefits. The first was that the sea provided financing. Vanni organized his small ships to pirate freighters, which were then used to make money through human and drug trafficking. He followed the example set by the Somali pirates off the Horn of Africa who attacked and captured nearly any ship they wanted and collected millions in ransom. Vanni's strategy had filled the LTTE's coffers.

The second benefit was the multitude of supply lines the sea offered to the Tigers. On land, trailers had to travel on roads between cities. In the air, planes had to follow certain routes. Even the oceans had distinct sea lanes—well-defined patterns that offered the shortest route between two points. But there were no sea lanes when it came to illicit trafficking. In fact, traffickers mostly avoided the more common routes altogether. Vanni himself had traveled to Myanmar, Singapore, China, and even North Korea on crew passports taken by his pirates. He made connections in the maritime underworld. That was how he contacted Hu's organization and became a part of its network. Intrigued by the description of Gala's hafnium weapons and their potential to destabilize the country, Hu provided shiploads of basic equipment for mining and military operations—everything from thousands of AK-47s to the contents of the latest shipment—a cargo of innocuous bicycles.

Hu was impressed by the accomplishments of the young scientist Gala and sent some of his own people to support Gala's laboratory—and to keep an eye on his investment in a weapon China could utilize itself one day. Vanni recognized this but chose not to tell Hu that the Chinese would never get the hafnium. If Vanni's plan succeeded, not even the Chinese would be able to get to him.

The third benefit lay in the fact that Sri Lanka was an island. The goods that entered and left the island's ports were vital to the nation's economy. During the first civil war the Sri Lankan navy had cut off the Tigers' supply lines. With the EMP weapons Vanni now did the same to Sri Lanka. There was no longer a navy to protect the nation's commerce, and merchant freighters and airlines now avoided the ports and airfields.

The fourth and final benefit was that the ships he intended to use to win this war could be his new capital as well, if needed. Cities like Mullaitivu, the former Tigers' last stronghold, were subject to attacks, invasion, and capture. Not so the great ships, which could always be on the move. After years of planning Vanni now had a fleet that far surpassed that of the previous Sea Tigers. He still had stealthy suicide boats, powerboats, and trawlers, but he had taken his pain and anger and had turned it into a new fleet with a new type of weapon that would take the Sri Lankans, the Chinese, and the Americans by storm.

Prior to the civil war, the LTTE had effectively governed its own state, but the Sri Lankan government had put an end to that following the defeat. Vanni wasn't certain he could reclaim all that he considered the Tamils' homeland, but he was certain he could prevent the Sri Lankan government from ever being capable of stopping the Tamils again. The plan was just days away from implementation.

As always, Vanni was dressed simply this evening in plain khaki clothes—the same sort of clothing he had seen in photos of Ho Chi Minh, Mao, and Pol Pot. He eschewed the gaudy medals and elaborate military uniforms South American dictators favored and Libya's Gaddafi had worn. The simplicity had two reasons: it suggested that he was above such tawdry government awards, and people who *did* value ostentation tended to underestimate him.

The building in which he now stood had been the last stand for many of his former Tiger brothers and sisters, the site of their final battle. Had he not been out on a mission, he would have been here with them and the Sri Lankan army would have executed him as well. "It is our time again, my friends," he said, his voice echoing against the concrete walls and tin roof of the large storage facility. The last rays of the sun lit up the windows on the west wall. In just a few hours the building would be full of people, and he would address his Sea Tigers as they prepared for their mission. And he would have two hostages to inspire their bloodlust.

He stooped and touched the wooden floor, passing his hand over the bloodstains that were all that remained of his compatriots and friends, including the Tiger who had first recruited him. By the end of the war she had commanded her own boat and had returned to Mullaitivu for its defense, thinking he was still there. She was gone, as were his family members lost to the Breakers or to the war and the mass executions by the Sri Lankan government. No international investigation ever uncovered all the bodies or determined who had killed those they did find. That was why Vanni felt no remorse when he told his own men to bury those he had butchered. They were just bodies for the earth.

A soldier entered from the other side of the building, calling loudly, "Vanni!"

Vanni rose quickly. "I told you not to disturb me."

One of Vanni's Tiger loyalists pulled a bloodied young soldier through the doorway. The conscript limped up to his leader to give his report. Visibly trembling, the man whispered, "The American hostages are gone."

"Tell me everything," Vanni said quietly.

The soldier stumbled over his words as he tried to describe the UAV that crashed into the truck and the helicopter that came out of the sun firing bullets. Then came the small boats onto the beach. They had taken the Americans away on the boats and back across the horizon.

"Who were these people?"

"Americans," the shaking man said.

"And how do you know what happened?" Vanni asked.

"The others were killed. Only I and another survived."

"Give me your gun," Vanni ordered. The conscript immediately did as he was told. Vanni checked that it was loaded then pointed it at the man's head and fired.

"Kill the other survivor as well," he said to the Tiger. "We do not want Americans involved in this. Perhaps they will leave now that they have their people back." He pointed at the dead man. "Get this thing out of here. I must prepare."

"Shall I have your boat readied, Vanni?"

"Yes. After the speech I will go back to the ship tonight. Send someone there now with orders to send out more small patrol boats. I want to know where the Americans are."

M/V Syren

When he had ordered the medical module for the ship, Connor Stark hadn't planned to be the first one treated there. His medic—a retired Navy corpsman—had outfitted the container with four beds, two stacked on each side, and a treatment table. Stark lay on his stomach as Doc—after first injecting a numbing agent—meticulously picked out debris from the deep abrasions on his back to reduce the chance of infection.

Connor had received fewer lashes from Vanni's man than some sailors received two hundred years ago, before flogging was abolished as corporal punishment. Given how much pain he had suffered he found it difficult to imagine what one of those floggings must have felt like. The wounds were open and raw. Some of the blood had dried while he was hanging from the pulley, but the wounds continued to ooze fluid.

In the reflection of one of the container's small mirrors he saw Damien Golzari standing with his arms crossed as he watched the procedure.

"Enjoying this?" he asked the Diplomatic Security agent.

"Just sorry I didn't have a chance to do it myself. The man was clearly an amateur. I would have made a perfect chessboard pattern. The Tiger's pattern is unfortunately haphazard. Shame, isn't it?"

"Oh, yes," Stark said sarcastically.

Golzari thought back to the locker room at the embassy in Yemen when he had first seen Stark's naked body as he emerged from the sauna. It was scarred with bullet wounds, stab wounds, and one or two others he couldn't identify. Now he would bear these unmistakable signs of torture for the remainder of his life as well.

"This is going to hurt a bit, Captain, even with the lidocaine," the medic said as he started cleaning out the wounds with peroxide. Stark tensed up and clenched his teeth with each application. The medic dressed the wound with an antibiotic ointment and then laid gauze over the wounds. He helped Stark up to a seated position, then wrapped more gauze around Stark's torso to keep the bandages in place.

"Thanks again for coming for me," he said to the two men, still clenching his teeth.

"Commander Johnson's plan was very effective," Golzari answered, "but we were lucky they didn't use an EMP rocket against the helicopter. They had three. We brought them back with us."

"What's the old saying? 'Success is where luck and preparation meet,'" Stark commented, still trying to block out the pain. "Why didn't they use one of them?"

"Most of them were looking at the wreckage of the UAV and didn't hear the helicopter coming until it was too late," Golzari said. "The helicopter took out about half of them. By then, our two boats had made it ashore and we eliminated the remainder of the opposition."

Once again Stark was struck by Golzari's ability to dissociate himself from those he killed in the line of duty. The Iranian American saw the opposition as simple targets, no different from those on a firing range.

"Where's Rossberg?" Stark asked.

"Ah, the admiral. Yes, well, he regained consciousness on the boat and said something about you trying to kill him," Golzari said. "We thought it best to send him directly to *LeFon*."

"I'm not on active duty anymore. Do I admit to that, Agent Golzari?"

"Best not to, I'd think. Bloody shame we couldn't leave the wanker behind. We knew there was another hostage, but we didn't know it was him."

"How'd you find us? Let me guess—Jay and his magic bag of tricks."

"Yes. He is quite useful, isn't he?"

There was a knock on the door. The medic said, "Enter," and Olivia Harrison walked in.

"Great job, Liv," Stark said to her.

"Great crew, Connor. How are you feeling?"

"Good enough to hear a report on what's happening out there."

For the next fifteen minutes, while the medic examined Stark's leg and knee, Harrison described the rescue's aftermath. As the RHIBs were leaving shore a few speedboats arrived on the scene and chased them for a few nautical miles until the other two RHIBs provided cover. Then *Syren* bore down on the speedboats and began firing on them from just beyond the range of their EMP rockets. *LeFon* was a few miles behind *Syren*, and her 5-inch guns began firing for effect in the proximity of the speedboats, which eventually turned around and returned to their base in the north. *Syren* picked up the four RHIBs, returned to station with *Asity*, and sent Admiral Rossberg to *LeFon*.

"So now he's Jaime's problem. God help her. Did he say anything?" Stark asked.

"Other than that you attacked him?" Golzari said with a smirk.

"He said he didn't remember the LCS going down," Harrison said. "The first thing he remembered was being held on a ship."

"Did he say what ship?" Stark asked.

"He had no idea except he saw some Russian markings on some pipes."

"Moving or stationary?"

"Stationary."

"Rossberg told me in the shack that he was brought to shore in a small boat. Six to eight knots for about an hour," Stark said. "And you said the speed-boats were heading back north?"

Olivia nodded.

"Let me guess—the Breakers," he said to Harrison and Golzari.

"That would make sense, Stark," Golzari said. "There are dozens of old ships and so much activity that the Sri Lankan government wouldn't have noticed a concentration of Sea Tigers there. Most of those ships are so large that you could hide anything in them."

"Including people, speedboats, an ore-processing facility, and a weapons laboratory," Stark observed.

"And logistics from the sea. Any ship could enter the anchorage and leave practically unnoticed," Olivia added.

"Looks like we've accomplished our primary mission and found the Sea Tigers' base," Stark said. "But the Sri Lankan navy is gone, the two replacement ships were sunk thanks to Admiral Rossberg, all our communications are down, and the Tigers are getting ready to mount a major offensive. Olivia, let's meet with the other captains as soon as possible."

"Aye, Captain."

"Am I good to go, Doc?" Stark asked the medic.

"Just be careful with those bandages, sir. I don't want you ripping open your wounds. You've got to take it easy. And here's something for you," he said, handing him a small bottle of pills from the cabinet.

"What are they? Motrin?"

"Motrin won't help enough. It's Percocet. Take one every four hours for the next few days. Then we'll taper them off. Strong stuff, Captain."

"Duly noted, Doc. Thanks. Let's get back to work," Stark said as he confidently jumped off the table, and then gasped in pain as his feet hit the deck. Golzari caught him before he went down.

"Like I said, Captain, take it easy."

Mullaitivu

There were no conscripts in the building when Vanni addressed the Tigers at midnight. Those men had only recently been trained in small arms, and Vanni realized that it had been unwise to have them guard the mine and the prisoners. But what choice was there? He had loyal, well-trained Sea Tigers prepared for seaborne operations, but they were all needed for the real attack. The conscripts served him only because he had executed their families or friends. Fear was a good motivator for recruiting, but fear did not guarantee a good, selfless soldier.

Hundreds of Sea Tigers had come for this last meeting before the operation. Many were from Mullaitivu, where they had slaved in the Breakers. Others had come from the Jaffna Peninsula in the north and the cities of Kilinochchi and Vavuniya. Some had been Sea Tigers in the last war. Many had simply heard of their exploits and been inspired by them. Some had emerged from hiding in southern Sri Lanka or other parts of the world. Vanni had recruited most of the hard-core loyalists at the Breakers. That they had turned that hellhole of bourgeois oppression into the stronghold from which they would destroy their oppressors made it all the more satisfying and inspiring for them.

A small stage was hastily arranged with shipping boxes for Vanni to stand on and be seen by the hundreds of men and women who made up the main force of Sea Tigers. Vanni had decided against a formal stage and sound system. Stacked boxes and a bull-horn lent an air of anti-elitism to the proceedings. Vanni wanted to emphasize that he was one of them, born of the Breakers and forged by a war for independence. His eyes met theirs with every word.

They had seen what he could accomplish in a short time. The attacks on the Sri Lankan navy had been but the start, he told them. They now had a weapon unknown and unavailable to any nation on earth. They—not the Sri Lankans or the Western nations—were the ones who carried the rockets of victory.

Some began to chant the name "Gala." Others joined in, repeating his name in unison until Vanni turned and beckoned to the young man standing in the shadows of the dimly lit building. Gala took Vanni's outstretched hand and awkwardly climbed up the boxes to stand beside him. The cheering intensified for the man who had created the new weapon that would be their salvation. A minute later, as the cheers waned, Gala stepped down and gave the stage back to Vanni.

"In the next two days we will gain back our country," Vanni said to the crowd, his voice building. "And their country will be the one left in ruins. As our armies march to the south, you, my Sea Tigers, will the instruments by which we achieve our victory." By now he was shouting. "Let no one stand in our way."

The Tigers erupted in cheers—yelling, stamping their feet, and cheering for their leader and the arrival of the day that just a few years ago had seemed impossible.

After a few moments Vanni raised his hands for silence. "Go to your boats and prepare."

Vanni's guards escorted him through the velvet-dark night to his personal boat, with Gala walking two steps behind him. Once the two men were safely on board, the guards cast off and joined the armada of small boats slowly making their way to the Breakers.

"What happens now?" Gala asked.

"It's simple, Gala," Vanni said, breathing in the cool, salty air. "The ships will take up stations before every coastal town in Sri Lanka and launch the weapons. Every town will be immobilized just as Trincomalee, Galle, and Colombo were when our ships attacked."

"But you have been sending the conscripts south in every vehicle we have," Gala pointed out. "The weapons will render those vehicles useless."

Vanni shook his head. "They are simply massing on the border right now. Do you know the story of how the Japanese army took Singapore from the British in World War II?"

Gala tried to recall something about Singapore's history, but it was not a subject that had interested him during his studies. Certainly he had had no time to learn about it during his visit there to pick up the extruder.

Vanni saw him struggling. "Bicycles. They rode bicycles into Singapore. In the past year we have received several shipments of them. Such a simple means of transportation. They have no electronics. They have nothing that can be affected by your weapon. As the Sri Lankan tanks sit silent and helpless, our conscripts will enter the south on bicycles. Others will arrive by ship."

"What then, Vanni?"

"Then it will be over. They will kill everyone, and we will have our nation back."

"Kill everyone? Millions cannot be killed by tens of thousands," Gala said, shocked.

"Gala, we have the guns and the ammunition and the people. We will not stop until the enemy has been broken—and broken forever. Look what a few men with guns have done in Mumbai, Paris, and America," Vanni said, referencing past terrorist attacks. He turned back to face the bow and his ships that lay beyond it.

Gala thought about what Vanni had told him. Gala had never intended the weapon to be used for such destruction. Vanni had told him it would be used to disrupt enemy forces and secure a new land for the Tamils. There was never any talk of genocide. "We . . . we don't need to do this," he said meekly, his voice barely audible above the hum of the engines.

"What?" Vanni asked turning back to him.

"We don't need to go to their cities and kill them. They would be fools to enter our territory. Any nation would. Even the Americans," Gala said.

"The Americans came."

"But only to get their people. How do we know they will attempt anything more? Vanni, we sank two of their warships and they did nothing!"

"You never learned how to swim, did you?" Vanni said coldly, and then ordered his guards to hold Gala.

"No, Vanni. Please don't," he pleaded. "I was just . . ."

"You were questioning my plans for our permanent security. You have served me well, Gala. But we have our weapons. Do we need you now?"

"Vanni! I have been loyal. We still have work to do. And the Chinese are still on the ship in the lab!"

"I am not concerned about them. They will all be killed. They must not be allowed to tell Hu and the others anything," Vanni said.

"Then who will be left to make your weapons, my leader? After the battle, we will still have the equipment and the ore. I am the only one who can build more, is that not true?"

Vanni was silent for several minutes as Gala feared every second for his life.

"Very well, Gala. You see how they cheered earlier for you? Remember that. But remember too that your life is mine."

DAY 16

Sea Tiger Command Ship *Amba*

The Soviet *Ugra*-class submarine tender that had served as the laboratory and manufacturing facility for their rockets, mine buoys, and suicide boats was nearly deserted when Vanni and Gala returned. The small boats were gone too, distributed to other ships, as were some of the rockets—three for each of the boats deploying.

Vanni had gone to sleep with two guards posted outside his stateroom. Before going inside he had instructed the guards to wake him if any of the patrol boats spotted the American ships. Gala wished him a good sleep and then went below, telling the guards that he needed to check on the laboratory before going to bed. No one was there, and the lights were out. He sat down at his cheap metal desk, made by Soviet laborers forty years before, and pulled a thumb drive from a drawer. He turned on his computer, inserted the thumb drive, and began to download all of his files. It took only a few seconds.

Then he pulled out the drive, slipped it into his pocket, and left the lab for the last time. He walked down the silent passageway, encountering only a couple of the crew on their way to the next shift. He went up two flights to the deck and came face to face with three people just coming on board. He recognized only one, a Chinese gunman named Qin from Singapore. Tied up along the starboard side was a ship familiar to him—*Nanjing Mazu*—the ship that had spirited him and the stolen laboratory equipment out of Singapore.

"Gala," the Chinese gunman said as he caught his eye.

Gala nodded in return. "Hello, Qin." He was certain he had never seen the two people with Qin, but the beautiful blonde woman seemed to recognize him. She said something to the burly man beside her, who nodded as if in approval.

"Did . . . did anything happen after I left Singapore?" Gala asked.

"Very little. The police were well paid. There was no evidence. A man attempted to gain a reward by informing the U.S. government. My agents killed him before he could say anything," the gunman said. "The Americans sent another agent to investigate the death of the one I killed for you."

"And what of him?" Gala asked fearfully.

"There is nothing to worry about, little man. My people were unable to kill him, but the police forced him to leave Singapore and to retreat to the United States. He has been rendered irrelevant."

"Good. That is very good. Then what are you doing here?"

"We are here to ensure that our scientists are working out well for you," said the burly man, who spoke with a heavy Russian accent.

"They have been very helpful," Gala said, though he doubted the strangers really cared about his Chinese assistants. Hu and Zheng R&D wanted the hafnium. *That* had been the deal Vanni had made with them in return for all the guns, bicycles, laboratory equipment, and other supplies.

"Where is Vanni?" the Russian asked.

"Sleeping. I'm sure he will see you first thing in the morning."

"We are not here to wait," Makarov said emphatically.

"Vanni . . . Vanni gives the orders here," Gala replied meekly.

"Very well. Then we will return at first light. No later. And I want to see the modified suicide boats I designed for the Tigers."

"Yes, of course," Gala said quickly. "Tomorrow. When it is light." He held his breath, hoping desperately that they would return to their own ship so he could enact his plan.

M/V *Syren*

Stark was gingerly pouring a cup of coffee when Bobby Fisk entered the wardroom and stepped up behind Golzari in the coffee line. Golzari courteously stepped aside to allow him to go ahead. They were the first to arrive for the latest war council. Some were still asleep or on their way. Bobby had been sent ahead with additional charts of the area.

"I hope that's the high-grade stuff, Captain Stark," the young officer said.

"Only the best on this ship, Bobby. You look tired," Stark said.

"Long night on the bridge dealing with our helmsman's personal issues."

"There are no personal issues when you're in the middle of the shit, Bobby," Stark said.

"This one's a classic, sir," he said as he added sugar to his coffee. "The night before we pulled into Chennai, the chiefs gave the crew the standard spiel about liberty, including a talk about the strip clubs."

"These stories never end well," Golzari said, taking a seat and beginning to butter a toasted English muffin.

"Yeah, well, the sailor tells me he fell in love in port and got married."

"Idiot!" Golzari exclaimed.

"It gets better. The kid says the worst part is that now he has to tell his fiancée back home."

"I had a chief petty officer who had a saying: 'Never fall in love with a stripper or a hooker,'" Stark said.

"And why is that?" the Diplomatic Security agent asked.

"Because, according to him, strippers and hookers are attractive, trained to manipulate people, disingenuous, and incapable of having a stable relationship," Stark said.

"Ah, we have a similar saying at the State Department," Golzari observed. "Never fall in love with a CIA case officer."

"Why is that?" Bobby asked.

"Same reasons," Golzari laughed.

"True," Stark said, "but at least some strippers and hookers have a moral compass that isn't frozen on the direction of Langley."

The door swung open and the rest of the council began to arrive: Harrison, Johnson, Johnson's XO, Ranasinghe, and Warren. Melanie Arden had gone to *Asity* to spend time with the rescued children.

"Where's Rossberg?" Stark asked.

"He was still asleep in sick bay when we left," Johnson said.

Stark snorted. "Small gifts. Okay, folks. All signs point to the Mullaitivu Breakers as the Sea Tigers' base. I've asked Jay to show us imagery from a couple of passes our first UAV made a few days ago and tell us the results of his analyses." Stark pointed to Jay, who brought up a video on the wide-screen television.

The video began with a grainy, high-altitude image of the coastline north of Mullaitivu as the UAV flew in a northerly direction. The hulks of scores of old freighters and passenger ships were either anchored off the coast or beached. Since they had not tasked the bird to zoom in live during its flight, they had to rely on the high-altitude imagery. Still, it told its own story.

"Take a look at how the ships are laid out," Stark said as he stood. Wincing in pain he pointed as Warren put the imagery into slow motion. A dozen ships were lined up on the beach, most of them in various stages of demolition. Approximately one hundred more were anchored just offshore. Most were by themselves, but at least three groups of five passenger ships were tied together, and there were six trios of freighters.

"Now look at the wakes in the area," Stark noted. "Those are all from small boats. Why all that offshore activity if the breakup work is done on the beach? Also, look carefully at the directions of those wakes."

It didn't take long for the others to see it. The boat wakes were like highways and off-ramps. Some were coming from the beach, but the main highway was between Mullaitivu and along the coastline between the beach and the anchorage. Some wakes showed boats turning into the lanes between the various ships. Most were heading for one of the groups of passenger ships. What better way to hide thousands of Sea Tigers than on board passenger ships?

"They're floating barracks," Golzari remarked.

"Right," Stark answered. "And if that's the case, there must be power on each of those ships to provide basics such as plumbing and cooking."

As they watched the images a few other speedboats made their way to various ships. Several, including a barge, went to a ship in the center of the anchorage.

"Any idea what's on that barge?" Johnson asked.

"Great question, Jaime. Jay ran a spectral analysis. It's earth with traces of hafnium. That's how they're transporting the ore from the mine to the processing facility. That ship has the most activity on deck of all the ships at anchorage. It's an old gray hull, so we went to the ship's copy of *Combat Fleets of the World*. That's an *Ugra*-class submarine tender from the old Soviet fleet. Admiral Rossberg apparently was held on a ship with Russian lettering. There are several other Russian freighters there, but even if we expand the search to every ship with Cyrillic lettering, this one is the most likely ship where they're processing the ore into weapons."

The others sat in silence for a moment, pondering the challenge of attacking a ship in the center of the anchorage with at least five ships on each of its four sides.

"That, ladies and gentlemen, has to be our primary target," Stark said. "The question is—how do we get at it?"

"Connor, I want to be perfectly clear at the outset," Johnson said. "We supported the rescue because we were under the impression two Americans were being held hostage. We got them out. Under the rules of engagement

Seventh Fleet provided, I have no justification to participate in an attack on the Sea Tigers."

"Perhaps there is one, Commander," Golzari answered. "As you know, I was assigned to find the killer of Diplomatic Security Agent William Blake. The Tamil scientist Gala was the only lead, and I followed his trail here, to Sri Lanka. It would make sense that he is with the Sea Tigers. Since he took lab equipment from Singapore, it's highly probable that he is on that ship as well."

"That's a reasonable deduction, Agent Golzari," Jaime said, "but it doesn't fall within my ROE. I have a chain of command. And I'm outranked by an admiral on my ship who is most unlikely to help you when he wakes up." She paused for a moment contemplating her choices. "I've brought charts for you and we're ready to refuel you. But it doesn't mean I'm going to leave you—as Americans—out there alone. We can't take the lead, Connor, but I will support the mission."

"Jaime, *LeFon* has served honorably here," Connor said. "You saved lives. You've done all you can do. I understand your restrictions. We'll accept a refuel. While we're at it, can we transfer the orphans to your ship where they'll be safe?"

"Absolutely. We'll take good care of them."

"Thanks. I suggest you get your crew and ship to Chennai. Captain Dasgupta will be able to help with the orphans. I'll have a letter to him ready for you before you get under way. Make repairs and we'll see you on the other side."

The two longtime shipmates, colleagues, and friends shook hands across the table before Johnson left with her team. Bobby Fisk turned back at the door to wish them luck.

Sea Tiger Command Ship *Amba*

Vanni sat cross-legged on the deck watching the sun rise on the day before their final glorious victory over the Sri Lankan government. His eyes were closed in meditation, and his nostrils flared each time he inhaled deeply the fresh sea air. This was his morning regimen regardless of what events he would face that day. Ten minutes was all he needed to clear his mind and sharpen his focus. When he finally opened his eyes, his personal guards allowed the three visitors to cross from *Nanjing Mazu* to the forward deck of *Amba*, the site of her forward 76-mm guns before she was decommissioned.

Vanni restrained a sigh and kept his face expressionless. These were the last people he wanted to deal with right now. They were minions of Hu and his firm. Had they arrived a few days later, everything would be done and Zheng Research & Development would no longer have the ability to interfere. He had given Hu one of the first pieces of hafnium, only raisin sized but less capable of producing a weapon with an effective range more than a mile in diameter. He had not given Hu the results of all the research Gala had conducted, although Hu had tried to get that from him.

The bleached-blonde American woman approached him ahead of the other two. She flashed perfect white teeth in a broad smile as she reached out for his hand and then gently cupped it with her other hand. He wondered how many people saw through her disingenuous veneer.

"What an incredible accomplishment, Vanni. We are all so impressed with what you have achieved," she said, the smile never leaving her face.

"What is it you want?" Vanni asked, pulling his hand away and clasping it with the other behind his back.

The smile stayed firmly in place. "I like your directness," she said. "I will be direct too. Mr. Hu is concerned. As you know, the firm has devoted a great deal of its resources to assisting you. He would like some payment."

"How much of the hafnium does he want?"

He was pleased to see her smile waver. She had not expected him to be this cooperative.

"Thirty pounds," she offered.

"I can give you twenty now. Two bars," he countered. "That will give you many weapons."

"What of the rest?" she asked.

"We are still processing it. Next week we will have everything finished," Vanni said stoically.

"Very well," she said. "That will be acceptable. We appreciate your flexibility."

Vanni looked away long enough to order a guard to get a box from his stateroom.

When the guard returned with the box Vanni told him to open it and show the contents to the three visitors. Inside were two silvery, brick-sized blocks of metal. The woman and the Russian man nodded approvingly.

"We will take this to Mr. Hu and return in one week for the rest," the man said.

"Vanni, it is a pleasure to do business with you," said the blonde. She offered her hand again.

Vanni merely looked at it. He turned away with his guards and entered the ship, leaving the threesome alone on the deck.

"Delightful disposition," Makarov said sarcastically.

The blonde sniffed. "And he's a charismatic leader?" she replied.

"In the land of the blind, even the one-eyed man is king," the Russian offered. "The people will follow anyone who offers them a glint of hope, especially when they are looking into the barrel of a rifle," he added dryly.

M/V Syren

The helmsman easily kept station off the less maneuverable *Asity* as Stark sat in the captain's chair sketching out notes about everything he had seen and heard at the Breakers. On one page he drew a rough map of Sri Lanka with an X to mark each of the ships anchored offshore, although there was a large photo of the anchorage taken by the second, now-lost UAV in the CIC. *Syren* had lost her eyes. She was befert of her UAVs, radar, and over-the-horizon communications. Only the hand-held radios were operational. Both RHIBs were out acting as pickets just over the horizon.

The sky was clear, but Stark and the bridge crew kept a weather eye on the sea and the horizon looking for telltale signs of a change. The wall-mounted barometer on the bridge and the beautiful old sextant on the navigation table, among the few old-school devices Stark kept around out of sentiment, were going to prove useful after all.

Most of the crew were resting because they didn't know when or how the next attack would come. Warren was below in his engineering module assessing the three captured hafnium rockets. Despite their rudimentary craftsmanship, he admired their design—crude but effective.

Golzari was on the helo deck conducting target practice with one of the security teams, including a few of the men he had led back in Socotra. Stark watched them for a moment, musing that Golzari would make a great successor to Gunny Willis. Their initial animosity toward each other had developed into deep respect, and then friendship. *Maybe I should offer him the job*, Stark thought.

Melanie was sitting on the UAV pad to starboard taking notes and recording her thoughts into her digital recorder, her camcorder at the ready. She was about to write the kind of story every journalist dreamed of reporting.

Stark adjusted the pillow that cushioned his back from the hard chair. His discomfort was increasing to pain again. He reached into his breast pocket for the Percocet bottle, took another pill, and washed it down with his ever-present coffee. Once again he went over the potential threats and his capabilities to counteract them. *Syren* still had plenty of ammunition but only two RHIBs. And they couldn't get close to the anchorage without being spotted and chancing more rockets, which would take out the spare cards they were now carrying and leave them dead in the water and alone.

One of the watch standers entered the bridge and reported two incoming contacts at high speed. Stark was about to give the word for battle stations when the radio crackled. "*MacDonough* to *Syren*, *MacDonough* to *Syren*. We are inbound accompanying another boat, unarmed. Stand by to receive in five minutes."

"*MacDonough*, *Syren* Actual. Message received," Stark said. "Notify the bay, helm. Let's get them refueled and resupplied while they're here. I'm heading down there." He exited the bridge onto the main deck, well away from the target practice starboard and aft, and remained briefly on the port side looking through his binoculars at the two boats just coming into visual range.

Melanie appeared behind him. "Captain? What's out there?"

"Not sure yet. One of our RHIBs is coming back with another small boat, not one of ours. The only other small boats I know of belong to the Sea Tigers. It may be *MacDonough* found one and is bringing it in."

"He shoots well, doesn't he?" Stark said as he caught her looking at Golzari.

"He's excellent at everything he does—except marriage," she answered.

"When you look at the statistics, few marriages succeed," Stark pointed out. "About 50 percent. Plus another 20 or 30 percent who wish they could get a divorce. Likely it just wasn't meant to be."

"It definitely wasn't meant to be," she said bitterly. "I'm not his type. I'm a South African woman, not an English man."

"He is who he is," Stark said simply. "I may not like him all the time—but he has my respect, and my friendship."

"Yes, he has many positive characteristics," she admitted. "He's an intrepid fellow, for one thing."

Stark snorted. "I've not heard him described as that. Cantankerous, opinionated, and arrogant, yes; but not intrepid." Stark's mind wandered from their conversation to the view astern. "Intrepid," he said again. "*Intrepid.*"

"Are you okay?" she asked.

"Yeah. I think I am now."

"Sir," said a crewman interrupting them. "Another call from *MacDonough*. They've requested that Doc meet them when they tie up."

Stark didn't bother to ask who was injured. It didn't matter. What mattered was getting his teams taken care of. "Stick with me," he told Melanie as he went down to the stern ramp.

The boats arrived just as they got there. *MacDonough* stood off as an unknown speedboat piloted by one of *Syren's* crew pulled alongside. Doc and a couple of others got a man off the boat. His white shirt bore a quarter-sized bloodstain. He was still conscious when Stark knelt beside him, just as Golzari joined them.

"Who are you?"

"My . . . my name is Gala."

Sea Tiger Command Ship *Amba*

Vanni felt a temporary sense of satisfaction when he thought of the two bricks he had delivered to Hu's hatchet men—and woman. Because hafnium was most often found with zirconium and was similar in color, it had been easy to pass off the two bricks Gala had formed of zirconium as hafnium. He had hoped that they would not assess the bricks right away. But if they had, he would simply order his guards to eliminate them. There were only three of them. Eliminate the opposition—and sometimes even reluctant allies—had long since become his mantra. Josef Stalin's history in the Soviet Union had taught him that.

Nanjing Mazu slowly pulled away to the north on the port side of *Amba*, which was, like the rest of the ships, facing east, the direction in which the previous night's breeze had gently pushed them. He could still see the Russian and the American on the deck watching *Amba* like a vulture watching over its eggs, waiting for them to hatch. No hafnium would hatch for Hu and Zheng R&D.

The breeze had picked up, creating tiny ripples on the surface indicating rising wind. The sea conditions were still good for the small craft but not optimal, particularly for the suicide boats. He had hoped for perfect conditions in the next two days as the trawlers and freighters got under way, bound for the southern Sri Lankan coastline to release the low-freeboard suicide boats and the speedboats that would launch the Gala II hafnium EMP rockets over cities and towns.

Soon the landscape—or rather the seascape—of the Mullaitivu Breakers would change. Vanni's long-laid plans were reaching fruition. He ordered one of his guards to bring the Chinese scientists to the starboard side of the ship and line them up against the rail. He sent another guard to find Gala. It was time for him to join the others whose usefulness had come to an end.

Some of the scientists were still in their underwear, clearly pulled right from their racks. They rubbed their eyes or shielded them with an upraised arm from the powerful sunlight. They were accustomed to working in the incandescent light of the laboratories below, and some had not seen sunlight in days or, in some cases, weeks.

When they were all lined up against the starboard rail, five Tiger guards quickly ran alongside, took up positions, and began shooting the unsuspecting scientists at close range. The force of the gunshots hurled some of the victims over the side. Others hung limply over the rail. The remainder simply crumpled to the deck. One guard walked along the line of bloody bodies and put two bullets into the head of anyone who moved. When all were dead, the guards threw their bodies over the side. Vanni watched it all from the bow. This was just the beginning of the violence. When his Tigers entered the cities, the death and destruction would rival Japan's rape of Nanking during World War II.

Vanni approached the murder scene, careful to avoid the blood and pieces of flesh that remained on the deck. He told the crew not to wash it down. The blood would whet their appetite for the slaughter that was about to come. He looked up to see one of his picket boats returning at high speed. Just as it pulled alongside the starboard ladder a guard ran up from below. "Gala is gone!" he shouted.

"What?"

"We have searched the entire ship. He is not here."

"Then search it again!" Vanni uncharacteristically shouted.

"Vanni," a weak voice said. One of his Tigers was climbing the final rungs of the starboard ladder. The man had blood on his fatigues. Vanni looked over the side and saw two bodies in the picket boat below.

"Report," Vanni said.

"One of the speedboats came through in the early morning when it was still dark," the man said. "It came from the direction of the Breakers so we thought it was either a message from you or supplies. A voice on the radio said that the boat was taking station beyond us. Our night-vision goggles showed only one man in the boat. He failed to answer when we asked who he was. Then he sped out to sea. We chased after him and kept shooting at him, and I think we hit him because he fell. A few minutes later, an American small boat came up and boarded the speedboat. And then the Americans attacked us— two men were killed."

"Gala . . . ," Vanni breathed, fighting for self-control. The Americans had Gala. If he was alive, then he could tell them a great deal that might damage the upcoming operation. The Sea Tigers still held the upper hand, but Vanni could not take the chance. An all-out attack right now was necessary.

"How soon can the Vels be readied?" he asked of one of his aides.

"They are all fueled and ready for tomorrow's deployment. We just need to order the teams to the boats."

Vel. The name meant "lance" in Tamil. In Tamil mythology Muragan, the god of war, carried a *vel* as he rode a great peacock into battle. The name seemed appropriate for the suicide boats that would lance into the heartland of Sri Lanka. A spar on the bow of each boat need only touch the hull of an enemy ship to detonate the shaped explosives it carried and severely damage or destroy the ship, along with the Vel. The weapon's effectiveness had already been proven during Muragan Day when the Sri Lankan fleet was destroyed.

"Now. Have them leave now." He pointed at the injured Tiger. "This man will lead them to the last known coordinates of their target. Here is what you will do . . ."

M/V *Syren*

Two of the crew put Gala on a stretcher and carried him to the medical module, trying to hold him steady as he groaned and twisted from the pain of his wound. The crewmen continued to hold him down as Doc gave him a shot of morphine, and Gala gradually relaxed. The two crewmen left, making room for Stark and Golzari to stand close enough to the bed to watch but far enough away to give Doc enough room to tend to the young Tamil scientist. Doc pulled some scissors from his pocket and cut off Gala's shirt, tossing it in a heap in the corner. Melanie remained at the hatch observing and taking photos.

Gala's breathing slowed and steadied as Doc washed the blood off.

"Bullet went right through him, Captain."

Stark raised his eyebrows questioningly. Doc shrugged. It could go either way.

"He's mine, Stark," Golzari said quietly. The softness of his voice merely emphasized his resolve. Golzari had taken a backseat to Stark's mission since the two had come together at Mount Iranamadu, but this was the man he had been seeking. The mission was now his.

"Go for it. Just don't kill him . . . yet. Okay?"

"I'll try not to," Golzari said. In a louder voice he asked Doc if he could begin the questioning. Doc nodded as he began to treat the wound.

"Gala," Golzari said firmly. Gala focused his eyes on the fierce-looking man with the large nose and black goatee. "Do you understand me?"

Gala's eyes showed fear. Were the Americans going to torture him now?

"Gala, do you understand me?" Golzari asked again.

"Yes," Gala responded.

"Good. Is your full name Viswanathan Gala?"

"Yes," he said, resigned to answer this man's questions. Whatever he endured here would be benign compared with what he knew Vanni had in store for him. Golzari had borrowed Melanie's audio recorder for his investigation after agreeing to her stipulation that she could use any of what Gala said for her report.

"Are you twenty-seven years old?"

"Yes."

"Are you Tamil?"

"Yes."

The questions were simple at first as the doctor continued to work on him. Golzari was a skilled interrogator. First the easy questions, then the difficult ones. Over the next fifteen minutes, and relatively painlessly for Gala, Golzari managed to extract the information he needed. The scientist discussed finding hafnium, told how Vanni and the Chinese had provided the resources to develop it into a weapon, and how he had stolen the American laboratory equipment in Singapore through a front company.

"Did you kill the American Diplomatic Security Agent William Blake?"

"No." Gala winced from the pain of the stitches Doc was putting into place. "The . . . security firm sent someone."

"What security firm?" Stark interjected.

"Zheng works with a security firm. They have people and ships."

"What ships?" Stark asked again.

"Some floating armories, some freighters. And they helped to design our new small attack boats."

"What's the name of this company?" Golzari asked.

"I don't know. They never told me. I knew only one of them. Qin—he is the most experienced one with weapons and has killed people, including the American agent in Singapore. I was told he used to be a top sniper in the Chinese army."

Golzari had a witness, a name, and a lead on a company.

"I know most of the firms with floating armories, Damien," Stark put in. "I'll make you a list."

"Tell me more about Zheng R&D. Who was your contact there?" Golzari asked.

"Hu," Gala replied, closing his eyes.

"Yes, who?" Golzari asked again.

"Wait a minute," Stark said. "That's not a question. That's a name. Hu. You don't think . . ."

"Hu?" Golzari said to Stark. "You think it's the same man we met at Eliot Greene's home in McLean after the episode in Yemen? I don't know. It's a common name in China."

"Describe this Hu," Golzari said to Gala.

Gala shook his head. "I saw him only once. He is a Chinese man. He is of medium age and has dark hair." Golzari asked again, but Gala couldn't think of any distinguishing characteristics that would be useful in identifying Hu.

"When we get back to civilization we need to do more digging," Stark said.

Golzari remembered what the detective in Singapore had told him. "They have a long reach," he said. "This Qin who works for Hu. He could be the same sniper who killed Abdi Mohammed Asha on Socotra." Golzari was still bitter about losing his prisoner. He had been questioning Asha about the murder of the deputy secretary of state's son when a bullet shot from a mile away blew the man's head apart.

Before Golzari and Stark could hypothesize further a voice shouted down from the bridge. "Battle stations! All hands, battle stations. Captain, we have incoming! Lots of them!"

"They have come for me," Gala said. "They have come for you."

"Find out what else you can from him, Doc, and let us know right away if you come up with something!" Stark raced to the bridge with Golzari and Melanie on his heels. As they arrived, Warren burst onto the bridge from the starboard bridge wing. Olivia was peering out the port side, holding binoculars in her right hand and offering Stark the hand-held VHF radio with her left. *Syren* was facing north, with *Asity* four hundred yards to starboard. "Report, XO," he said.

"*Somers* is inbound, balls to the wall, about twenty-one nautical miles off our port bow, about two-eight-zero degrees," she responded. "They're being chased by three low-freeboard, high-speed boats painted in a blue-gray camouflage pattern. *Somers* saw at least fourteen boats, but there may be more. It looks like they've formed a line stretching over thirty or forty nautical miles."

"They were chasing Gala and hunting for us. They found us." Stark switched the radio to channel one-seven—the channel *Asity* was monitoring.

"*Asity*, *Syren* Actual. Make flank speed course zero-nine-zero immediately." *Asity* responded instantly and pulled away to starboard, but Stark knew that the old freighter was only capable of fifteen knots at best. She was a sitting duck if the incoming boats got past *Syren*.

"Helm, all ahead flank, steer course . . . steer course zero-eight-five," Stark ordered. The great T-foils below the pilothouse and the trim tabs dug into the water, and *Syren* surged forward like a thoroughbred on the home stretch. The wind was rising, but the seas were not yet high enough that Stark had to worry about slamming the ship in between two waves. He had learned that lesson as a young Navy commander of this ship.

At thirty knots the ship could turn 180 degrees in less than a nautical mile. *Syren* was just picking up steam at twenty knots and turned easily toward the inbound *Somers*. Unlike mono-hull ships, *Syren* didn't heel when she turned, so the crew and security personnel about to enter battle had a stable and level platform.

Somers was keeping just ahead of a pack of three small boats. Another four were closing in, and several more were popping up north and south of the grouping. Stark counted twenty altogether. Although the seas weren't kicking up waves, the small boats couldn't operate at their best speed. Their shallow draft made them too unstable. That was the only thing saving *Somers'* crew as the RHIB struggled to rendezvous with *Syren*.

The boats must have been sent out in a picket line like World War II German U-boats, Stark thought. As soon as one of the ships sighted an enemy surface ship it notified the others and the wolf pack closed in on its prey. Vanni couldn't have known *Syren's* location, but he did know the direction Gala's boat had gone. From there he had simply sent out a line of boats a few nautical miles apart, giving them an effective search line of fifty or sixty nautical miles, like a giant net. *But U-boats have to communicate with each other to search effectively. And so do those small boats.* "Jay, can you set up two of those rockets aft of the pilothouse?" Stark asked.

"Easy, boss. Shouldn't take more than five minutes."

"Then do it now. Set both at a forty-five degree angle, both astern, with one facing our port quarter and the other our starboard quarter."

Warren raced down the ladder to his module.

"Don't forget what Gala said," Golzari warned. "If a spar on one of the suicide boats taps our hull it will rip it apart."

"We're going to play chicken," Stark said, keeping his eyes trained on the boats. They were close enough now that he didn't need binoculars.

"You know, Stark," Golzari muttered, "sometimes you're the exclamation point at the end of a really shitty sentence."

Stark ignored him. "No offense, Treat, but step aside," he told the helmsman. "I have the helm. We'll be maneuvering too quickly to issue commands."

Treat got up and Stark took his place, strapped himself in, and quickly refamiliarized himself with the control panel. Harrison got into the OOD's chair to his right.

"XO, tell *Somers* to maintain their heading as zero-nine-zero," Stark ordered. Harrison quickly complied. *Somers* acknowledged, and they could hear gunfire in the background. In another two or three minutes *Somers* would approach *Syren*'s port quarter and pass along her port side. Two groups of three Tiger boats had closed their formation and were changing direction. They were now on a direct course for *Syren*. Harrison reported eight more boats several miles off their starboard bow and another six well south of the closest grouping.

"Golzari, tell me when Jay says we're ready." Golzari took up a post where he could watch the scientist set up on the aft helicopter pad. Warren's head popped up only to watch *Somers* pass by.

All the security teams had been issued hand-held VHF radios, the only way of communicating locally. Harrison ordered them to stand by.

"Sir, first formation of six boats now two nautical miles," Harrison said.

"Very well, XO. Turning to port." Stark pulled the joystick to the left, forcing it until it would go no further. *Syren* began her 180-degree turn at fifty-two knots. As soon the ship's starboard security teams saw the small boats, they began to fire.

"Tell security teams and Warren to hang on," Stark told Harrison. Then, "All stop." Stark had experienced rapid deceleration on the original Navy *Sea Fighter* before and knew exactly what to expect. When the gas turbine engines tripped off, the 1,600-ton ship would stop abruptly, creating enormous inertia. A rapid restart combined with a wide-arc turn would harness the inertia and transfer it to the water, and a huge wave would form and radiate out toward the oncoming boats.

As *Syren* completed the turn and sped away, the six closest boats lost their limited sea-keeping ability. Three did not try to avoid the wave and simply flipped over. The other three decelerated but were still swamped, allowing *Syren*'s gunners to train their weapons on the Tigers themselves.

The other two groups of boats managed to avoid the wake and were coming up astern of the ship on either side. *Syren* had lost the advantage of distance when she decelerated and turned, allowing the Tiger ships to overtake her.

"Dr. Warren indicates he and his assistant are ready," Golzari said, returning the scientist's wave through the Plexiglas window.

"Get him in here."

One of *Syren*'s original weaknesses—and one reason the Navy *Sea Fighter* program was canceled—was the shadow zone around the ship; anything closer than 130 yards astern was invisible to those on the bridge. An enterprising young *Syren* crewmember had taken a commercial off-the-shelf camera and designed a monitoring system that gave the helmsman a full view of the ship's surroundings. Stark was benefitting from that now as he fought to keep the ship away from the attackers. As Golzari had said, a single strike on the ship would at the very least slow her down enough for the others to pounce.

"Jay," Stark said as soon as the scientist entered the pilothouse, "what's the range of the rockets at a 45-degree angle?"

Warren shrugged. "I think about two miles, airspeed about two hundred yards per second. These aren't exactly like the Palestinian Qassams, though, so I can't be sure.

"I need it to be closer than that," Stark said.

"Closer? R-squared is our friend, Captain. It gets closer and . . ."

"Jay, I want the range to be one mile."

"Boss, we're within the pulse's effective envelope at a mile and a half!"

"Damn it, Jay, get the elevation so that it's one mile and signal when you're ready to launch." Warren left the pilothouse and adjusted the rocket launchers.

"Sir?" Harrison asked quietly. "The sea state's changed. Looks like the Tigers are gaining on us, trying to vector in on each side."

"He's ready, Stark," Golzari said.

"XO, pull up the aft bridge camera on the second screen."

"Aye."

"Launch!" he ordered, and Golzari waved to Warren.

As soon as the cameras showed the two rockets launch, Stark checked the time on his watch and then increased *Syren*'s speed to fifty-five knots. Back when he had commanded the ship in her incarnation as *Sea Fighter*, with Jay Warren as one of the ship's designers, that had been maximum speed; the gas turbine engines had been limited to the RPMs required for fifty-five knots. Warren, always trying to improve the ship, suggested they change the governor settings to allow for higher RPMs, and that boosted the speed. On her best day now, with good sea conditions, *Syren* was capable of sixty-one knots. Fortunately for Stark and the crew, that day was this day.

Stark made three quick zigzag turns to create enough wake to slow down the suicide boats. Most were now only a few hundred yards behind them. He began a mental countdown. *Five . . . four . . . three . . . two . . . one.* The rockets exploded over the Sea Tigers' suicide boats.

Stark had managed to speed *Syren* up enough to get her to the edge of the mile-and-a-half radius effect of the hafnium rocket, though a few systems around the stern were fried, including the hand-held VHF radios on *Somers*. The EMP bubble did, however, envelop all of the suicide boats, immediately shutting down their systems. Stark turned *Syren* again and slowed her to fifteen knots as he offered targets to the gun teams on deck. They hit one boat, then another and another until they had destroyed all of them, and their crews as well.

Stark popped another Percocet like it was a Pez candy as he sat in his rack. At least his hand had stopped shaking. He had taken a huge risk and won. The Sea Tigers' suicide boats had been destroyed at the cost of a few minor injuries to his ship and crew. Stark had shown the Sea Tigers as much mercy as they would have shown him and his crew. If their goal was death in battle, then he had allowed them to achieve it.

Olivia was back in command as they returned to station with *Asity*. Commander Ranasinghe had been informed of the outcome via hand-held radio. He offered congratulations but expressed his regret at not being involved. It was his friends and colleagues who had died when the Sea Tigers destroyed the Sri Lankan navy, and his country that was now in grave danger. He wanted into the fight. Stark promised that if the next plan worked, Ranasinghe would get the fight he wanted and the revenge he sought.

For now, all Stark wanted to do was to lie down on his side and rest, to recover from the lack of sleep, the torture, and the exhaustion that followed the adrenaline rush. He looked longingly at the framed picture of Maggie on his desk and vowed—not for the first time—to stay in Ullapool with her after this was over. A knock at the door brought him out of his reverie.

"Come," he said loudly.

The door opened a crack. "No time to rest, old man," Golzari said. "I'm going back to talk with Gala. You should be there."

"I will rise and fight again . . . ," Stark began.

"What?"

"Nothing. Let's go."

Gala was sedated but conscious. Stark looked at him impassively. *This man created the new weapon we've been forced to fight. He is the one responsible for so many deaths, including Gunny's. Why not just chuck him overboard right now?* He shook his head. That was the fatigue speaking. Or maybe it wasn't.

"The captain here fended off your colleagues in the suicide boats," Golzari said.

Gala merely nodded.

"How many of them are out there?" Stark asked.

"There were twenty in the trawlers."

"He might be lying," Stark said to Golzari, "but that is the number that came after us."

Golzari methodically interrogated Gala for the next fifteen minutes about Qin and Blake's murder, but there was little the scientist could add to what he had already said. Golzari had resigned himself to accept that when Gala mumbled something about his pants pocket. Golzari reached in and took out a thumb drive.

"What's on this?" he asked.

"Most of my research on the applications of hafnium," Gala replied weakly.

Golzari was stunned. The small object in his hand was a treasure trove of information that would level the playing field. "Does anyone else have this information?"

"No. I deleted the files after I copied them so the Chinese wouldn't get them. When I escaped, I took my laptop with me and threw it overboard just in case. There were several Chinese scientists helping me, but they were not allowed to leave the ship or communicate with Zheng R&D."

"Why did you do this? And why did you leave? You must have been a hero to Vanni and the other Tigers," Golzari said.

"The weapon was only supposed to help us regain our land. I knew nothing about Vanni's plans to use it to attack and murder as many people as possible in Sri Lanka."

"When we were leaving Mount Iranamadu we saw convoys of soldiers headed south," Stark said. "Were they the main attack force?"

Gala shook his head. "Vanni and the others spent months refitting fifteen freighters at the Breakers. The rockets will be distributed among them. The ships are to leave one by one and go to ports and towns on the southern coast. Once they have used the weapons, the ships will land soldiers to complete the destruction. The Tiger army heading south is a decoy to lure the Sri Lankan army away from the coast."

"Which is your command ship?" Stark asked. "What kind of defenses does it have? How many soldiers defend it? What is the layout belowdecks? And where is the hafnium kept?"

The rapid-fire questions seemed to bewilder Gala, who was clearly growing weaker, but he did his best to answer. "Most of the hafnium has already been used or is in the rockets we built for the final attack, but all are on a ship called *Amba*. Vanni restricts access to the rockets. He trusts no one. They are to be distributed just before the ships get under way."

"When is that?" Stark asked.

"Tomorrow at noon," Gala replied.

"Where is the remaining hafnium?" Golzari asked.

Gala explained the layout of the laboratory deck. "The hafnium is in a storage room next to the second lab. There are about forty bricks."

"All right, Gala," Golzari said. "I think we're finished. You will remain in this room under guard, and then you are coming to the United States to be tried as an accessory to the murder of Special Agent William Blake."

Stark and Golzari walked out together.

"Think he's telling the truth about everything?" Stark asked.

Golzari turned up his hands. "Who knows? He may have been intentionally shot and sent to give us false information, but I think what he said is factual."

"If that's the case, then we have less than a day before that first ship gets under way and a lot to do to prepare. It's 1300 now. Don't worry, though, I have a plan."

"My God, how I cringe whenever you say that."

USS *LeFon*

Rossberg berated Jaime Johnson and every other officer on the ship for two solid hours. He had stormed out of sick bay and up to the bridge, where he announced that henceforth he intended to review every command given on *LeFon*. He countermanded every decision Jaime Johnson made on the bridge, even simple orders. The ship was on a direct heading to Chennai when he asked how much fuel they had.

"Thirty percent, sir," she responded.

"Why so little, Commander?"

"Because, Admiral," she said, standing up from the captain's chair, "we offered assistance to *Syren* and provided fuel."

"Is *Syren* a U.S. Navy ship, Commander?"

"No, Admiral, *Syren* is not a U.S. Navy ship; however, under the circumstances—" she began to explain.

"Stop right there. *Syren*'s commander attacked me—an admiral in the U.S. Navy—and you didn't take him into custody. I am the senior officer on station. He is an enemy. And you aided and abetted the enemy. Furthermore, you provided military assistance to people who were interfering in a civil war in a foreign nation contrary to the rules of engagement you were given. And you did so to release Mr. Stark from the Tamils."

"Sir, I did," she admitted. "But had I not done so—"

He cut her off before she could add that he would still be in their hands. "That's enough, missy. I relieve you of command. I am now captain of this ship. Am I clear?"

"Yes, sir." Jaime Johnson was an inch shorter than Rossberg, but in the eyes of the crew who had worked side by side with her for nearly six months she towered over him. Only a few of them knew that the president of the United States himself had put her in command of this ship—as a result of Connor Stark's influence. Among those few was Ens. Bobby Fisk, who stood on the bridge as officer of the deck. She loved her country passionately. She loved this ship. She cared for this crew like a mother. She regretted leaving *Syren* and *Asity* to fend for themselves, and she had nothing but contempt for the craven flag officer standing on her bridge.

Her eyes remained fixed on Rossberg as she stepped aside to the shipwide intercom and picked up the mike. "*LeFon*, this is the captain," she said slowly. "As you know, this ship has been caught in the middle of a civil war while trying to remain out of it. I have made decisions that directly affected the lives of Americans, and I stand by those decisions. Rear Admiral Rossberg has just advised me that he is relieving me of my duties as CO of *LeFon* and taking my place. Sometimes, ladies and gentlemen, we have to step aside for the greater good."

She took a deep breath, then continued. "This is not one of those times. Admiral Rossberg is not in my chain of command. I am bound by my duties as a naval officer under the Uniform Code of Military Justice not to obey an unlawful order. I am placing Admiral Rossberg under arrest for dereliction of duty." She straightened to her full five feet four inches. "For strength," she said proudly.

"For courage!" a thunderous chorus rang throughout the ship, including the bridge.

"Master-at-Arms, report immediately to the bridge and take Rear Admiral Rossberg into custody," she said.

"What? You can't do this. You can't—" Rossberg lunged at her in mid-sentence.

Ensign Fisk grabbed him by the arms and threw him to the deck, then threw himself on top of him so Rossberg couldn't move. "Remember when I warned you about the threat to *Bennington* and you wouldn't let me warn the others?" Bobby whispered into the admiral's ear. "You had the sailors hold me back. I could have saved them if you hadn't done that. You killed them, you son of a bitch."

Rossberg continued to struggle until the master-at-arms slapped the handcuffs on him.

Johnson ordered Fisk to inform the air boss that the ready helo would be taking off within fifteen minutes, and discipline, good order, and morale returned to the bridge.

DAY 17

As dawn broke over a cloudless morning off the eastern Sri Lankan coast, Vanni sat on the deck in quiet meditation. This was Sri Lanka's last day as a nation. Already Vanni and his men had resurrected fifteen freighters and tankers from the Breakers and given them new life. Smoke billowed out of their stacks, and all swung slowly southwest with the morning breeze. Just as these ships had risen from certain death, an independent homeland for his people would rise from the ashes of the south.

He had no political structure in place yet. Only the Tigers served him. But anarchy would follow the destruction, and the people would accept the order brought by Vanni and his most loyal men and women. The Vels had not returned from their mission, but that did not worry him unduly. They were either successful or unsuccessful. It was out of his hands. But he doubted that the few enemy ships had been able to withstand the attack of twenty Vels. If the ships somehow had survived, they had certainly been dissuaded from attacking. And yet . . . there was Gala. If he had survived to pass on what he knew . . . Vanni drew another deep breath and then rose to his feet.

The Breakers was bustling with activity. Small boats were transferring soldiers from the cruise ships to the fifteen freighters that would take them to the southern provinces. The final stores of ammunition, guns, knives, and hatchets were being distributed to each ship. A small boat from each of the fifteen freighters sat idle and unmanned. It would still be several hours before Vanni gave permission to transfer all the rockets.

None of the freighters was supposed to be under way yet, much less heading toward the Breakers, so it was with considerable interest that Vanni saw a small freighter steaming slowly toward *Amba* from the east. The ship was typical of the five-thousand-ton steamships he had become accustomed to seeing after decades in this region. Its paint was long gone, though a few green patches indicated its former color.

Two of his picket speedboats were escorting it. One zoomed ahead and pulled alongside one of *Amba*'s ladders. The boatman called up that the ship was one of the Tigers' supply ships that had been delayed a week because of engine problems. Vanni signaled his approval to get the freighter's munitions on board *Amba* and left to consult with his top aides in the wardroom. A handful of guards remained on deck, mostly in the stern watching the coastline prior to what might be their last mission.

The freighter decreased speed to three knots and prepared to sidle up next to *Amba*. The captain was on the starboard bridge wing, but only his upper torso was visible above the metal shield plates. He was shouting orders to the crew, who were preparing the bow and stern lines and the bumpers to keep the ships apart. The captain ordered the engines to full reverse as the starboard side of the freighter pulled up on *Amba*'s port side. The freighter's propellers produced a backwash as they struggled to stop the ship's forward momentum.

Two *Amba* deckhands forward and astern prepared to accept the lines, then passed them through to the cleats and secured them. The freighter's captain ordered the engines to be cut and looked at his watch. *Amba*'s deckhands helped attach their ship's gangway to the supply ship, though the old submarine tender displaced nearly two thousand tons more than the recently arrived freighter and rode higher.

One of *Amba*'s deckhands crossed over to *Asity* to ensure that the freighter's deckhands had secured the gangway properly before preparing for the transfer of the ammunition and guns. Just as he was about to check the open cargo hold closest to the three-story superstructure, he saw the main deck hatch swing open and a gun barrel pointed at him. It was the last thing he ever saw.

Highland Maritime security teams poured out of the freighter's hatches, finding every target of opportunity on *Amba*'s deck and in the pilothouse. *Asity*'s captain donned his cover—that of a Sri Lankan navy commander— and pulled out his own pistol to fire at the pilothouse across from him. A two-man team hidden behind the metal plates stood and set up their 50-mm gun and began raking *Amba*'s stern. Taken by surprise, the guards fell one by one.

Eight three-person Highland Maritime teams crossed the gangway onto *Amba*'s now-cleared deck and took up positions. One team went to the stern to keep watch for other ships and small boats, and two other teams took up positions amidships. The others covered the hatches of the superstructure to wait for more guards to come up from below.

Commander Ranasinghe picked up a flare gun and fired one shot to signal *Syren*, now seven miles away and approaching out of the rising sun. He threw the flare gun aside, picked up a hand-held radio, and issued an order to the cargo hold. A few seconds later the Tigers on the ships surrounding *Amba* saw the fiery plume of a Qassam rocket emerge from the hold and rise half a mile into the sky above *Amba*. Four seconds later—predetermined by Jay Warren's modifications of the third and last captured rocket—a blue-green explosion silenced nearly every piece of electronic equipment within a mile and a half. Speedboats, patrol boats, freighters, and tankers—none were immune to their own weapon. Smaller boats sat helpless in the water.

The first phase of Operation Intrepid had begun.

During the First Barbary War, President Thomas Jefferson sent a squadron of ships to Tripoli under the command of Commo. Edward Preble on USS *Constitution* with orders to maintain the blockade of Tripoli harbor. The commanders of the sloops in the squadron—daring young officers such as Stephen Decatur, Richard Somers, Charles Stewart, and Isaac Hull—would later be remembered as "Preble's Boys."

The Tripolitans already held one U.S. Navy ship. In October 1803 the frigate USS *Philadelphia* under Capt. William Bainbridge had gone in too close to shore and run aground. Bainbridge tried in vain to free the ship, even throwing the guns overboard and cutting off a mast to lighten her. When *Philadelphia* remained firmly grounded, Bainbridge surrendered ship and crew. The Tripolitans salvaged the guns, rearmed the grounded ship, and used her as a battery to protect the harbor. The crew were sent into slavery.

Preble was ordered to retake *Philadelphia* or, if she was no longer seaworthy, destroy her. Young Stephen Decatur came up with a daring plan. Preble's squadron had captured a local sixty-foot ketch named *Mastico* during the course of the blockade and had renamed her *Intrepid*. On the evening of February 16, 1804, Decatur took seventy men, most of them hidden belowdecks, and sailed *Intrepid* right into Tripoli harbor. They boarded *Philadelphia*, determined that the frigate was no longer seaworthy, and blew her sky high. Providing operational support to *Intrepid* was the brig *Syren* under the command of young Lt. Charles Stewart.

Admiral Horatio Nelson described the raid as "the most bold and daring act of the age." For his action Decatur was promoted to captain at the age of twenty-five—the youngest Navy captain in America's history.

M/V *Syren*

The new *Syren* steamed into an anchorage bereft of operational ships after the EMP detonation. Five thousand feet above her Starfire One-Eight, an SH-60R helicopter from USS *LeFon*, stood watch. *LeFon* herself was now just eight nautical miles from the anchorage, which was well within the range of her 5-inch gun. She was already providing suppressing fire as shells from the main gun landed among the outermost anchored ships.

Syren pulled along the port side of *Amba*, and Stark and Golzari led the last security team up boarding ladders and onto the old sub tender's main deck. One team member fired a grappling hook up three decks to the blown-out window of the pilothouse, and Stark and Golzari scampered up the attached rope ladder, each carrying an FAL-308 slung over his shoulder and a nine-millimeter pistol holstered on his belt. Ranasinghe's fire support team motioned the all clear to the two as they reached the deck of the pilothouse.

"Ready for the rattlesnake's den?" Stark asked Golzari.

Golzari gestured, "After you."

Stark waved to one of the teams below that they were ready. Team members placed enough C4 on the outer hatches to blow them from their hinges in preparation for going in. The explosions both provided a distraction and masked the entrance of Stark and Golzari into the pilothouse above. As he went through the door Starke noticed a freighter about ten miles to the north that clearly hadn't been affected by the EMP. He hoped Jaime and *LeFon* would handle that one.

Stark and Golzari raced down the ladder to the main deck. A gun battle had broken out astern. With Golzari covering his back, Stark slowly made his way aft until he could see several Tigers in the next compartment with their backs to him firing at the security teams. Stark pulled a flash-bang canister from his vest, pulled the pin, and threw it into the middle of the group, then began firing into the shooters, dropping most of them before the security teams could push through.

With the security teams now behind them, Stark and Golzari turned around and headed forward. They passed several staterooms, a wardroom, and a galley before they found another ladder that would take them down one deck. If Gala had been telling the truth, this would be the deck with the laboratories.

Another gunfight between a security team and the defenders was going on in a passageway on the starboard side of the ship as they stepped onto the lab deck. They inched their way forward, looking for traps and defenders. The first lab they came to was empty, although coffee cups and tools on the tables indicated that the scientists who worked there had left suddenly. Two overturned cups suggested the departure might not have been voluntary.

Bullets flew from the next compartment as they approached. *The rattlesnake's den,* Stark thought. Two Highland Maritime security personnel followed Stark and Golzari as they considered their options. Stark tossed a flash grenade through the hatch, and all four men sprayed bullets haphazardly after it. Golzari threw in another flash-bang for good measure. Silence followed. Stark, Golzari, and the team entered the second lab, peering through the smoke for tiger-striped uniforms. Some were there, but the guards were down and dead.

Seated cross-legged atop a pile of metallic silver bricks at the back of the room was a small, dark-skinned man in khakis. He smiled at the intruders, his deep-set eyes unfathomable. Golzari pointed his weapon at the man as Stark approached him slowly.

"Hello, Vanni," Stark said.

The man acknowledged the greeting with a nod. "I was hoping to have you and the admiral with me for the final attack," Vanni said. "Now, alas, it seems there will not be one."

There was a bustle outside the room as security team members made way for Commander Ranasinghe, who entered and took a position at Stark's left. "It is time to surrender, Vanni," the Sri Lankan naval officer said.

"No. I will not surrender to you."

"Very well," Ranasinghe said. He drew his pistol and put two bullets in Vanni's head. Vanni slumped backward, his blood spilling over the hafnium bricks.

DAY 18

Trincomalee Harbor

Syren, *LeFon,* and *Asity* were tied up at adjacent piers in the harbor where the war had begun, joined by *Amba,* which had been taken as a war prize and towed into port by *Asity.* The Sri Lankan government was already making repairs to the ships' communications and radar systems in appreciation for finding the Sea Tigers' base and eliminating the threat. Vanni's death and the capture of the rockets had thwarted the seaborne assaults, and the conscript army coming in from the north was easily repelled. Order was being reestablished in Tamil-held territories.

Warren had secured the EMP weapons and the hafnium in one of *Syren's* modules by Stark's order. A security team relieved hourly stood guard over the module, even in this safe port.

Ranasinghe had already said his goodbyes and expressed his gratitude for being allowed a part in Operation Intrepid. As one of the few surviving Sri Lankan navy officers, Ranasinghe had been told that he would be promoted to admiral—bypassing captain—and stationed off Mullaitivu with the next navy ship Sri Lanka acquired.

A limousine bearing the official seal of the government of Sri Lanka swept up to the pier. A guard opened the rear door, and out came Ambassador Adikira, the man who had given Stark the letter of marque at the outset of the mission. Stark still wondered if he would have accepted the mission if he had known the cost to Gunny Willis and others.

Adikira was smiling broadly and accompanied by someone even more familiar to Stark and Golzari. She was barely five feet tall, and her lavender dress made her dark complexion glow.

"I believe you know Ambassador Sumner," Adikira said.

"C. J.," Stark said with a rare smile. He had known her when she was a young foreign affairs aide in the Senate and later when she served as ambassador to Yemen. She was now the president's national security adviser.

"Connor," she said warmly. "And Agent Golzari. My apologies. I didn't realize that releasing you from my protective detail would force you to work with Commander Stark again."

Golzari tried to hide a smile. "Someone has to keep him out of trouble, Madame Ambassador," he said gravely.

Adikira spoke again. "Captain Stark, my government is so grateful for your efforts. We are now prepared to transfer the hafnium."

Stark shook his head. "No."

Shocked by the lack of respect toward a senior government official, the ambassador nevertheless managed a forced, diplomatic smile and said, "Perhaps you did not understand . . ."

"Oh, but I did, Mr. Ambassador. No. I will not transfer the hafnium," Stark replied. "That's a hell of a weapon. Can you tell me unequivocally that you will be able to secure it appropriately?"

"That is not the issue. You were operating as an agent of the Sri Lankan government, and therefore the hafnium is ours," Adikira said, his false smile having long since faded.

"I'm sorry, but you are incorrect. I was operating under a letter of marque issued by you for specific work. Under international law going back hundreds of years, a ship operating under a letter of marque can claim as its own any captured ship and materials on that ship," Stark answered.

"Unacceptable! Unacceptable!" the ambassador sputtered. "You have not heard the last of this." He stormed back to his limousine.

"Still making friends, I see," C. J. observed. "So, what's your price?"

"You think I'm for sale?"

"Nobody who knows you would think that. But you do have costs associated with your business. You have to sell the hafnium to someone, Connor. We both know the Chinese played a part in this. I wouldn't want it to fall into their hands. I also know that you believe in a balance of power. The Chinese might find another lode. If you sell the hafnium to the U.S. government, then this is that balance."

Stark thought about it and realized she was right—again. "I have to operate this ship and maybe more like her. I want twenty-five million a brick, and I can sell you twenty."

"Twenty million, and you'll sell me thirty," she countered.

"Done," he said, shaking her hand.

Golzari realized he had just witnessed Stark's transformation into the mercenary he had accused him of being at their first encounter.

"What of the remainder?" Golzari asked.

"I'm not looking for more bidders. The material will be well protected."

"Thank you, Connor," Sumner said. "It was good to see you again. Our people will be in touch. For now, I have to stop by *LeFon*. I'll be escorting Admiral Rossberg back to the States personally and then trying to sort out this mess." She sighed. "It won't be easy. He has influential protectors."

"Take care of Jaime. She did the right thing."

"I know that. Don't worry. We'll watch out for her," Sumner said. With that, the president's national security adviser returned to the limo, which sped away.

"Sorry you didn't get your killer, Damien," Stark said, reaching into his pocket for another Percocet.

"I have Gala, who was an accessory. And I have a name—Qin. It's a start."

"What about Melanie? I haven't seen her since we came ashore."

"She has already started filing her reports about Vanni and the war. She did ask me to thank you for giving her access to the information. She decided not to include a lot of what happened on *LeFon* and *Syren*. She thought you deserved to keep some anonymity for now, and her real story was about Vanni and the mass murders."

"She'll win a Pulitzer for it," Stark said.

"Very likely, but she has other work for now. She said she was taking the orphans and a Buddhist monk to Mount Iranamadu to reestablish the monastery there," Golzari replied.

"Did you at least make peace with her?"

"The damage was done a long time ago," Golzari said emotionlessly, then mused, "I wonder how much hafnium is still there. The Chinese may come after it."

"Not much, I think. Jay did some additional testing further down the mineshaft past the transfer station. Looks like the Tigers got most of it out. But Ranasinghe told me that he'll be posting guards at the paths to the monastery once he takes command of the region, just in case someone else tries to come after what might be left."

"What's next for you, Stark? Must I plan on getting you out of another situation?"

"Home, Damien. Just home. That's all I want right now."

"Very well, old man. Always a pleasure. Until next time." Golzari shook Stark's hand and then disappeared into town.

DAY 33

Hong Kong

I n his office high above the streets of the city, Tao Hu leaned back in the two-thousand-dollar ergonomic chair his wife had demanded he purchase if he was going to spend so much time there. He swung around toward the floor-to-ceiling glass windows overlooking the harbor and Kowloon and thought about the team of three individuals who had just left his office. He could fire them, but they still had value and had accepted their mistakes. They would seek redemption for having accepted two bricks of worthless zirconium from the deceptive Vanni, and they would work twice as hard on their next assignment. Despite this error, all had proven their real worth too many times for him to dismiss them.

His problem now was the board of directors. He had invested in two major projects that had failed. He could not fail a third time and retain his position. Fortunately, his scientists were already exploring a new weapon that would change the face of naval warfare in the twenty-first century and catapult the Chinese navy to its rightful place as the undisputed hegemonic force in the world.

He turned back to his glass desktop and looked one more time at the nugget of hafnium as he closed the lid of the velvet-lined black box.

Ullapool

Syren still had two weeks before reporting for patrol duty in the Gulf of Aden. Stark advised the authorities in Yemen that the ship would arrive at the agreed-upon time. Meanwhile, *Syren* slowly glided back to Scotland and Highland Maritime's island off Ullapool, where she would resupply and Jay would have time to work on some of the ship's modifications. The rain was driving hard off the coast of Scotland, but Olivia Harrison had expertly piloted Royal Navy ships in far worse weather.

Doc was satisfied that Connor's back was healing properly, though Stark still hadn't decided how to explain it all to Maggie. It would work out or it wouldn't. She would understand that he had done what he had to do, or she wouldn't. He would do his best to convince her that she mattered more to him than any other person on earth—and then wait and see what happened. He knew she would see the scars—how could she not—but she would never ask about them. He looked again at her framed picture knowing he was now only hours away from seeing that red ponytail. He picked up a half-full pill bottle, looked at it for a moment, then tossed it into the waste can and reached for her family's *sgian dubh*. Without thinking he unsheathed it, and reddish-brown flakes of dried blood fell on his desk. In the weeks since he had been taken prisoner, he still hadn't cleaned the dagger of the blood.

ACKNOWLEDGMENTS

Just as John Donne wrote that "no man is an island unto himself," no author writes without learning about the world through the friends, acquaintances, and colleagues with whom we all travel in life. I am indebted to the following people who supplied answers or put me on the right path.

For information about EMPs I turned to a friend and fellow officer, Cdr. James "Milhouse" Calpin, USNR, who discussed the effects of a possible EMP rocket. When I wanted a rare earth element, "Big Al" Zalewski, a real Youper, narrowed it down to hafnium. Although hafnium does not exist in the state discussed in the book, interesting work was done on it by then-captain Hyman Rickover at Clinton Laboratories in 1947. Readers seeking more information may be interested in U.S. patent number 5,160,482, "Zirconium-Hafnium Separation and Purification Process" and "Applications of Liquid Anion Exchangers for the Separation of Zirconium and Hafnium," by Manjusha Karve and Srhipad Khopkar; "Separation of Hafnium from Zirconium and Their Determination: Separation by Anion-Exchange," by Lawrence Machlan and John Hague; and "Corrosion of Hafnium and Hafnium Alloys," by D. R. Holmes and A. T. I. Wah Chang. "Big Al" also helped me understand more about mines.

Although the Breakers in this book is a fictional place, readers can learn about a real breakers in Bangladesh in the May 2014 issue of *National Geographic* magazine. Other sources included the November 24, 2014, issue of *Atlantic* magazine. There are also several excellent documentaries on this subject.

Lucien Gauthier worked with me in war-gaming one of the scenarios in the book. Greg Harris and Whit Hauprich read an early version and, as they did with *The Aden Effect*, offered helpful suggestions. Cdr. Josh Brooks also lent his expert advice.

Don Preul, ship model curator at the Naval Academy Museum, showed me an early model of FSF-1, *Sea Fighter*. I was intrigued by the ship's design and capabilities and was even more convinced that this ought to be the ship commanded by Connor Stark when I spoke to two experts. I am deeply indebted to Vice Adm. Jay Cohen, USN (Ret.), the former chief of naval research who conceptualized, designed, and built this ship. I am also very grateful to Cdr. Brandon Bryan, *Sea Fighter*'s first CO. Our discussions helped me understand some of the realities of the ship, her capabilities, and small details. The Navy is very fortunate to have had these two officers. If I have deviated from their specifications, it was either in the interest of the story or because I simply got something wrong.

My thanks also go to Cdr. Paul Povlock, professor at the Naval War College, who spoke to my maritime security and irregular warfare class at the Naval Academy several years ago about his research on the Tamil Sea Tigers. I recommend his paper in *Small Wars Journal*, "A Guerilla War at Sea: The Sri Lankan Civil War."

As always, I appreciate the outstanding work of those at the Naval Institute Press—Rick Russell, Claire Noble, Adam Nettina, Mindy Conner, Emily Bakely, and Judy Heise—as well as other U.S. Naval Institute staff. I am especially grateful to Mary Ripley, the "Borg Queen."

Mary LeFon is a gracious woman, and she kindly allowed me to continue in this book with the USS *LeFon*. As I noted in *The Aden Effect*'s acknowledgments, I named the fictional Navy destroyer after her late husband, Capt. Carroll "Lex" LeFon, a military blogger and superb writer who blogged as "Neptunus Lex." The ship's name is a tribute to his talent and character. For strength, for courage.

NOTES

Readers will struggle to find Mount Iranamadu on any map of Sri Lanka. This is fiction, and I needed a little leeway with geography. In the original draft the mine was set at Mount Ritigala, but that range is too far south for the purposes of the storyline. The same is true of the Mullaitivu Breakers, which is actually based on similar breakers in Bangladesh and India. For more information on these, watch National Geographic's *Where Ships Go to Die*.

Jay Warren's UAV has several sensors on board. In one scene the sensor is able to detect the cairngorm quartz crystal on Stark's *sgian dubh*. In reality, the UAV's fly-by would be a problem because of the size and weight of a transmitter and detector, the maximum payload, communications, electrical power, drag from outboard sensors, response time, etc. But as with much of "science fiction" technology, it's likely just a matter of time before these are all resolved.

With the publication of *The Aden Effect* I held an online contest. I would name two characters in the book after the winners. Jay Warren and Melanie Arden won with the best photos of readers with a copy of the book. Neither character in any way resembles the real Jay and Melanie.

ABOUT THE AUTHOR

Claude Berube has taught at the United States Naval Academy, worked at the Office of Naval Intelligence and the U.S. Senate, and served as an officer in the Navy Reserve deployed overseas. He has been a fellow with both the Brookings Institution and the Heritage Foundation. He is the author of three nonfiction books and the Connor Stark novels.